STEAL MY MAGNOLIA

LOVE AT FIRST SIGHT BOOK #3

KARLA SORENSEN

WWW.SMARTYPANTSROMANCE.COM

COPYRIGHT

DEDICATION

For the reader who might be looking for hope in the midst of something scary.
I promise, whatever it is, you have the strength inside of you to get through it.

PROLOGUE

GRADY

*I*n the end, it was my complete lack of organizational skills that ended up being my downfall. Or my savior. Depended on how you wanted to look at it.

And there was a long list to choose from, ways that I could have easily messed up the entire scheme of moving to Green Valley from California. Trading out a tech job that I was good at (but hated to the very depths of my bored soul) for a fledgling idea of a guided hiking and camping business on the cusp of the Smoky Mountains came with a host of ways to monumentally screw up.

But I was the kind of person who refused to dwell on a single item on that list.

Which was how I found myself in a leased office space that was probably too big for my needs, with gear and inventory that I most likely didn't need until I got my business up and running, and without a single employee to help me with the mess I was quite literally buried in.

"Holy hell, Grady," my twin sister, Grace, muttered as she surveyed the disaster that housed the brand-new business. "What have you done?"

1

"It's fine," I insisted. "You know that when you're organizing, it always looks worse before it gets better."

One eyebrow, the same dark gold color as my own hair, lifted slowly, rife with disbelief and the slightest hint of pity.

"Don't give me that look."

She sighed. "I just think ... I think maybe you should take a step back, you know? You've got all these amazing ideas, Grady, and no one can fault your enthusiasm."

But.

I held my breath and waited for it. I didn't want to hear the *but*. I didn't want to hear all the ways this could go wrong, or how I may have bitten off just a tad bit more than I could chew.

"But," she continued, "if you'd let someone help you, you could focus on the parts of this you're so, so good at."

Using the edge of my booted foot, I pushed a box of hiking gear to the side to clear a path back to the paper-laden desk. "I'll hire someone." Rifling through papers, I grimaced when I couldn't find my laptop. "Eventually."

"Tucker can help you," she said, referencing her boyfriend and my only actual friend in Green Valley.

"I know he can. But he still has a lot of responsibility at the law firm, and that's okay because once we're up and running and I get some customers, then Tucker will have more time to help with the fun stuff. The 'let's spend our time in the beautiful outdoors' stuff that we both want to do."

Grace had followed my lead when I decided to move to Green Valley, even though I'd been the one with the grand plan. So, it was with no small amount of irony that my twin sister was running a successful photography business in town. She'd also fallen head over heels in love with literally the first man she met once she passed the city limits.

"Can I help you find some office help, maybe?"

"No," I said firmly. "I will hire my own employees, thank you. Besides, shouldn't you be packing?"

She grinned. "Yes. I can't wait for Mom to meet Tucker."

"What if she hates him?"

Grace slugged me in the shoulder. "You know she won't."

I wanted to rub at the spot where she nailed me, but if I did that, she'd know it actually hurt. And that was my own fault because I'd taught Grace how to throw a jab when we were fifteen and some guy at school had a terrible habit of grabbing her ass when I wasn't around. She'd clocked him in the left eye, and I caught him behind the school and threatened to pull his balls off with a socket wrench if he ever touched her again.

"I know," I agreed, "because he's perfect."

Her answering smile was dreamy and happy and so lovesick that I wanted to roll my eyes.

"He is." She sighed. "It doesn't even seem right that I'm so happy." Her eyes turned devious. "You know that means you're the last single Buchanan left standing, right? It's only a matter of time."

I pointed a finger at her. "Don't you start with me."

"Keep your eyes peeled, Grady," she said in a singsong voice. "You never know when she's right around the corner."

"Which is why I keep my eyes straight ahead when I walk anywhere in this town."

It was true. Unless I was forced into conversation with any woman under the age of forty in Green Valley, I pretended they didn't exist.

And like the jerk my sister was, she cackled. "You can't avoid it, Grady. Didn't you learn anything from me and Tucker?"

I rubbed the back of my neck. "Grace, I know because you found your perfect match that you think our juju family love curse is real, but ..."

"It is," she cried. "Mom and Dad didn't work out because they didn't meet here. I'm telling you, when you meet her, Grady, you are going to know it in the depths of your soul, and there will be no avoiding the fact she's your soul mate."

A growing sense of unease gnawed at my gut. Her surety was something I'd been trying to avoid ever since she met and fell in love with Tucker Haywood. We'd grown up with stories about the Buchanan love curse, something buried deep in the southern lore of our family tree. Grace and I never believed it, not even for a little bit, because our parents had divorced years earlier and were much, much better people because of it.

It almost felt like a betrayal that my twin sister now believed this with every fiber of her being.

"Can we go back to talking about my lack of help, please?" I begged. "I'd take any subject except this one."

She laughed. "Fine. But bro, you need help, and you need it bad. Please promise me you'll work on finding someone to whip your sorry ass into shape while we're gone."

I held up one hand. "I do solemnly swear."

Once more, she glanced around the space at the stacks of unopened boxes, the shelves I wasn't sure how to fill in the most efficient way, and the empty filing cabinets that would eventually hold ... papers and shit, if I could get a better system than the one I currently favored (piles on the desk). "You sure you've got this, Grady?"

Her tone wasn't light or teasing anymore. It was chock-full of sisterly concern and a slight edge of pity that I seemed to be drowning in my own grand idea.

"I have this," I told her, then shoved her gently toward the door. "Now go. And give Mom a hug when you see her."

She nodded. "Hire someone good," she called over her shoulder.

"I'm sure it'll be a match made in heaven."

The door closed behind her, and I sank back into the chair by the desk.

A match made in heaven.

No, it turned out to be something else entirely, and if I'd known just how complicated it would be, I might never have answered the phone when she called.

CHAPTER 1

MAGNOLIA

*W*hen I younger, I used to think my family was perfectly normal. But isn't that the way of most children? We know what *our* life is like, and it's hard to imagine, until you grow up and experience a bit more of the world, that other people know life in a different way than you do.

It wasn't until my daddy had the etiquette coach for my cotillion class fired—she had the unmitigated gall to tell me I was breaking a dress code rule—that I had any inkling that the family dynamic wasn't supposed to work that way. Young ladies being bred into the life that I was accustomed—wealthy southern families who valued a certain life-style—did not glare mightily across the room at each other, but the day that J.T. MacIntyre stormed through the doors like an avenging angel and informed her that her time of teaching the young ladies of Eastern Tennessee was unequivocally over, I received looks that made my eleven-year-old heart feel pinched and cold.

Of course, as we left classes that day with my daddy's arm wrapped around my shoulders, he promised me something that I'd heard a hundred times since that day: "Don't you worry about a thing, Magnolia. I'll take care of this for you."

My whole life, I knew that truth like it was printed on the pages of the family Bible, the one that used to sit on my grandma's nightstand.

God is good, and Daddy would remove any obstacle in my way by sheer force of his will. Amen.

Only it didn't seem so funny on that particular day.

The glares of those girls niggled at something in the back of my head that I couldn't shake until we got home and he told my momma what happened.

They didn't know I was listening because I was told to go read in my room, but I tucked myself up at the foot of the stairs and listened because I thought maybe I could learn why those looks bothered me so much. I'd done nothing wrong, right? Black tights looked pretty with the dress I'd been wearing, prettier than boring old white tights, and when I stuck my leg out, the delicate pattern of the material made me happy. They made me feel like a princess.

"J.T." My momma sighed. "You can't fire anyone who corrects her."

"That woman embarrassed her in front of all those little girls." He sighed, and I knew that sigh of his. It always preceded a good rant, paired with frantic pacing around our kitchen. "And nobody—I don't care who she thinks she is—embarrasses our daughter and gets away with it. You should've seen her face, Bobby Jo."

"Embarrassed Magnolia or you?" she asked quietly.

I pressed my hands to my cheeks, because even now, they felt hot to the touch.

The kitchen went quiet, and I knew my momma was either giving him a hug or giving him that steady look of hers that she was so good at. That was the difference in my parents. Momma was the steady one. Sometimes, I thought she had more pragmatism in her veins than blood. But Daddy was a bit more unpredictable. Especially when it came to the two most important people in his life: me and Momma.

Even back then, I knew he'd burn cities to the ground for us without a second thought.

"I didn't have her fired because she corrected her," he said, voice a bit calmer. "I had her fired because of the way she spoke to her. Like she was less. Like she couldn't have possibly known what the rules were. And ..." His voice trailed off.

"Ah," Momma said. "Well, we can't have that."

"Damn right."

"But," she continued gently, "life is going to be full of hard lessons for Magnolia. There will always be people like that woman who don't care her daddy is white because I gave Magnolia enough of me. You can't protect her from all those people."

He was quiet, the kind of quiet that was tense and scary, because it usually preceded a storm.

"I know that." His voice was rough. I looked down at my arms, a deep golden tan, a color I loved because I always felt like God must've poured a little bit of Daddy and a little of Momma into one giant paint can and mixed it up until He found the perfect blend. "But, by God, I will not sit by if I see it happen. Anyone who makes our daughter feel like she's less will have the full wrath of hell brought down upon them."

My heart didn't feel pinched or cold when I heard him say it like that. I felt loved and protected. I knew I'd always have someone to face the world on my behalf. Wasn't that what daddies were supposed to do?

Momma laughed under her breath. "Maybe you could teach her how to fight some of her own battles."

"Why would I do that? If I can fight them for her, doesn't that make her life easier?"

His genuine confusion had my face scrunched tight with the same feeling. My life had been pretty easy, and I knew now, it was a byproduct of the fact that both my parents came from families so wealthy that it was tacky to bring it up in public. But back then, I took it for granted. That was my normal, and kids can't be faulted for the way their parents raise them. All we can do is try not to let them twist us up if their own issues bleed into those choices.

Thinking about that day, when the eleven-year-old me sat on the stairs and listened to my daddy ask that question, I should've known I was in trouble.

I should've known that when I became an adult and was trying to find my foothold in this life I was born, I'd still be bearing the weight of my father trying to make my life as easy as possible for the simple reason he didn't want to witness me struggle.

Not only was that not normal, but by all the saints and apostles in heaven, I knew exactly how downright unhealthy it was.

Which is how I found myself at the age of twenty-six, working for my father and wondering how I'd let things get this far.

He was pacing my office, hat ripped off his head and clutched tight in his fist. "It's not right, Magnolia."

"Daddy," I said calmly, "why don't you take a few deep breaths, and I'll explain to you why it's perfectly fine."

That hat pointed in my direction like an accusing finger. "She shouldn't have undermined you in that meeting. Anyone working in that office knows you're in charge. You run the show, and if you say that we're coming in over budget, then we're over budget."

The hands I had resting on my lap flexed for a moment. I wanted to scream at him for being such an overbearing ass, but I took a deep breath of my own and schooled my facial expression. Those cotillion etiquette classes—once I got a new teacher—came in handy just about on a daily basis. Ironically, I needed them most in dealing with my father.

"She was right."

"She was ..." His voice trailed off, and he gaped in my direction. "No, she wasn't."

I stared at him, the same steady look that my momma was so good at. Finally, I saw his shoulders relax. "I ran the numbers wrong in one spot when I was doing the bookkeeping. I forgot about one invoice that was paid when I thought it wasn't. It was a simple mistake, but she noticed, and it was perfectly acceptable for her to let me know before anything was approved by the board."

Daddy's face turned an unattractive shade of purple, which, for as handsome as he was, was not a good look for him. If I'd been able to give that color a name in a paint fan deck that they kept down at the Eager Beaver Hardware store, it would be something like Unreasonable Eggplant or Authoritarian Aubergine.

Something you need to understand about my father is that he loved me. He loved my mother. And he loved running the Green Valley Chamber of Commerce. Those three things defined him almost entirely. The problem lay somewhere buried in the first two things because he'd allowed that love to become something it shouldn't be.

Ever since I graduated with a degree in business administration four years ago, I'd been my father's office manager, and for all four of those years, he'd systematically cultivated a work environment where I, alongside him, reigned supreme. Anyone who challenged or disrespected me was dispatched with alacrity. Not by me, of course, but by my father, who wouldn't tolerate such things.

Not that it had happened a lot, but occasionally, a puffed-up peacock waltzed into our office demanding something for their business in town, and without knowing the politics of who I was, who he was, or what families I belonged to in the Green Valley hierarchy, they'd treat me as nothing more than a glorified coffee-maker.

That man, I can hardly remember his name now, called me "Girl" and told me how he wanted his coffee fixed. No "please." No "thank you." (He had a Northern accent though, which I feel is important to the story.)

Suffice it to say, he was dropped ass first onto the concrete outside the Chamber of Commerce after Daddy cursed him up one side of the sidewalk and down the other. He decided, quite wisely, not to move his business into Green Valley after that.

But this was different, and I couldn't help but add it to the list of things that made me certifiably insane about my father.

"She undermined you in a staff meeting where everyone was watching," he said. Bless his heart, he was trying to keep his tone even because we'd had this discussion a thousand times over the past four years, and he knew my will matched his own. I just wielded mine with a lighter touch and a sweeter smile, like every good southern belle does.

"A gentle correction is not undermining, especially when I could have presented incorrect information to the Chamber board. You should be thanking her." I unfolded my hands and smoothed them down the front of my pink and white gingham skirt. "I will speak to her, which is appropriate as her superior. You will stay out of this, Daddy."

"This is my office, Magnolia, and I will not tolerate disrespect of my main administrator."

I let out a slow breath and stood from behind my desk. The surface was immaculate, my laptop closed and centered on the gleaming walnut. A small vase of pink peonies sat in the corner next to an antique lamp with an ornate golden base. But the way my daddy filled the space, he eclipsed everything about it that I loved. Because it turned the neatness, the order, the carefully cultivated mood into something ominous. Like I'd been watching an angry thundercloud roll in for the past few years but never even considered raising my umbrella in case of rain.

"I am the person who Candy reports to," I told him, my voice firming and my spine straightening. My temper took a long time to rise to the surface. It usually hovered out of reach, where I couldn't grab it easily, and he knew that. He knew it, and if I was honest, he used that to his advantage. It took me longer to reach anger, and when his was so readily accessible, it usually turned to quick action that he refused to second-guess. "And if you fire her without my permission, then you are also disrespecting my position within this office."

"She took a tone with you, Magnolia," he warned. "I saw it in her eyes. That woman took great joy in correcting you in front of everyone else."

The thing I hated most, as I watched my father work himself into a righteous frenzy, was that he wasn't wrong. Candy had looked mighty pleased with herself when she pointed out my error. But it wasn't a fire-able offense, not to me.

There would always be people who looked at me and judged. Always. My skin color, my age, the fact that I was given my job simply because I shared my father's last name. My mere existence was fodder for judgment.

The door of my office was open, and our intern walked past, watching my father and me unabashedly.

My cheeks heated as I turned my attention back to Daddy. "I'm done with this conversation."

Daddy rocked back like I'd pushed him. "I'm not. It's unacceptable, Magnolia."

"It's fixable," I told him. "And as your administrator, I will fix it how I see fit. End of discussion."

The set of his strong jaw told me exactly how done with this he wasn't. His shoulders, broad and strong, straightened, and his eyes, the same golden green that I'd inherited from him, narrowed in determination.

"Daddy," I warned him. "Don't you even think about undermining me in this. I will handle it."

"You will let her get away with it because you're afraid to be firm with someone who looks at you like she does."

It stung, partially because it was true. I'd come up against more than one person in my time who I wanted to eviscerate because of something they'd said or done. Instead, I channeled every etiquette lesson and killed them with kindness and a sweetly spoken reprimand. A steel bat wrapped in lace was still a formidable weapon, and my father often forgot that.

And sometimes, I had to wield that weapon with the man who loved me more than anything on this earth, with the exception of my mother. "Daddy, stay out of it, or you will not like the consequences."

His eyes narrowed farther but not in determination. This was a subtle gauging of how serious I was. What he couldn't see was the maelstrom whipping fiercely under my skin, the furious energy that I felt when I thought about him going against me on this.

"What exactly are you threatening me with, Magnolia Marie MacIntyre?"

The full name, hefted like a weapon of his own, should have sent me cowering. My parents never, and I mean never, used my full name unless they were cross with me.

I kept my face even, just like my momma did, and I begged him with my eyes to let this go. To let me fight this battle on my own because, God Almighty, being the only child of J.T. MacIntyre and Bobby Jo Boone gave me enough determination that he should have been thrilled to unleash me on the world. Except all he wanted to do, even as I rounded the corner to thirty, was wrap me in Bubble Wrap and protect me from the ugly.

His chest expanded on an inhale, and just as he was about to speak, Candy popped her unfortunate head into my office.

"Magnolia?" she said sweetly. "I have that corrected finance report all ready to go for the board meeting tomorrow." Her thin lips, covered with a frosted pink lipstick that should have been outlawed in 1999, curled up in a victorious smile. "You're welcome, by the way."

When I caught a glimpse of my daddy's expression, I exhaled slowly.

Unaware that she'd just sealed her own fate, Candy smiled a little bit wider. "J.T.," she said. "I'm sure she'll never do it again. She's such a good girl, isn't she?"

Daddy set his hands on his hips, looked up at the heavens for a moment, and I sucked in a breath.

"Candy," he said, sending me one brief, apologetic look before he turned toward the door. "You're fired."

She blinked. Then blinked again.

"Excuse me?" she whispered.

There was no stopping him now, and to speak up would only make this worse. I clasped my hands in front of me and watched the carnage unfold.

Daddy pointed at the hallway where a couple of people had stopped to gawk. "You have one hour to pack up your desk, and if you can manage to do that without a single word denigrating my daughter— who is your superior—then I grant you a month of severance pay. But if you open that condescending mouth of yours one more time, you won't get a dime."

Unreasonable Eggplant didn't look very good on Candy either. With the slight graying to her blond hair, it made her look ill.

She pinned me with accusation in her eyes, and I kept my face even. Even before she opened her mouth, I knew it would be bad.

"Good luck getting anywhere in this life besides the four walls of this office, Magnolia."

"Out!" Daddy yelled, pointing in the direction of her own workspace. "Pack up and go, Candy."

She stormed down the hallway with Daddy in her wake.

My hands were shaking as I sank back into my chair, and I gripped my fingers together so tightly that my knuckles turned bone white. As people walked past my office, I felt their stares, heavy with so much that I didn't want to identify. If they were able to separate me from my father, they all liked and respected me. But that was an "if" bigger than the Smoky Mountains, and just as formidable to traverse.

I didn't even pretend to work as I sat there, trying desperately to make sense of what I should do next. When I warned Daddy of consequences, I'd meant it, but I wasn't exactly sure what those consequences were.

Candy's parting words echoed through my head, and I had to pinch my eyes shut against the sheer force of what they did to me.

My job paid well, and I was good at it. Even if Daddy hadn't handed it to me on a silver platter, I would've run that office seamlessly. Some people had callings in life, right? Mine was something like this. The pleasure I gained from a color-coded spreadsheet was probably on par with how most people felt about Death by Chocolate cake or good sex or a shopping spree with someone else's money. For my eighteenth birthday, I'd asked for a label maker that cost as much as nice jewelry, and I cried when I opened that box.

But this wasn't about me being good at my job.

For the second time that day, Candy wasn't wrong. Every time Daddy swooped in to fix something he defined as a problem, he knocked my legs out from under me.

Swiveling my chair to the side, I stared out the large window of my office overlooking downtown Green Valley. Each business lining those streets held a connection to us by way of Daddy's role and my own. I thought of how many people glanced at me sideways because of the way he bulldozed his way through life under the guise of granting Momma and me every happiness. Momma had hers, carved out in the backbone of Green Valley, as the owner of the Bait and Tackle shop. She was well-respected, loved by the people who worked for her, and by the customers who kept her business thriving, even if my parents' marriage was viewed as some sort of oddity.

No one really understood him except us, and normally, I was okay with that.

As a young girl, it was something I loved about him. Something that made me cherished and loved and precious.

But as a woman who was feeling locked down by that part of him, the part that wanted to take on the world if it meant he could make things easier on me, it didn't feel so precious anymore.

Outside my window, I saw a dirt-covered SUV pull up in front of the office space across the street. The man who stepped out of the driver's seat was tall with dark golden hair in need of a cut and had a swimmer's build—broad and muscular without the bulk I was used to seeing on men my age. I didn't recognize him right away, but when he turned and smiled at someone walking past him, my eyes narrowed.

Grady Buchanan.

New to town in the past few months, he was not someone I'd met yet. I was, however, very acquainted with his twin sister, Grace. Also known as the woman who moved to town and managed to upend my carefully constructed life when she proved too irresistible for my longtime boyfriend, Tucker.

Despite how maudlin that sounded, there was no real drama behind it. He and I had been together too long and had gotten far too comfortable, so his breaking up with me to pursue a relationship with Grace had probably been a good thing. I didn't hold any ill will against Grace, per se.

All I knew about Grady was that he was trying to start a new business in town, though I'd prejudged him a bit for not immediately joining the Chamber. I also knew he'd struggle to find a foothold doing what he wanted to do; run guided hikes and camping trips in the greater Green Valley area. Our tourist numbers weren't high enough to sustain something like that.

As I watched him unload a massive box from the back of his vehicle, hefting it easily into his muscular arms, an idea lit somewhere in the darkest parts of my brain.

It felt like freedom and held a dangerous edge that I'd never dared to approach.

He'd have no preconceived notion of who I was. No built-in bias of how to handle the daughter of J.T. MacIntyre.

And as he struggled to open the door to the office space, almost dropping the box in the process, I found my lip curving into a slight smile. He'd also need help. A lot of help from someone who knew this town, knew this state, had been born with the gift of organization, and had the Lord's own patience.

Something unlocked behind my chest. Something rusty and unused. Almost like a bird who was trying out its wings after a long rehabilitation.

It was hope. And it looked an awful lot like Grady Buchanan.

CHAPTER 2

GRADY

"Where did you go, you little asshole? You were right here a second ago," I murmured. The empty office space didn't answer me. Neither did the pile of crumpled receipts as I rifled through them.

One large purchase order had up and walked away. It was the only explanation. And that was not acceptable, because if I was going to start this business, I was going to start on the right foot.

In theory, I was doing well. But that theory was flimsy, and I refused to think about what might happen if it crumbled under the weight of reality.

The money I'd been saving for years was my jumping-off point. The springboard I'd slowly built for the past five years while I slaved away behind a computer.

I had a partner in the form of Tucker, even if that was a nominal partnership at best, given that we had approximately zero customers. But those would come, I had to believe. I just needed someone to do ... everything else that I sucked at. Like figuring out how to organize all this bullshit.

Did I want clear bins?

Or inventory straight on the racks?

How much inventory did I really need?

That depended entirely on the number of customers I managed to bring in. If I would be focusing more on small day hikes with groups or if I could build a steady stream of overnight trips that included camping too.

My thumb tapped against the surface of the desk, and I struggled to breathe through the press of panic on my chest. "This wasn't a mistake," I said for the hundredth time that week. "This is a good idea."

The panic, something I could normally push down with two hands, built into something bigger and heavier, and I felt it spread to the back of my neck and down to the stretch of skin between my shoulder blades.

If this failed, I'd have to go back to doing a job that I hated.

If this failed, and I had to face people like Tucker or Grace or my dad and admit that moving to Green Valley had been a mistake, I couldn't handle it.

I took a deep breath and repeated something I'd always heard Memaw say. "Lord, if you're listening, save this wretch from the wreck I've found myself in."

No sooner were the words out of my mouth than my cell phone rang.

Blinking stupidly at the small piece of plastic, I couldn't help how the hair on the back of my neck lifted. The timing was probably coincidence, but still, before I hit the screen to answer the call, I found myself glancing up at the heavens.

Or ... the ceiling, at least. Nothing was out of the ordinary, no sign from above that my salvation was imminent.

The number was local, and before voicemail picked it up, I carefully tapped the button to connect the call. "This is Grady."

There was silence on the other end. I pulled the phone away from my face to make sure I'd answered.

"Hello?" I said.

I heard a deep breath before she spoke. "Hi, I'm here, sorry."

My head tilted to the side when I heard her voice. It was soft and low with the curling accent that I'd gotten used to in the past month and a half. But it ... I shook my head ... something about it made the hairs lift slightly on my arms.

"Did you mean to call my number?" I asked carefully. Inexplicably, I found myself holding my breath, waiting for her to answer.

"I heard you're looking for help. Administrative help," she clarified.

My head went back. "Did you?"

She was quiet for a second. "Small town," she explained. "People talk."

I laughed under my breath. "So I'm learning." It made me shake my head. The darknet had nothing on the Green Valley information pipeline. "So," I continued, "tell me a little bit about yourself."

"Of course." For the second time since I picked up, she let out an audible breath. "I have my BS in Business Administration, an MBA from Vanderbilt, and other than college, I've lived in Green Valley my whole life."

Scratching the side of my face, I glanced around at the horrific state of the office and tried to imagine someone with an MBA wanting anything to do with it. My face was bent in a grimace.

"I've spent the past five years as an office administrator for my ..." She paused. "For a local business, and I'm looking to change things up. Fresh start."

21

I sat up slowly. "I can understand wanting a fresh start. That's why I'm here."

"I know. I, umm, I heard that. In town." She stumbled slightly over her words, and I smiled. "I'm not very outdoorsy, and I know that's what you'll be doing, but I'm the most organized person you'll ever meet. My label maker is my favorite accessory, and I have lists for my to-do lists. And I know every single business owner from here to Merryville."

I laughed. "You sound like you're already in your interview."

She laughed too, and I grimaced when my chest tightened. It caused a strong enough physical sensation that I glanced down at my body, like it was separate from me somehow.

"I can come in and fill out an application, if you'd like," she said.

I laughed under my breath. "If I had applications, I'd say yes." I glanced around the mess surrounding me. "But ... I'm not quite that prepared yet."

"That's also why you need someone who knows how to get an office up and running."

"That's true," I agreed. "Can you come in tomorrow so we can talk a little bit more? Since I don't have an application."

"That would be great," she said firmly. The stumbling was gone. I found myself wondering how old she was. What she looked like.

If I had a calendar, I would've glanced at it. But that was also buried in a stack of papers.

"How does nine sound? Do you need the address?"

"Sounds perfect," she answered. "And uh, no, thank you. I know where to find you."

I shook my head.

"Small town," we said in unison. She laughed, and my smile took up my whole damn face.

"Then I'll see you at nine tomorrow ..." My voice trailed off. "I'm sorry, I didn't catch your name. I'm still working on my southern manners."

She laughed. My chest did that thing again. It wasn't the heavy press of panic. It was a lightening. A lifting of whatever pressure I'd been feeling before she called.

She spoke slowly, like she was thinking carefully about her answer. "You can call me Lia."

"Lia," I repeated. "I look forward to meeting you."

She paused. "You know, if you're free this afternoon, I could come over later today if you wanted."

Surprise had my eyebrows lifting. My day was hardly packed, given that the most pressing thing I was working on was trying not to panic that I'd made a massive error in uprooting my life and trying my hand for the first time at being an entrepreneur. "Oh, umm, I'd be fine with that." I laughed. "The office is a mess, though. I have to warn you about that."

"A mess is just an organization project waiting to happen, and that's my favorite kind of opportunity, Grady."

Her response had me tipping my head back with laughter. Maybe this phone call, and she, was really an answer to a prayer. "Well, you lost me on that one, but I'm glad there are people like you in the world." I glanced at my watch, then back at the mess. "Do you want to swing by in about an hour? Or is that too soon?"

"An hour is great." Her eagerness was a breath of fresh air on a day that had rapidly been deteriorating. For the first time since I started loading my car with boxes of inventory I wasn't even sure I needed, I could take a deep breath. "I'll try to leave the mess intact for you."

"You are too kind." I heard the smile in her voice. "I'll see you soon."

Why did my stomach flip when she said that?

"I look forward to it," I told her.

I disconnected the call and hardly realized that my hand was gripping my phone so tightly that my knuckles were going white. It took a concerted effort to relax my fingers before I set it down, my head tilting to the side as I replayed the conversation.

Digging into my pocket, I pulled out a butterscotch candy, which I carried with me at all times. The yellow cellophane crinkled when I unwrapped it, and as soon as the sweet, hard candy hit my tongue, I felt my body relax. A little.

Something ... something felt peculiar inside my head. To be honest, I wasn't sure I'd used the word peculiar to describe anything in my entire life because I wasn't the sort of guy who used words like that.

But it was the only word that fit.

Maybe my jokingly uttered prayer had found a foothold somewhere, or maybe I was truly losing my mind. For a few minutes, I did nothing except stare out of the large window facing downtown Green Valley. Because I was a couple of blocks off Main Street, with a field behind the building, the foot traffic was lighter. Only the occasional person slowed in front of my space to gawk inside.

I smiled when I saw one such person approach the window, except she took it a step further and cupped her hand against the glass to see if anyone was inside. Maxine Barton, one of my sister's favorite people in town, caught sight of me and nodded in satisfaction when I lifted a hand in greeting. There was no jingling bell on the door when she opened it. But I'd be remedying that soon, simply because I liked the idea of it.

"Young man," she said.

I stood and jogged to the door, holding it open so she could push her walker through. That earned me a grunt.

"You may not be from the south, but I can't fault your manners. Your momma must have done something right."

I smiled. "She did a few things, ma'am. What can I do for you today, Miss Barton?"

She waved a hand. "Call me Maxine. I've practically adopted your sister as one of my grandkids, so I think we can move forward on a first-name basis."

"Maxine, it's an honor."

With a roll of her eyes, she started to walk farther into the space and then stopped when her walker pushed up against some boxes. "Good Lord Almighty, Grady. This place should come wrapped in caution tape."

"Yeah, uhh, I'm still settling in." I rubbed the back of my neck and fought an embarrassed flush crawling up my face at the way she studied the sad-looking room. Just like that, the pressure was back on my chest. What had I been thinking, telling Lia she could come here in an hour? I needed a week not to look like such a mess.

"And you think this'll work?" she asked skeptically.

"I sure hope so."

"Your sister leave on her trip yet?"

The change of subject was welcome, and I nodded. "They left early this morning."

"Your momma ever plan on visiting here again, or is she gonna make you kids always cross the whole damn country when you want to see her?"

Another thing that took some getting used to was the absolute unerring way elderly southern women had no compunction about speaking their minds.

I gave her a lopsided smile. "I don't know if I like you bad-mouthing my mother, Maxine. She's the only one I have, you know."

She sighed. "Fine. Can't be easy with her and your daddy being divorced as long as they've been. I probably wouldn't want to come back here either, what with it being his home and all."

"Green Valley was never home to my mom, but she's glad that Grace and I are happy here. I'm sure she'll come to visit eventually."

Maxine looked skeptical.

I let out a deep breath. "Maxine, as much as I love being able to spend some time with you, I have someone coming for an interview in less than an hour, and I'd like to tidy up a bit before she gets here."

Her focus sharpened on that little tidbit. "What's her name?"

"Lia ... " My voice trailed off. "Actually, I didn't get her last name. But she heard I needed some administrative help."

Maxine's mouth pulled to the side. "Can't think of a single Lia who'd want to work here with you doing this."

"Thanks," I said dryly.

"Oh, don't go fishing for compliments. It's not attractive." She turned her walker. "Grab the door for me, will ya?"

When I pulled it open for her, she glanced up at me, wrinkled face thoughtful. "Lia, you said?"

"Yes, ma'am."

"Huh." She pushed forward until she was almost clear of the doorframe.

"Maxine?"

"Yes, young man?"

"Is that why you came? To ask if Grace left on her trip?"

She gave me a mysterious little smile. "Of course not. Someone from church asked me why it looked like a crime scene in here, so I wanted to see for myself that you weren't doing anything illegal."

I was still shaking my head as I watched her make her way down the block and turn the corner.

"This is a weird place," I muttered.

A gust of wind blew down the street, making tree branches sway, and I shivered. Given that I was raised and spent most of my life in California, the mid-forty days of an early Tennessee winter were something I was still getting used to. Some of the leaves had fallen, now that October was finished, and for some reason, it made everything look a little bit colder than it actually was.

When I was back inside, I took a hard look at the space and knew I couldn't do much to make it look any less terrifying for my first potential employee. Whoever she was, there was a good chance she'd walk in, decide the "organization opportunity" wasn't all that exciting, and walk right back out.

Absently, I pushed the sleeves of my Henley up past my elbows and started stacking the boxes a little bit ... neater. The desk took a bit more time, and I was hunched over the surface, reviewing a piece of receipt that had gotten smudged in the stack. Was that a five? I turned the paper to the side. No, it was an eight.

When the door opened, the change of angle in the glass caught the sun, and for a moment, I couldn't see a thing. She was bathed in that bright, golden light, and it framed her like she was meant to be under a spotlight somewhere, hanging on the walls of a famous museum.

Something whispered through the back of my brain as the door swung shut, and I got my first look at her. I hardly heard what that whisper was because the second her face came into focus, everything went static and quiet. An eerie calm that I'd never felt before spread through my body like an ink stain.

"Grady?" she asked.

I think I nodded. Maybe I said something. I wasn't entirely sure because that peculiar feeling from the phone call ... I knew what it was.

"Oh, shit," I whispered.

Her head tilted, a confused smile frozen on her face. "I beg your pardon?"

Shit. Dammit. Why were my palms so sweaty? What was wrong with me?

"Sorry," I said on a rush, "just ... I wish I'd been able to tidy up more."

Her shoulders relaxed.

The dress she wore was bright yellow, and it made me think of the lemon tree in my mom's backyard.

My mouth watered instantly.

Her lips looked soft and sweet, and oh my hell, I was going to get sued before all this was over because now I'd probably do something stupid like hire her on the spot. Even if she turned out to be a serial killer.

When she extended her hand, yes, I absolutely looked for rings, and my shoulders did some relaxing of their own when I didn't find any.

I should have been thinking about lawsuits.

About inadvisable hirings.

About anything except how long her eyelashes were. How high her cheekbones were. How soft her skin looked. What her middle name was, and why she loved to organize messes, and how she chose her major, and if she'd get coffee with me. If she even liked coffee. I'd get tea. Tea was great. I *loved* tea.

She continued to hold out her hand, and if my stunned silence freaked her out, then she was doing a damn good job of hiding it. "It's a pleasure to meet you."

When I took her hand in mine—the most beautiful woman I'd ever seen—my heart stopped, and in that suspended moment, I knew I'd never be the same.

CHAPTER 3

MAGNOLIA

*I*n hindsight, I wasn't sure what I expected from Grady Buchanan. After a moment's pause, he shook my hand.

His eyes held mine, and for some reason, my cheeks went slightly warm at the intensity I saw there. There was no way he could know who I was because I'd purposely not given him my last name when we spoke on the phone.

Slowly, I pulled my hand away, and that seemed to snap him out of ... whatever it was.

My eyes wandered away from the man in front of me—God blessed the Buchanans with a healthy dose of attractive genes, that was for sure —to the space around us.

If there was a name for the thrill that ran through me at the idea of bringing a system to the stacks and stacks of boxes in front of me, I didn't know what that word was. I was smiling before I knew it, a real smile too. Not the polite, southern "bless your heart" smile I had to use often in my day-to-day life. People who were annoyed by something Daddy had done got that smile. Coworkers like Candy often found themselves on the receiving end. People who never even wanted to take the time to get to know me for who I actually was.

As sad as it was, I knew how to wield that not-so-real smile so much more easily than I did any other kind. And it was a good sign that within minutes of walking into this horribly messy office space, it came out of hiding.

"I wasn't exaggerating on the phone, unfortunately," he said ruefully. Grady shoved a hand through his hair—an undeniably nervous gesture —and I felt my smile twitch at how it sent his golden-brown hair into messy disarray. "I need help."

"Yes, I can see that." I wandered past him and ran my finger over the edge of one stack of boxes. The desk was cluttered with papers, and there was only one chair. I tilted my head to the side, my mouth opening to ask where I should sit, when he darted past me.

"I'm sorry, here." He tripped over the corner of some boxes and caught himself from pitching forward by bracing one hand on the desk.

I swallowed a shocked laugh.

Grady exhaled loudly, and I caught a flush of embarrassment splash across his chiseled face.

I tried to see the similarities between him and Grace when he slowly, carefully pulled the chair out from behind the desk and found a spot for it close to where I was standing. It was in their coloring, to be sure; all the Buchanans had that golden look to them. It was in the eyes too, hazel and green, similar to my own, but his tended more golden brown, and mine looked like the trees in my backyard as they started changing color in the fall.

And I saw it in his smile. Grace had a pretty smile too, I remembered. We'd only spoken a couple of times because it wasn't easy to see the woman who'd made your ex-boyfriend fall in love with her.

That brought me up short, and I had to swallow past a rush of anxiety that I was not accustomed to feeling.

What was I *doing* here? I never made rash decisions. But when he answered and actually agreed to meet me in an hour, I'd refused to give it a second thought when I rushed home and put on my favorite yellow dress. Overkill for an interview, but the Peter Pan collar and wide ribbon around the waist made me feel pretty and feminine, and I knew the color made my skin glow.

In that dress, I felt powerful. Like I could conquer the world. And I needed a little bit of that reassurance before I had my first blind interview in my entire life.

Thankfully, Grady was so busy trying to push a couple of boxes behind the desk for a makeshift chair of his own that he didn't notice my mental freak-out. I took a seat on the chair and let out a deep breath. He did almost the same thing, and again, I found myself smiling at how off-kilter he seemed.

"Okay," he said, and grabbed a pen from the desk, but no paper on which he might write anything down. "So, business school, huh? That's ... good."

"I think so," I told him. "Vanderbilt is a great school."

He did that intense eye contact thing again, then blinked down to his desk. "Right. It is. I've heard of that one."

"I was on the dean's list every semester during my bachelor's and master's." Carefully, I folded my hands in my lap and thought of what else he might want to know. "And the only thing I love more than finding ways to make things work efficiently is seeing this town thrive."

Grady smiled differently this time, like my answer pleased him, but he didn't want to show it too much. "You said you've lived here your whole life, right?"

I nodded. "I have. Other than going away for college, of course."

He scratched the side of his face, mouth opening and closing like he wasn't sure what to ask next.

"Is this your first time interviewing someone?" I asked.

His grin was lopsided and full of self-deprecation. "Am I that obvious?"

"My grandma used to say that obvious is only a character flaw if you're a cheater or a liar."

"That sounds like something my memaw would say." He tapped the pen on the side of his leg. The way he was looking at me was disconcerting but not uncomfortable. Like he just wasn't quite sure what to do with me.

"Are you officially open to take bookings yet?" I asked.

"Ahh, yes." He looked around at the boxes. "Sort of."

"And you've already connected with the park rangers, right?"

"A former one, yes. I, uhh, I had a conversation about my idea with Jethro Winston when I first got into town, and he had some pointers for me, but ... I wasn't ..." The pen clattered to the floor when it fell out of his hand, and he swooped down to pick it up. "I was still gathering information at that point."

I hummed. "Good. I think there's a market for what you're doing." The boxes, so many boxes, captured my confused gaze again. "May I ask, though, what exactly do you have for inventory? I was under the impression it would be guided day hikes, that sort of thing."

Grady grinned. It was so happy, so boyish, that I found myself unexpectedly charmed by the sight of it.

"You know, I probably shouldn't admit this, but just before you called, I was wondering why I had all these boxes too and was thinking maybe

I needed someone to help save my sorry self from getting too many ideas that I couldn't execute."

My laughter wasn't much more than a soft exhale. Only a man who was crazy or incredibly secure in who he was would admit that to a person he was trying to hire.

He continued, pointing at a few of the stacks. "I have packs in there. Boots and gear over here. My thought was that I could have a bit wider range of offerings than just the day hikes that most companies do."

"Such as?"

"Well, say you have a company that wants to do some team building or maybe even an overnight trip. If they had someone they could call to handle all the logistics, rather than make their employees purchase all new gear, we'd have things built right into the package price, and all they'd have to do is show up."

My brain immediately switched into a higher gear. It would take substantial tracking to maintain that sort of thing, but as long as you had the right person in charge, it was doable for a smaller operation. "Food, too," I said. "You'd have to contract with one of the restaurants around here to make sure you could provide meals for larger groups that didn't break the budget."

He leaned forward. "Exactly."

"I could help you with contacts there. Like I said on the phone, I know every business owner from here to Merryville."

Please don't ask how, please don't ask how, please don't ask how.

Grady seemed like a levelheaded guy, if not a little flighty, but if he knew I was Tucker's ex-girlfriend before he hired me, my fantasies of starting fresh somewhere that had nothing to do with my father would disappear right before my very eyes like a horrible magic trick. With nothing more than a wave of his hand, this opportunity would vanish into thin air.

"And you said you were an office administrator?"

I nodded. "Since I graduated college. I've done it all: scheduling, payroll, managing the books, HR. You name it, and I've done it in some capacity or another in the past five years. I've managed budgets and foundation disbursements, and I've had to organize events, big and small, so logistics are no trouble." I leaned forward in the chair. "When I say that spreadsheets are my favorite things in the world, I'm being perfectly serious."

He laughed, a big booming sound that filled the room. It was a happy sound coming from a man who smiled as easily as he did. I got the sense that Grady Buchanan loved life, and he probably wouldn't apologize for it. After the past year of mine and my growing frustrations with Daddy, it was that kind of freedom that I was craving with a fierceness that surprised me.

We were going about this interview in every way except the right one. I had no references typed up, no letter of recommendation, and there was a good chance that if I filled out a payroll form right now and he saw my last name, he'd usher me straight out the door.

"I'm ready for a change, Grady," I told him. "And I'd be thrilled to help you make sense of this mess, if you let me."

His face changed a bit as he studied me, and I got the sense something internal was going on, some decision he was trying to weigh, and he wasn't quite sure how to puzzle it through. This man, tall and handsome, had a face that didn't hide much. And I found that I liked it.

Maybe that should have been my warning, that it was all far too complicated to be anything but a mess. But the warning went unheeded, and I held my breath to see whether he'd agree with me.

CHAPTER 4

GRADY

This was, without a doubt, the worst, most unprofessional interview in the history of the world. I'd hardly asked her anything of substance. Within two minutes of my bumbling attempt to recover myself, she'd effectively started interviewing me.

Steamrolled. I'd been steamrolled, and I couldn't even be mad about it.

She was so beautiful that it became increasingly hard to meet her gaze without feeling like I was gawking at her. On the phone earlier, I remember wondering what she looked like and how old she was because the tone of her voice was so soft and low, she could've been anywhere from thirty to sixty, and it wouldn't have surprised me.

But this woman—with her sharp questions, and her talk of spread-sheets, and her degrees that far outshone anything I'd managed to accomplish—was right around my age, and that was something horrible and wonderful.

I'd fully and completely doubted the existence of the legendary tales in my family about how quickly the Buchanans fell in love when they met The One. Yes, a huge part of that came from the fact that my own parents' marriage hadn't lasted, but even when my twin sister moved to town and fell ass over teakettle for Tucker and proclaimed him the unequivocal love of her life, I thought all the stories were total and complete bullshit.

But I couldn't deny a single part of it anymore.

Not with her sitting across from me, prim and proper in her bright yellow dress, while I managed to catalog the different smiles I'd seen in the past twenty minutes. Each smile, each shift and change and degree of realness I saw uncovered in them as we talked was like a dart that landed with unerring accuracy in the center of my chest.

The polite one when she walked in.

The excited one when she talked about her spreadsheets.

The amused one when I dropped my pen and couldn't form a single intelligent word because her presence had me so fucking tied up in knots.

Thunk.

Thunk.

Thunk.

Each one pinned my heart down just a little bit more with their sharp edges.

And as she stared at me expectantly, waiting for an answer, I knew it would be monumentally stupid to hire this woman. Because how was I supposed to be around her every day, see those smiles, and try to uncover the hundreds of others she kept locked up behind her southern manners without staring at her like a whipped puppy dog.

Yet knowing all that, having processed through it the entire time she easily manhandled this interview, I said the dumbest thing I could have possibly said at that moment. "The job's yours if you want it."

Maybe I should have taken it back. Maybe I should have told her that I needed to talk to Tucker first. But every single fiber of my being relaxed knowing that I'd be able to spend time with her, get to know her, and see her.

And the smile she gave me? I almost had to clutch at my chest to make sure I was still breathing. It was like watching a sunrise unfold over the mountains. There was slow disbelief to it, a warmth, and a sheer, bright, blinding happiness that she couldn't hide.

That smile didn't waver in the slightest when she spoke. "Have we both lost our minds if I say yes?"

"Probably," I admitted.

Her smile disappeared slightly in the wake of my honesty, but in those eyes, I could tell she was still excited. "Maybe we should talk things like salary and benefits."

Right. Because that's the kind of stuff normal business owners did when conducting a professional interview and not hiring people on the basis that they may or may not have just experienced a probably-made-up-phenomenon of love at first sight.

I could hardly stifle my horrified groan, which I quickly covered up by clearing my throat. "Yes, uhh, yes. Good idea."

I yanked open the drawer on the desk where I'd jotted down notes from my phone call with Tucker about this very thing. He and I had worked out some preliminary numbers based on how much the business had in savings, because we were both aware that having someone on hand full-time to manage the logistics would be the most important first step. In order for him to come on full-time someday, we'd need steady bookings. Not just steady, but more than I could handle on my own. And in order to do that, we'd need someone capable to run everything else. Both he and I were willing to forgo a salary upfront in order to make that happen.

After glancing through my notes, I snagged a piece of paper from the desk, scrawled out a number, and handed it to her. "This is what I can offer you right now."

She stared at it.

"As the business grows," I continued, like her silence demanded an explanation from me, "there's room for that to grow too, if you're worried about that."

Glancing up at me, she smiled again. "I wasn't."

"Good."

"That'll be just fine for me."

The way her accent curled around the words was adorable. *That'll be* became one word. *Just* was dragged out longer than I would've said it. And I wanted to sit like a freaking creep and listen to her talk all day. I could already imagine Tucker's face when he walked into the office to find me doing nothing except listening to her answer the phone. Talk about the weather. Recite the alphabet.

This was *awful*. No wonder my sister had turned into such a basket case over Tucker. I felt like little heart-shaped aliens had taken over my body, cranking the wheels of my thoughts into these strange directions that I hadn't even known existed before she walked into this office.

"Good," I said. That one simple word was all I could manage without looking like a fool. Or more of a fool, at least.

I shifted on the box, and that distribution of weight proved too much for the sturdy cardboard. The tape popped, the corner caved, and my ass sank into the middle, lifting my feet off the ground.

Lia stood off the chair. "Oh heavens, do you need help?"

My face must have been bright red for how hot it felt. Really, in twenty-six years, I'd never fumbled my way through an interaction with a woman like I was fumbling through this one. If she looked at me with anything other than abject pity, I'd be fortunate.

"No, I'm fine." And I was. Once I pushed up off the side of the box, it fell forward, and I tipped onto the floor. I laughed under my breath at the look on her face. If my sister were here with her camera, and she snapped a shot of that one facial expression, it would be titled, "bless his heart."

She'd schooled her face when I finally managed to stand, and again, with the way the light was streaming into the front windows of the space, she practically glowed. There wasn't a single flaw on her that I could see. Like someone, somewhere plucked individual traits from a catalog and crafted an impossibly perfect human being. Or at least my definition of one.

And now, I thought with a dawning sense of horror and excitement, I was her boss.

Lia glanced over my shoulder at the mess, and I chuckled at the look of anticipation I saw in her face.

"Am I that obvious?" she asked.

I held up my hand, pointer finger and thumb only about an inch apart. "Only a little."

"I can't start today," she told me, cheeks pinking slightly from my observation. "And I'll need to transition out of my other job over the next couple of weeks, but ... I'd love to come back tomorrow afternoon and start working through these boxes."

I scratched the side of my face. I really should've shaved. I probably looked like a hobo. "Sure. That works. Do you think we'll need actual inventory software?"

That sounded expensive, but of course, I had no gauge for most of this.

Thankfully, she shook her head. "No, a spreadsheet should suffice since I'll be the only one tracking it for now. But what would be great is if you could have a list of vendors for me on all this, login info for wherever you ordered, and I'll need access to all the places you're running ads so we can make sure we're hitting all the right places. And do you have a connection with *Made in Tennessee*?"

"I ..." My head tilted to the side. "What?"

She smiled. "The visitor's bureau publication. It's called *Made in Tennessee*. We should contact their office and see about placement in their booklets and on the website."

My heavy exhale made her eyes twinkle.

"I'm not overwhelming you yet, am I?" she asked.

This ... this was a question I could answer with the utmost honesty. "Only in the very best way, I assure you."

"Good." She lifted her chin. "I don't fail, Grady. I promise."

"I feel like I should salute you right now."

She laughed. "Let's check that impulse for now, all right?"

"Yes, ma'am."

She appraised me, and I found myself standing straighter, holding her gaze in a way I probably shouldn't.

"I'll be back tomorrow at three."

"I can't wait." Another truth. Another admission, and she had no idea.

I found myself holding my breath until she was clear of the door, and it had swung shut. She walked in front of the window, looking like the queen of Green Valley for the way she held herself.

"Oh, shit," I muttered. "What the hell did I just do?"

CHAPTER 5

MAGNOLIA

*I*t was a terrible habit, one that betrayed nerves and horrible decision-making skills, but I was wringing my hands like they were a dirty dishtowel as I walked slowly through downtown.

"Oh Lord, what have I done?" I mumbled.

Mumbling.

When Magnolia MacIntyre wrung her hands and mumbled in public, it was a sad day indeed.

A young couple from church passed me, and I brightened my smile. And with all the force I could muster, I forced my fingers to unclench. "How y'all doing today?"

With his arm wrapped firmly around his wife's shoulders, he nodded. "Miss MacIntyre."

"Magnolia," the wife said, "the dress is pretty as a picture."

"Thank you, Darlene." I waved.

As our paths intersected and then diverged, I felt my body relax. That state of tension—smile pretty, be pleasing, don't give them a single

43

shred of ammunition not to like you—was a state I was very accus-tomed to. Working for my father, I didn't have much of a choice.

That was about how it felt to live in this town. People liked me despite who Daddy was. People loved my mother in the same way.

But in the safety and comfort of the home I'd been raised in, there was love. So much love. And I was about to walk into it and tell Daddy that I quit. Or ... give him my notice, if he didn't fly straight off the handle and land himself into complete irrationality.

The Chamber offices were dark. Whoever had been left behind after Candy's unexpected demise probably got the heck out of Dodge when I'd left to change before my meeting with Grady.

My smile now, thinking about that disaster of an interview, was easy and unforced. Working with him wouldn't be like working with Daddy. Underneath that fumbling charm, I got the sense that Grady was a man at ease with himself. And the idea of that was something I liked.

Unlocking the front door to the office, I found myself glancing behind me to make sure Grady wasn't out for a stroll himself. A guilty pang knocked through with the force of an out of tune church bell being hit with a sledgehammer. He wouldn't be happy with me. He might even fire me.

No. My chin lifted in determination. I was not a hand-wringing, mumbling girl who worried about getting fired because I withheld my last name in an interview. He hired me on my merits. And I'd keep that job, that low-paying job, because I was damn good at what I did.

As I walked back to my office, I kept the lights off. It was still bright enough outside that I didn't need any, and it made my life easier if I could manage to do this without any interruption.

My laptop fired up quickly as I crossed my legs under my desk. While it pulled up a new document file, I looked across my office to the framed picture of my family. Taken at my high school graduation, my diploma clutched in my hands and flanked by my parents, I was beaming.

My valedictorian speech had made the mayor cry, and my family made the most obnoxious display of whooping and yelling as I crossed that stage to move the tassel to the other side of that silly hat. They got away with it because my momma's side—the Boones—and my daddy's side—the MacIntyres—both had more money than God. No one would dare to chastise either of those families, giving my daddy a sense of power that he drank a bit too freely from, unfortunately. But no matter if he did or didn't, the smiling faces of my parents in that picture were full of pride, full of love.

My momma, in one of the rare instances I'd ever seen her dressed up in something other than jeans and a T-shirt, looked so glamorous it almost hurt. Like an actress walking a red carpet somewhere, effortless and stunning. My dad, clean-shaven at that time, was smiling so wide it seemed like his cheeks might crack open.

I sighed. This wouldn't be fun.

But my fingers flew across the keyboard, eyes focused on the screen now, because waxing nostalgic about a picture wouldn't help me.

It didn't take me long to finish, and when the printer slid the finished product into my waiting hands, I felt lighter than I had in months. Maybe even years, if I was honest.

The drive out to my parents' house probably should have filled me with dread, because as sure as Dolly Parton would be a saint in heaven someday, my daddy would lose his ever-loving mind at what I was about to tell him. But there was no band of pressure tightening inexorably around my chest. No sense of dread crawling with sticky legs up the back of my neck. Those were feelings I was accustomed to and had been for years.

In a strange way, Tucker ending our seven-year relationship was the first time I'd truly experienced that feeling of unexpected freedom from expectations. Not in a million years had I seen that coming. Because we'd planned everything out (all right, *I'd* planned everything out) from the age of seventeen, how our life would unfold together, when he saw a different path for his life, I'd been the one left blindsided.

The girl who prepared for *everything* was left stunned by a fork in the road she hadn't seen coming.

When the road curved toward my parents' house on Bandit Lake, the trees towering over me, I realized when I'd hit that fork in the road— single and surprised by it—I no longer had to conform to someone else's definition of what was right or wrong for my life, for fear of making an irreparable mistake that would somehow reflect poorly on me. That that mistake might make me look bad in the eyes of whoever decided to judge.

Even though no cars were behind me, I flipped on my blinker before I made the turn onto my parents' driveway. At the base of the gently curved driveway, the log cabin home I'd been raised in rose up like it was trying to compete with the trees around it. The peak of the roof was impressive. Maybe not in comparison to the Smokies, but it was a home that made you stop and stare nonetheless. From that angle, you couldn't see the best part, though, which was the side of the house that faced the lake and made almost entirely of windows.

Momma and Daddy paid someone to come in to clean those windows every other week because they wanted a clean, clear view of all that space they owned. People born into money, I was convinced, all had strange little quirks and foibles.

A wall of perfectly clean windows was theirs.

The house was quiet when I let myself in the front door, and I took a second to stare out all those windows. My daddy liked to tell the story that when he finally convinced my momma to marry him (after they'd been together for around fifteen years, and at the realization that they'd both enter their fortieth year on the planet as parents for the first time), she said she would as long as they lived somewhere where she felt like she was outside all the time.

I smiled because I saw her out on the end of the dock by the lake, casting her line into the smooth water. Other than the Bait and Tackle, it was the place we always knew we could find her.

Glancing down at my bright yellow dress, and then back out to her, in her standard outfit of faded jeans and a simple T-shirt, I marveled that she and I came from the same gene pool. She'd given me the color of my skin, my bone structure, and a healthy dose of her determination. Everything else was from my daddy and those etiquette classes I'd sat through.

"Magnolia," my daddy said, startling me as he appeared from down the hallway that led to their bedroom. "Didn't know you were coming by, sweetheart."

I let out a shaky breath and set the paper down on the granite, blank side facing up so that he couldn't see it.

He kissed the top of my head and opened the fridge. "Tea?"

"Please." I took a seat at one of the stools and watched as he poured two glasses of sweet tea.

"Your momma and I didn't have anything fancy planned for dinner, but if you're gonna stay, I'll whip something up."

My daddy was handsome, I thought, as I watched him peruse the contents of the fridge. His hair was dark with shades of silver growing in along his temples, his jaw strong and determined. When I was younger, I used to think that he looked like a movie star from the forties and fifties with a barrel chest, strong arms, and shoulders broad enough to carry the weight of the world.

And he had too. For both me and Momma.

"Don't go to any trouble for me." I took a sip of the tea and exhaled. Sometimes I thought sweet tea contained restorative powers.

He shook his head. "Nothing's trouble when it comes to my girls. How about breakfast for dinner? I can do pancakes and some bacon."

I closed my eyes and fiddled with the edge of the paper. "I need to talk to you about something, Daddy."

"Well, we can talk while we eat." He never pulled his gaze from the fridge. "Where you'd go this afternoon? I got out of my meeting with the mayor about the park cleanup day and your office was empty." Daddy stuck a finger in the air. "Remind me to go over the budget for that tomorrow. I told him we'd sponsor the supplies again this year, even though he promised he'd start getting donations. I told him he waited too long to get that rolling, but he never listens."

"Daddy," I interrupted smoothly. "Can you please close the fridge and look at me?"

"I could've sworn we had bacon," he mumbled. "Well, sausage will be just as good."

"Daddy."

He yanked open a drawer and pulled out a package of links, studying the package carefully. "Lord, who stamps the dates on these things? They ought to fire whoever does their quality control."

"Daddy," I snapped. "I am trying to talk to you."

His whole frame went still because I could count on one hand the number of times I'd ever raised my voice to him. I could count on one hand the number of times I'd raised my voice at anyone.

The fridge door closed quietly, and he set the sausage on the counter, his eyes assessing me. "Normally, I'd tell you to watch your tone when you address your elders, but since you don't make a habit of it, I'll let it slide."

I don't know if most people know how hard it is for a proper young woman raised in the south to hide an eye roll. We all do it in our heads, but we're taught to fight the impulse as though someone is holding

48

tight reins on our facial expressions. The mental eye roll I just executed would've gone down in record books.

But I kept my face smooth, kept it even, and I slid the paper across the counter so that he could reach it. "This is for you."

He made no move to pick it up. In fact, he didn't so much as glance at it. His eyes stayed on my face, and I knew he was trying to search out what I was doing. I might've inherited a few things from Momma, but my poker face came straight from J.T. MacIntyre.

"What is that?" he asked.

I didn't answer, simply held his gaze steadily. His cheek clenched when I didn't blink. But then again, neither did he.

"Magnolia," he said quietly, "why don't you just tell me what this is about because I don't like that look in your eye."

"Please just read it, Daddy. I could've waited to give that to you tomorrow at the office, but I decided that this would be best."

He slicked his tongue over his teeth. How he knew with surety that whatever was on that paper was something he didn't want to read, I had no idea.

The slider connected to the sprawling deck slid open, the only thing that could've broken our stalemate. Daddy's gaze landed, unerringly, onto my mother. It always did when she entered a room.

"Magnolia," she greeted quietly. "Wasn't expecting you tonight."

"Hi, Momma."

If anyone truly questioned whether my father was born without a soul, all they had to do was spend five minutes in my parents' company. It wasn't until Tucker broke up with me that I started studying my parents as carefully as I was now. I'd always taken their relationship for granted, but in the wake of my only long-term relationship ending, I saw them in a different light.

The way my daddy looked at my momma when she walked into a room was how I wanted a man to look at me. I wanted him to feel a peace so deep that it settled him down to his core when he simply shared space with me. That was what my daddy looked like right now.

And even though my mother had a quieter nature about her, she was the same way with him.

They were magnets, drawn together simply because they couldn't not be.

She walked over to Daddy, slid a hand up his chest, and kissed his cheek. He wrapped an arm around her and set his nose against her temple, drawing in a deep breath. I glanced down at the counter, feeling like an intruder on this quiet moment between them.

"What's that?" Momma asked, reaching for the paper.

I held my breath and found Daddy's gaze. "Something for Daddy."

She handed him the paper without a single glance because it wasn't in her nature to pry if we didn't ask her to.

The muscle along his jaw jumped, and he finally reached out to take the paper from her hands. He gave it a quick glance, and I held my breath.

"What the hell?" he whispered. His eyes, wide and confused, jerked up to mine. "Is this a joke?"

The paper floated to the counter, and before she picked it up, my momma's eyes moved from me to Daddy and back again.

"It's quite serious," I told him. I lifted my chin, but my insides were vibrating dangerously. The reality of quitting the job he'd given me, and the security it provided, was far scarier now that he was actually looking at the words I'd typed. I felt like a kettle set to boil without a way for the steam to escape. The water boiled and bubbled inside with nowhere to go.

"You're quitting?" he thundered.

Momma set her hand on his arm, her eyes still on the paper. Only briefly did she lift them to me, and they gave away nothing. If there was anyone in the world who could handle him, it was her, but maybe because I was ready to boil over myself, I didn't want her to. I wanted to handle this myself, without interference.

"I'm giving you my notice," I corrected. "For the next two weeks, I'll help transition Marcia to handle my duties as she's more than capable."

Marcia had worked in the Chamber office a solid ten years longer than I had, and she would take over the reins seamlessly. Not only that, but she wasn't afraid of Daddy, and that was invaluable.

"It's not Marcia's job to manage my office." He flung his hands out. "How can you do this to me, Magnolia? Is this the treatment I've earned as a father?"

"No, of course not."

My easy agreement had him pausing. His arms fell to his side.

"This comes as a result of you as a boss, not a father. You undermined me today with Candy when I was perfectly clear that I wanted to handle her. As per the chain of command in that office, it was my right as the office administrator. You took that choice away from me and opened us up to a wrongful termination lawsuit because she's only been written up once, not twice like the HR handbook mandates."

His face slowly turned redder and redder as I spoke in direct correlation to the increasing firmness of my voice.

"I have asked you so many times, Daddy. I've asked you to let me handle things as I see fit, and every time, you do whatever you want."

He slicked his tongue over his teeth again but didn't respond. Maybe because Momma still had her hand on his arm.

Carefully, she set the paper down, gave my father a long look, and then glanced back at me. Again, I marveled at the inscrutability of that gaze. Maybe the poker face came from both of them.

When he still didn't speak, I kept going, the words I'd practiced in the car flowing easily now. "It's past time for me to try something new, and I think you know that. I can't keep crafting a life for myself in the confines of what you say is acceptable."

"Try something new?" he asked. "You have a new job already?"

That tone was as dangerous as a coiled snake, and I probably should have sidestepped. But I tipped up my chin, met his gaze, and nodded.

"Who hired you?"

"Someone awfully smart, considering how damn good at my job I've been," I snapped.

"Don't you sass me, young lady." I saw the wheels in his head start to turn. "You're not working at the Lodge, are you?"

"It's no one you know, so you can quit trying to figure it out."

His eyes widened. "No one I know? Impossible."

My mom's eyes narrowed thoughtfully.

"They paying you more?" he asked.

Of course, he thought it was about money. But the answer was no. Not even close. Grady's opening salary, and my ability to accept it, was resting solely on the fact that I'd crafted myself a budget at the age of sixteen and stuck with it religiously. Dave Ramsey should've taken lessons from me.

"That's none of your concern."

"None of my concern?" His tone was sheer incredulity. "I'm your father, Magnolia. Everything I've done for the past twenty-six years has been out of my concern for you, to make sure you've got a good life."

"How am I ever supposed to know what's good and right *for me* if everything's dictated by you?"

"I'm not dictating your life, Magnolia. You chose what you went to school for. You chose where you went to school. You chose that house you live in."

"You gave me lists, Daddy. Lists of majors, and lists of colleges and neighborhoods and homes, and yes, I got to pick from those, but that's hardly freedom."

"Look around this place, young lady." He swept an arm out, to the home that housed our family, the land they owned, the view that unrolled in front of us like a beautifully crafted painting. "Your mother and I built this life with our bare hands, but we didn't turn our noses up at the support of our families either."

A laugh burst out of me, startling them both. I couldn't help but gape. "Are you trying to be funny? Is this a joke? You two didn't listen to a damn thing anyone had to say about your life, or your relationship, or how you should or shouldn't do things." I leaned forward. "And I love that about you. No one—not your family, Momma, or your family, Daddy—kept you two from being together."

That softened him, just slightly. But the hurt in his eyes almost killed me.

Theirs was the bedtime story I was raised on, instead of princesses locked in a tower, waiting to be rescued. My parents were almost forty when I came into the world, and as he told it to me, he'd asked my momma to marry him at least a hundred times in the fifteen years leading up to the positive pregnancy test. Sometimes, he said two hundred, and the truth was that I wouldn't have doubted it if that turned out to be the case.

When you had a woman from one of the wealthiest Black families in town and a man from one of the wealthiest white families in town, both of those families were relieved every time Bobby Jo Boone turned down J.T. MacIntyre. But what he saw in my momma, from the first time he took her out on a fishing date and she caught a bass three times the size of his own, he knew in his gut that he'd love her for the rest of his life. According to him, she knew it too. She just liked to play coy since everything else in his life came easily.

And it was the hundred and first time he asked (or two hundred and first, depending on the telling) when she finally said yes. Their marriage blazed a trail as the first interracial marriage that Green Valley had ever seen. Even though the Boones and the MacIntyres would've both picked different partners for their kids, they embraced the new family immediately.

When I came into the world at six pounds and nine ounces, with a shock of black hair, I was the jewel on the top of their crown, according to my daddy. And he'd never let me forget that. Not in how he treated me or the people who dared cross me.

"Daddy," I said wearily, "you and Momma walked down that aisle with your middle fingers waving, and you know it. You never let anyone tell you that you shouldn't marry her because she was black. And Momma did the same to you. So, don't tell me that I haven't earned the right to do the same thing in this world, simply because you've erected some sort of shield around my very existence."

I stood, and he watched me with careful, suspiciously shiny eyes.

"I'm not trying to keep you from the world, Magnolia," he said, voice gruff. "But I can't protect you when I'm not around."

"I don't need you to protect me. I need you to trust me. Trust that I know what's right for me."

He opened his mouth, but Momma slid her hand over his. "Let her go, J.T.," she said softly.

A shaky exhale of relief escaped my mouth, because as much as I loved my momma, and I did, we didn't often find ourselves agreeing on things. For the handful of physical features she gave me, our personalities were night and day different. She'd spend all her time outdoors, fishing rod in hand, if given the choice. And while I respected that about her, it didn't always leave room for a strong maternal instinct.

But this was a moment I needed her to take my side, and my heart beat erratically that she had.

I came around the corner and gave her a brief hug, which she returned with a brief squeeze of her lithe, strong arms.

Daddy was staring down at the counter, like he didn't dare look at me. The color was still high in his cheeks, and I found myself tearing up, simply because he was wearing his hurt like a neon sign.

It was unfathomable to J.T. MacIntyre that I might crave something outside of the life he built for me.

But I did.

"I love you, Daddy," I whispered.

He wrapped me up in a fierce hug that stole my breath, and I pinched my eyes shut against the warmth of his chest.

"Love you more," he said into my hair. "Now go before I change my mind about allowing this."

Since no one could see my face, and something about small rebellions felt right, I rolled my eyes.

CHAPTER 6

GRADY

*T*oday would be better.

Today, I would not look like a fool.

I parked my car in an open spot by the curb and took a deep breath. I'd hardly slept the night before, so while I might not look like a fool, I had dark circles under my eyes that couldn't be hidden.

What was I supposed to do? My whole body was a giant mass of nerves and anticipation.

It was her. I was going to go to work and see her every single day while trying not to make an idiot of myself when I'd generally never had a problem with the opposite sex.

With one last glimpse of myself in the rearview mirror, I just had to hope she didn't ask why I looked hungover as hell. Imagining my answer was an exercise in misery. "Oh, no, I didn't have a single drop of alcohol last night. I laid in bed, thinking of you, how I can find out every single fascinating detail about you, earn your heart and your respect, while starting a successful business and trying to figure out if you're going to fall in love with me in the process or if I'm doomed to love you from afar for the rest of my life."

I groaned, dropping my forehead onto the steering wheel. This was awful.

I'd avoided all contact with my family the night before because I couldn't handle a single *I told you so* moment when they realized that I'd no longer be able to write off the Buchanan curse as bullshit.

Oh, it was bullshit, all right.

Heart-shredding, start-writing-poetry-about-her-eyes-and-her-lips, soul-too-big-for-my-body-because-all-it-wanted-was-her bullshit.

Resolutely, I lifted my head from the steering wheel and stared at the front of the office space.

I was more than capable of managing this.

Every member of my family had experienced these feelings, and no one had died from them yet. If Lia was my perfect match, then I didn't need a pep talk from Grace, or my cousin Levi, or anyone else. All I needed to do was calm down, be patient, and know that anything that was good and worthwhile in life was worth being patient for.

Just as I had that thought and felt the calm certainty of it, I saw her walking down the street. There was no bright yellow dress today, but I smiled at her outfit all the same. *Southern belle does unpacking in a dusty office* had a whole different vibe to it than anything I was used to from California girls.

Instead of jeans and a T-shirt like I was wearing, she was wearing bright pink slacks that hugged her curves. Around her feet were bright yellow heels with a thin strap around her ankles. Her shirt was a loose white blouse covered in small pink flowers that she'd tucked into the front of her pants. Her dark hair was twisted up in an elaborate knot, and around her head, she'd knotted a white and pink handkerchief.

She looked like Rosie the Riveter, if she'd dressed in pastels.

My heart turned in a backflip, and I rubbed at the spot on my chest, willing it to calm down.

Before she beat me to the door, which was still locked, I grabbed the spare key I'd had made for her at the hardware store and hopped out of my car. "Hey," I called out.

She stopped, shading her eyes from the sun. "Afternoon."

A tractor rumbled down the street, and the man driving it gave us both a lazy wave.

I jogged across the street once the behemoth had passed between her and me. "Still not used to seeing stuff like that," I said, hooking a thumb over my shoulder at the tractor.

"Y'all came from California, right?"

I nodded. "Yeah. My mom is still outside LA."

She peered at my face. "Must be quite a change. Do you miss it?"

I fell in step beside her as we approached the office. "Not really." I pushed the key in the lock and held the door open for her. "After you."

Her smile was sweet and quick, and I felt another telltale flip in my heart. I liked that smile. If this kept going, I'd have to start a log in my phone of all the different ways her lips curled up and the things they told me about her.

"I miss my mom," I continued, flipping on the overhead lights. "Miss some of the restaurants. But I hated so much about LA. The traffic. The smog. The traffic."

She laughed.

"I'd sit behind my computer every day at work, no window to look out, and feel like I was trapped in a cage. I'd sit in my car for hours on the drive home on my way to an apartment that was hemmed in on every side by other buildings." Where these words came from, I wasn't even sure. I found myself leaning up against the wall, admitting my unhappiness to someone other than Grace, and it was happening so easily, I could hardly believe it. It was the kind of stuff I never said out loud except for a random joke here or there. I shook my head. "That's why I haven't been in here yet today. I woke up and found myself wanting to spend some time in the mountains."

"You sound like my momma," she said. Setting her purse on the edge of the desk, she perched a hip there. "She'd spend all her time outdoors if she could too."

"Yeah?"

Her answering nod was slow, and she stared out the window, her eyes unfocused. "When they drew up the plans for their house, my daddy put in as many windows as he could facing the mountains and trees because then she could still feel like she was outside, even when she wasn't."

I hummed. "Sounds like he loves her a lot."

She blinked, standing abruptly from the desk. "He sure does." Then she clapped her hands. "All right, if you've got a box cutter, let's open these up and get moving. They won't unpack themselves."

The abrupt end of the conversation had my head spinning a bit, but I guess normal people took time before jumping into the 'tell me all your thoughts' portion of a workplace relationship.

"Uhh, yeah. In that middle drawer. I think."

Again, she laughed as she took a seat at the desk chair and opened the drawer. Instead of the box cutter, she pulled out a butterscotch candy. "Now ... this is not what I expected to find."

My face went warm. "Yeah, I keep those everywhere. They're my favorite."

"That cannot be true," she said. "These are no one's favorite. They're the candy you grumble about when you go trick-or-treating as a kid."

I leaned over and snatched one. "Unless you're me and have excellent taste." Unwrapping the candy, I popped it in my mouth and hummed happily. "Help yourself."

She shook her head and pulled out the box cutter. "That's quite all right, thank you."

"How do you want to do this, oh mistress of the spreadsheets?"

Her face lit with a pleased smile, and if I hadn't been so enamored with the change it brought to her already beautiful face, then maybe I'd have reacted quicker when she tossed the box cutter in my direction. Instead, I was staring at her like a goon, so I didn't even attempt to catch it. The box cutter hit me square in the middle of my chest and clattered to the floor.

I stared down at it. "Right."

Lia covered her laughter with a conspicuous cough. "You open, I'll enter it in, and for now, just label the box with what it is so we can figure out a shelving configuration once I know what we're dealing with."

My thumb pushed the razor out on the top of the cutter, and I sliced open the first box. "Just shelves? I wasn't sure if you'd want racks for shirts or anything."

She flipped open a MacBook and typed efficiently, then she pulled out a Bluetooth mouse from her bag and clicked a few times. I may have left my tech job behind, but if watching her maneuver through software was not the sexiest fucking thing I'd ever seen, I didn't know what was.

She was like a flower, blooming bright and pretty, in the middle of the concrete-colored office space, sitting at a drab desk and chair, on top of drab floors. Almost like I'd picked everything about this boring space simply to highlight how beautiful she was.

"I don't think we'll want racks," she said, eyes still on her screen. "If customers get apparel, it'd be nice to have it still in the wrapping so they know it's clean and unused." She glanced at me. "But we don't need to talk about that yet because I'm still trying to figure out where you'll be getting those corporate clients."

"Yes, ma'am." I grinned and tore into the first box, then started listing off what I had. "Four medium long-sleeve windbreakers. Four large, four extra-large."

She tsked her tongue as she typed that in. "Now what do you need all those windbreakers for, Grady Buchanan?"

"I love that southern tongue cluck." I kept the piles neat, and then read off the next few items in the box. "I've got big plans, Lia. I know it probably doesn't seem like it now."

Her eyes flicked to mine over the top of the computer. "Let's hear 'em."

"Two pairs of men's hiking boots, size ten," I told her, flattening the first box and tossing it behind me. "When I was still in LA, we used to do these awful team-building days. They were cheesy and expensive for the company to put together, and figuring out the logistics was always a pain in the ass for the person in charge. Trust falls and 'stand in a circle and let's share your feelings.' Wouldn't you rather call a company that can pick up your employees from work, and you can spend the day out in the fresh air and sunshine, learning about the outdoors, and learn from each other how to navigate the wilderness? Maybe it's a daylong hike. Maybe it's a camping trip for a couple of nights."

She was quiet, and her fingers had temporarily paused their fast-paced tapping.

"It's a good idea," she said after another moment. "Takes time to build up regular clients, though."

"It does," I agreed. "Two pairs of women's hiking boots, size seven, and two in size eight."

After adding those, she got up from the desk to pick up the newly flattened boxes I'd been tossing to the side, sliding them between the wall and the desk where they'd be out of the way.

My grin couldn't be helped.

She picked her way through the boxes, back to her seat at the desk. "There's not much of a tourism industry in Green Valley. People who come here are visiting a friend or visiting family. Maybe driving through and stopping for lunch at Daisy's on their way to Gatlinburg or Knoxville or Nashville."

"There's so much good hiking and fishing," I said. "People *should* visit here."

"Not much in the way of lodging to build up that kind of business. You've got to have cabins like Gatlinburg, hotels, that sort of thing. Green Valley is an accidental stop if you catch it on the way to your destination."

"Maybe that's why my ads haven't done much," I heard myself say. "I thought it would be easier to get bookings at first, get some cash flow while I built up corporate clients."

"People who live here," she said quietly, leaning back in the chair as she watched me unpack some more boots, "they don't need anyone to tell them what hikes are good and what aren't, nobody to point out trees and flowers. But people renting all those cabins in Gatlinburg should hear why they can take a day trip out to a small town, do some beautiful hiking, eat some delicious, locally made food from Donner Bakery, and get a break from the tourist traps that overflow with people every year. Breathe in the mountain air away from the crowds while on your favorite hikes because the love you have for all that space you were missing, that's what'll make them talk about it when they go back home to the concrete prison you left behind."

As she spoke, my hands slowed their movements, and I found myself relaxing with each word that came out of her mouth. I wanted to hear

63

her voice every single day for the rest of my life.

Something elemental happened in my body when I listened to her. A poet, I wasn't. Nor had I ever considered myself a romantic. But as I watched her lips, full and soft-looking, form each word, I felt soothed. Comforted. A hand running down the back of my neck and calming anything tense that was being held in my muscles.

"Tell me about your favorite place," I said. "Where would you take people so they could talk about it when they left?"

Her face gave away surprise at my question. I hadn't even thought before asking it. Probably because it wasn't a 'new boss' kind of question.

Her eyebrows, those dark, graceful arcs over her expressive eyes, bent in for a moment. "Oh, I don't think it would interest anyone all that much."

I kept my answer simple, because really ..., that's all I could do at that point. I was as much of a stranger to her as she was to me, and I wanted that to change. With one question, one answer at a time, we'd get to know each other.

So, I told her the truth. "I'm interested."

Her eyes locked onto mine when I said it, and for a millisecond, I saw the question buried there.

"My home," she answered with a shy smile. "It's my favorite place in the world."

"Why?"

She didn't answer right away, and I unpacked another box while she typed in the contents.

"It's one of the few spaces that's mine," she said. "The yard isn't big, but I have some flowers that I've managed to grow. And I don't have to try to please anyone else with what's inside those walls."

Resting an arm on my bent knee, I leaned my head against the concrete pillar and listened to her answer. I wanted to ask all about it but curbed that impulse. Just barely. "How long have you lived there?"

She smiled. "Five years." Her eyes flicked to the next box, and I took the hint, opening it slowly before telling her what was inside. "Where are you staying since you got here?" she asked.

"Not a place that's my own," I said with a dry smile. "My aunt and uncle have a converted garage apartment on their property. It's small, but it does the trick. And it's hard to argue with a rent-free bed."

"They're good people," she murmured. "Fran and Robert are. Your daddy too."

While she typed, I was able to watch her facial expressions. "It's so odd to me how everyone knows everyone."

She paused, giving a meaningful lift to her eyebrows. "Small town."

I laughed, sliding the next flattened box onto the pile she started.

"You'll get used to it," she promised.

"Will I?"

"Eventually."

"How well do you know my pops?" I asked. Maybe I could ask him about her.

"Not all that well." Her smile dimmed, just a touch. "I think you've asked me more questions just now than you did in the entire interview, Grady."

I laughed easily. "I wasn't ready for you yesterday, that's for sure."

Again, it was the truth. She just didn't know exactly what truth that was.

CHAPTER 7

MAGNOLIA

I wasn't wrong often when it came to strategic business patronage within the city limits.

The reason I decided to get coffees for Grady and me at Donner Bakery was because I knew the likelihood of running into some of my extended family members were much higher out at Daisy's, given that my aunt owned it. My uncle ate there for breakfast every single morning, and he was just the first on a huge list of possible suspects who'd hound me about Daddy the second they saw me.

But my choice of location hadn't made much difference. The whispers inside Donner Bakery started the moment I walked through the doors.

My smile turned on, polite and sweet and *you just whisper your hearts out because I'm not bothered in the slightest.*

"Connie," I said as I passed the first table. "How's that grandbaby doing?"

"Just fine, Miss MacIntyre," she answered. Her eyes looked me up and down, searching for ... flaws? Who knew? Maybe a blinking sign that'd explain why I quit working for my daddy because if that wasn't what they were whispering about, I'd eat my favorite pink leather Marc Jacobs purse. "I saw your daddy at the Eager Beaver." She clucked her tongue. "He feeling all right?"

I laid my hand on her shoulder. That color of red really did nothing for her complexion. "Aren't you sweet for asking? He's as healthy as a horse."

She hummed. "I'm so glad to hear it. I thought maybe he'd been ill. He just looked so exhausted. Like he hadn't slept in days."

This time when I smiled, I imagined what it would feel like to rip that fake hairclip off her head because we all knew she'd been wearing it since 2005. Connie took the saying "the higher the hair, the closer to God" a bit too literally if you asked me.

"I'll be sure to let him know you were worried."

Her blue eyes searched my face. "You do that. Nice seeing you, Magnolia."

I wiggled my fingers at her daughter, who gave me a pained, uncomfortable smile in return. *Yes, your mother was a passive-aggressive busybody, and I'd be embarrassed if I were you too.*

Only a southern woman could convey all that in a finger wave.

I stepped into line and took a deep breath. My daddy had avoided the office the past two days that I'd stopped in to work with Marcia. Bless her, she hadn't asked me any questions about why I was doing what I was doing, just patted my back and listened carefully while we went over some things. The two weeks I'd given him wouldn't even be necessary for my transition out because half of what I went over with Marcia, she already knew.

Managing the allocation of the funds that went back into city improvements and events was the only piece she'd never dealt with, so we spent the most time on it. And while I'd kept my head down at the office with Marcia, all of Green Valley had been whispering my name.

If anyone knew I was working with Grady Buchanan at the newly minted Valley Adventures, they hadn't shown up at the office to gawk. As I waited in line to grab some coffee and a few treats for the two of us, I found myself excited to get back to the boring gray office.

He'd mentioned offhandedly that we should paint the place, and I loved the idea that this new venture could bear my stamp. It was easy to envision masculine colors on the walls to match the logo he'd had drawn up.

A table and some comfortable chairs up by the window where customers could sit and chat if they stopped by to book something. Hardcover books about Tennessee wildlife lining a bookshelf next to it. Maybe even a mural in blue and green tones with the majestic profile of the Smokies to cover our walls.

The last time I'd been able to daydream about anything like this was probably back in high school, and I wanted to snatch the feeling to my chest and protect it.

I was still smiling happily when it was my turn at the counter. Joy smiled brightly in return. "Magnolia, you look like you brought the sunshine in all by yourself today."

"Thank you, Joy," I said. I touched a hand to my yellow cardigan, probably my favorite article of clothing. "Would you believe my Mawmaw Boone crocheted this back in the seventies?"

She shook her head. "It looks brand new."

"She made it for my momma when she was high school," I told her with a smile, "but my momma never wore it on account it was too easy to get a fishing hook snagged on the design, so it sat in her closet until I found it three years ago."

"Well"—Joy sighed—"it makes you look like spring itself." Her smile brightened again. "What can I get for you this morning?"

I leaned over to look at the case, unsure of what Grady might like. Then again, he was a man. And the way he towered over me with all that lean, lanky muscle, he could probably eat half the baked goods in here and not gain an ounce. "Why don't you bag up a couple of those wild blueberry muffins, and I'll take two medium coffees. One black and one with a splash of cream and two sugars, please."

Her eyes gleamed speculatively at my order, but Joy was too sweet and too polite to ask who I was buying for.

Maxine Barton had no such filter, unfortunately. She pushed her walker up next to me and watched Joy work over the rim of her glasses. "Two coffees, eh? You trying to smooth things over with your daddy, or is that for someone else?"

"Maxine, you never did master the art of subtlety, did you?" I asked good-naturedly. Unlike Connie, who was still watching me like a hawk, Maxine wasn't prying to be able to spread her newfound information around town. She was just happier knowing everyone's business and keeping it to herself like a pot of treasure she'd stumbled on.

"Subtlety is about as useless to me as unsweetened tea." She studied my face. "You sure pissed him off, didn't you?"

When I glanced over my shoulder, every set of eyes I could see was watching our exchange, and I sighed. "Is this what everyone else in town feels like when they've made him mad?"

"Yup."

"Wonderful," I said under my breath. She heard me, though, because Maxine Barton had the hearing of a bat.

"He'll get over it." When Joy approached the counter with my items, Maxine handed her some cash before I could protest. "Let me get this for you, Magnolia."

"Awfully kind of you." I took the drink holder from Joy and tucked the bag of muffins into my purse. "You certainly didn't have to."

"Of course I did. First of all, you had the good Christian nature to stay and talk to Connie and not stare at the dead cat hair she wears on her head and calls an updo. Second, standing up to your daddy takes more guts than half this town has, young lady. He might worship the ground you and your momma walk on, but that doesn't mean he doesn't need his head yanked out of his ass on occasion."

I exhaled a shocked laugh, because on the one hand, I still had to stifle the urge to defend him. I'd defended him my entire life because his first instinct was to steamroll anyone and anything who might stand in Momma's or my way. But on the other hand, having someone recognize my gesture for what it was did something strange to my heart.

A part of me wanted to earn the respect of people like Maxine. Or their notice, at least, in a way that I'd never had it simply by doing whatever Daddy had planned for me. News of me working for Grady, and the inevitable complications that it would bring with Tucker and Grace, still wasn't common knowledge. Once it was, the whispers would start for a whole new reason, but I'd be prepared for that.

"Thank you, Miss Barton." I lifted the coffees. "For these and the compliment. Change isn't always easy, is it?"

She hummed. "Wait until you're as old as me. Then you won't give two solitary shits what anyone thinks about what you do." She tapped a finger on my arm. "You care right now because you're young, and your family gave you whatever you wanted, and your whole life, everyone has watched what you're going to do next."

We stepped out of the line so the person behind me could place their order, and I nodded slowly. "They certainly have."

It was never easy to swallow the bitter pill of someone reminding you that you'd been spoiled rotten. But I had been. By the MacIntyres, by the Boones, and most of all, by my parents in their own way. Momma spoiled me by never interfering, never imposing her will onto me even though we were so different, and because of that, I never had to fight with her on what I wanted. She was forty when I was born and already set in the way she wanted to live her life.

And Daddy spoiled me by smoothing out any obstacle in my way. Tucker used to tell me that all the time, that I'd have a hard time with reality if it ever intruded, after being raised as a Southern princess in both of those families.

Maybe reality hadn't quite intruded yet, but I liked to think I was stepping out into it on my own accord. Figuring out what it meant. And if this exchange with Maxine proved anything, it was that I still had a ways to go.

"You have a good day, Magnolia," she told me. "They'll find someone else to whisper about soon enough."

"Yes, ma'am."

The bell on the door jingled happily when I exited onto the street and started toward the office. It was a cloudy day, and the wind zipped right through my cardigan. I shivered when I thought of the coat I'd left in my car. My hair slid into my face because it was down today. I'd washed it last night, deciding to iron it out for the first time since Tucker broke up with me.

I felt pretty.

And that was a dangerous sensation as I took light, quick steps toward work and Grady.

I was no fool, and the look in his eye when he told me he was interested couldn't be mistaken for anything other than what he meant.

Grady Buchanan was attracted to me.

And today when I'd dressed to go back to the office, there was a foreign feeling swirling at the base of my belly when I pulled the bright yellow cardigan from the back of my closet. When I slid it over my white silk tank and stepped into the dark pants that made my behind look like one of God's most glorious creations.

The swirling was anticipation, not because I was ready for anything with anyone, but because a wonderful feeling accompanied when someone's eyes lit with appreciation when you walked into a room. Even if his appreciation was based in gratitude because I was helping him, it was a balm to my soul after what happened with Tucker.

As I approached, I could see lights on in the office but no sign of Grady. The door swung open before I had a chance to grab it, and there he was with a wide, bright smile on his handsome face.

"Great minds," he said by way of greeting.

I set the drink holder down on the desk and started laughing. Next to the coffees from Donner Bakery was a similar drink holder holding two coffees from Daisy's Nut House along with a neatly folded paper bag, which probably held something sugary and sweet and delicious.

"Well, we won't go hungry."

He snatched the bag from Daisy's and opened it. "Let's see who did a better job of picking the treats." With a flourish, he produced a donut wrapped in crinkly paper. "I don't want to brag, but I feel fairly confident in my choice. I present to the judges an eggnog donut brushed with bourbon butter and covered in spiced sugar."

I sighed heavily. "I cannot compete with that." Digging into my purse, I pulled out the bag from Donner Bakery. "So, I'll just keep the wild blueberry muffins to myself then. They're still warm, I believe, and topped with a cinnamon crumb streusel."

The skin outside of his eyes crinkled when he smiled, and I liked that telltale sign that showed he did it often. "I think we can call this one a draw."

I handed him a muffin and took the eggnog donut. As I took my first bite and tried not to emit a desperate, wholly unladylike moan at my first taste of the donut, I had to fight the urge to tell him that he'd probably seen a dozen of my family members that morning when he stood in line for some of Daisy's deliciousness.

I glanced around the office. He'd made excellent progress in the two days I'd been gone. The shelves I ordered from Merryville were already up and lined up neatly in the back.

"Shelves look wonderful," I told him. "Sorry I wasn't here to help."

"No problem." Before he dug into his muffin, he hefted a heavy box into his arms, the rounded curve of his bicep flexing wonderfully underneath his shirt. When he lifted it up onto the top shelf, the hem of his shirt lifted, and I caught a glimpse of a flat, muscular stomach and a line of dark hair disappearing into the dark waistband above the line of his jeans that had my face feeling hot.

"Lord have mercy," I murmured.

Grady turned with a grin. "The donut?" he asked.

"Mm-hmm."

He snatched the baked good I'd brought for him and finished half of it in one wolfish bite. Grady did not hold back his groan. "Amazing."

Grady wiped his hands on his dark jeans, and I stifled a smile at the streusel crumbs he had stuck to the golden stubble lining his jawline. He glanced down. "What?"

"Nothing."

"It's something. You're trying not to laugh at me." He patted his shirt. "Did I spill something?"

"I don't think you chewed that muffin long enough for anything to hit the ground," I teased, then made a vague gesture at his face. "You've just got a little stuck ... on your jaw."

His cheeks flushed as he wiped it away. "Ahh. Yeah, I've always been a fast eater. Drives my sister crazy. I'll have my meal finished before she's finished with her third bite."

The casual reminder of Grace had me turning away from him. What was it about this whole thing that made it so easy for me to forget how much I still had to tell him? I took a deep breath and thought about what I wanted to say.

Grady, I have something a little crazy to tell you, but I think it'll be fine.

Grady, please don't fire me, but I spent the past seven years of my life and all my formative early adult years with your sister's boyfriend, but I promise it won't get awkward.

The next bite of donut stuck in my throat like cardboard. I couldn't leave today without telling him. I just ... had to make sure the timing was right.

"I thought if you wanted to work on some ads today and getting some new targets like we talked about, that would be great. And maybe work up some package descriptions for guided hikes that include a picnic lunch. I'm going to fill those shelves before I go do a hike. I think it would be good for younger families or inexperienced hikers."

I nodded. "That sounds just fine."

He waited until I looked back at him to speak again. "Wanna come with me?"

My answer came out before I could even question it. "Not even if you quadrupled my pay."

Grady's smile broadened, and I saw a hint of a dimple. "That so? Not much of a hiker, huh?"

With an embarrassed laugh, I tucked a piece of hair behind my ear. "Ah, no. Me and the outdoors"—I waved toward the window—"we don't go together so well."

"Someday," he murmured, "someday I'll get you out on a trail. I think we can find something to your speed."

"Well, it won't be today," I told him and lifted one foot behind me. "Not in these shoes."

Grady pointed at the shelves. "I've got boots."

I gave him a long, loaded look, and he was chuckling the whole time he walked back toward the shelves. I took a seat at the desk, which was much neater than it had been the first day, and pulled my laptop out of my purse. While it booted up, I took a sip of the coffee he'd brought me. My lips curled in a smile, because somehow, he'd picked the same one that I would've bought for myself and had from Donner Bakery. Black with a splash of cream and a couple of sugars.

"Oh," he piped up, his head sticking out from behind the first row of shelves. "There's a convention in Nashville in a couple of weeks for outdoor retailers, and I thought it would be good to go meet some vendors. You up for a company road trip?"

Something was entirely too infectious about Grady Buchanan's energy. Joy had told me earlier that I had brought the sunshine with me, but he was the one who seemed to harness its power.

For some reason, that made it even harder to imagine admitting my duplicity. I knew it would dim some of that powerful spirit. My momma would probably be going to that convention or sending someone from the Bait and Tackle, at the very least. Where his daddy worked. For my mother.

"Sounds great," I told him weakly. His head disappeared back behind the shelf again, and he started whistling along to whatever music he had playing over a Bluetooth speaker in the back.

A car slowed in front of the office, the sun glinting off the side mirror, and my heart stopped when I saw who was driving.

Grace Buchanan.

Just like everyone else in town, I knew they'd gone out to California so that Tucker could meet Grace's momma, and for some reason, I hadn't even thought about the fact she'd stop by and see her brother as soon as she returned. I stood from the desk so fast that the chair clattered backward.

"You okay?" Grady asked.

I rubbed my forehead and set the chair back to rights. "Yeah, just ... need the restroom. Stood too fast is all."

Walking past him, I struggled not to sprint back to the safety of the small room. I refused to look at his concerned face because even that one pause could spell disaster for me.

Just as I was pulling the door shut behind me, I heard Grace walk in through the front.

I clicked the lock shut and sank against the cold metal with a groan. "Oh Magnolia, you have got yourself in a pickle now," I whispered miserably.

CHAPTER 8

GRADY

"Well holy shit, what miracle happened in this place?" Grace asked. She'd barely made it in through the front door when she jerked to a stop, set her hands on her hips, and gawked at the organized glory that was now Valley Adventures.

I adjusted a fake tie and waltzed toward her. "Not too shabby, huh?"

She nodded. "I'm impressed. It actually looks legit in here."

After she leaned over for a hug, I ruffled her hair. It earned me a narrowing of her eyes, which made me laugh. "Welcome back. Just get home?"

"Yeah. Tucker had to go into the law office to help his dad with something that came up with a big case, so I decided to come make fun of your mess again"—she turned in a slow circle, arms extended—"but lo and behold, you've stolen my thunder."

I scratched the side of my face. "I wish I could take all the credit, but I finally got some help."

Her eyes landed on the coffee and bakery bags. "How many people did you hire?"

"Just one," I said around a smile. "We both decided to be nice and bring caffeine and sugar this morning."

"Mom said to send you this." She slugged me in the shoulder.

"Ouch," I muttered. "What was that for?"

Grace peered around the space. "Because you suck at calling the woman who birthed us."

"I've been a little busy."

"Mom was good, thank you for asking. She loved Tucker, who has now replaced you in her heart."

I rolled my eyes.

Her fingers touched the edge of the pink leather purse sitting on the corner of the desk. "Whoever you hired has excellent taste."

I wanted to sigh like a moron when I thought of telling Grace about everything that had happened in the short week since she left. The words crowded into my mouth, but I swallowed them down because with Lia just a dozen or so feet away in the bathroom, it wasn't the time or place to tell Grace.

"It's been working out well so far. She's still wrapping up at her old job, but I think she's exactly what this place needed."

Grace's eyes sharpened as she watched me talk.

"What?"

Then they narrowed. "What's up with you?"

My shoulders rolled, trying to release some of the tension at her scrutiny. Twins were the worst. "Nothing, why?"

"You're being weird."

"How am I being weird? You've been in here for less than two minutes, and I've hardly said anything!"

"Exactly."

That was the problem, wasn't it? I wanted to say something. I wanted to tell my twin sister, my best friend, that I met her. Met the one.

And she was smart. Driven. Gorgeous beyond belief. She had good taste in muffins and treated her laptop like it was her prized possession. She was refined, but underneath it, I got the sense she craved to shed that Southern belle image like a snake shed its skin.

But my sister would never be able to hide her feelings about it, even if I managed to get my story out before Lia returned from the bathroom. Grace would study her like a specimen, inspect her from head to toe, pepper her with questions, and try to decide if she was good enough for her brother.

"Soooo, where is the owner of the beautiful purse?" Grace asked. "Since you're not going to tell me why you're acting like this."

I threw out my arms. "I'm not acting like anything! I just didn't know you'd be stopping by, and we were trying to get some work done." I sighed because I did, in fact, sound like a crazy person. "She's using the bathroom."

Grace hummed. "Fine, I'll leave you alone. But I'm not happy about it."

"And that brings me great joy." This time, I blocked her punch before it landed. I pinched behind her arm, which she hated about as much as I hated her punching me. "You're so violent. How does Tucker put up with your bullshit?"

She smiled sweetly. "I keep him exceptionally happy in bed."

"Out." I pointed at the door. "Get. Out. Now."

Grace flipped me her middle finger on her way out the door, and I sank into the chair. Generations of Buchanans before me had navigated this insanity just fine, but that didn't really make me feel better. All week, I'd thought about her. Replaying our conversations, I tried to glean something new and important about her from what I remembered.

But the truth was that it wasn't about getting to know her. That was the easy part, especially once we were seeing each other every day. The hard part was that she worked for me. It wasn't as simple as asking her out on a date because I wanted to, even if she seemed interested too.

I stared at her purse while I thought about that. What if she wasn't interested?

My cousin Levi waited five years before his friendship with Joss turned romantic even though he loved her the entire time.

Grace didn't have to wait nearly that long to be with Tucker, but when she moved to town, he was still in a long-term relationship. Nothing happened between them until Tucker broke that off and sent the whole damn town into upheaval. None of it had been easy on Grace while she waited patiently for all that to resolve.

I hadn't understood it when she kept defending Tucker. Kept defending their decision to keep it quiet. But I understood it now. It's easy to stand on the outside of someone else's relationship and say you'd do something different. That you'd conduct yourself correctly, that you'd never let anyone keep you from your happiness.

No wonder Grace punched me all the time. What an unsympathetic dick I'd been to her. Here I sat, less than a week as Lia's boss, and I had no idea how to function with these feelings. Leave it to me not to just ... tell her I'd call her back and let her know about the job. If I'd taken even one day to think it over, I would have known that hiring her would only box me into this immovable space where asking her out was not an option for serious consideration.

I came from LA. Abusing the dynamic of power in the workplace was nothing to joke about, and I was the last guy who'd ever force a woman.

Bracing my elbows on the desk, I speared my fingers through my hair and took a few deep breaths. When I opened my eyes, I saw her keys sitting next to her pink bag. There was a matching leather tag attached to the key ring, embossed with a giant M.

My finger traced the edges.

Then I laughed. I didn't even know her last name.

"What a joke I am," I whispered.

I'd hired her for a few valid reasons, yes, but holy shit, Tucker had every right to ream my ass over this. I'd lucked out that she was actually as good at this stuff as she'd said.

Sitting back in the chair, I dangled the keys off one finger and stared at the M. The bathroom door opened, and I heard her steps approaching from behind. I turned with a smile, and she stopped dead in her tracks, eyes frozen on the keys in my hand.

"Oh, sorry," I said, setting them back on the desk. "Not trying to pry."

Liar.

She tried to smile, but it came out more like a grimace. "It's ... fine."

With a vague gesture toward the keychain, I gave her a self-depre-cating smile. "Just marveling that I hired someone, and I don't even know your last name. Pretty impressive actually."

Her eyes were so big in her face as she watched me that she actually looked a little lost.

My head tilted. "Are you okay?"

"I have to tell you something," she whispered unsteadily.

I was out of the chair before I knew what I was doing, my hands gently gripping her upper arms. "Seriously, are you feeling okay? Here, take a seat."

When she was in the chair, hands rubbing the tops of her thighs, I crouched in front of her. "Do you feel lightheaded?"

She shook her head. "No, no, it's not that. I feel fine." Her hand swept over her face. "Well, I don't ... I feel awful but not physically."

When she dropped her hand, she looked at me in a way that I didn't really understand. It was a pleading look, when there was no way she could have known that I would've given her whatever she wanted.

What I wanted was to soothe her, lay my hands on top of hers so that she knew it would be okay, whatever was bothering her, but I made sure to hold myself back when I spoke. "You can tell me, whatever it is."

"Grady, I—" Her voice caught on whatever was going to come next. She took a deep breath, closed her eyes, and when she opened them, it was like she flipped a switch. "I have something to tell you, and it might sound a little crazy. But I think, if we do this the right way, it'll be just fine."

My eyebrows bent in confusion. "Okay?"

Honest to goodness, as long as she wasn't about to tell me she was married or moving across the ocean, I could handle whatever was going to come next.

"My name isn't actually Lia," she said slowly. "Or it's not my full name, at least."

"Okay," I repeated. "It's no crime to go by a nickname."

She pinched her eyes shut, and yet again, my hands ached to reach out to touch her. Smooth my thumb along her face so that those worried lines would disappear from her forehead and rub along the knuckles on her hands until she stopped clenching her fingers together so tightly.

"It'll be okay, I promise."

Her eyes opened. "I didn't want to lie to you, I swear. I just knew you wouldn't hire me if I told you the truth. And I really, really want this job, Grady. I'd be devastated if you fired me, but ... you'd be well within your rights if that's what you decided to do."

Everything inside me went a little too still, a little too quiet, because I knew whatever she was about to admit wasn't good. The truth of what she was saying was stamped all over her face, I didn't doubt that. The lines on her forehead smoothed out as she took another breath.

Don't say it, I wanted to scream, without even knowing what it was. The sense of foreboding I felt crawling through my gut was awful—cold and muddy and sticky.

Her chin lifted, and as the light from the window hit that glorious face, she looked so regal, so composed, and I knew that I couldn't ask her to hold in whatever truth was bothering her so much.

"My name is Magnolia MacIntyre."

There it was. The bottom fell out, like an anvil into a cardboard box.

"Oh, fuck me," I whispered.

Magnolia MacIntyre, as in Tucker's ex-girlfriend. His first love. The daughter of the man who almost ruined his law firm, which was why he was even partnering with me at all.

The woman he left for my sister.

I sank to the floor, my legs no longer able to support me, and for the second time that day, I speared my hands into my hair. But this time, my gaze held hers, and I couldn't find a single word to say in comfort.

Because not only was it a horrible, terrible idea for her to work here, I couldn't even begin to process the fact that she was the one. That, according to my family's stories—generation after generation of them —I'd love her until my dying breath.

"I'm so sorry, Grady," she said.

"That's why you ran to the bathroom," I said numbly. "You saw Grace."

Slowly, miserably, she nodded.

Her hand reached out, like she wanted to comfort me, but I held up my own to stop her. If she touched me ... no, I couldn't handle anything close to that with how my mind was racing. My brain was like a messy car crash, each scenario piling higher and higher on top of each other.

I stood abruptly, knocking over a small side table in the process.

Magnolia covered her mouth with her hand.

"I have to go," I said. "I ... I have to go."

"Okay." Her voice was quiet. She started gathering her stuff, blindly shoving her keys and laptop into her purse. I saw a sheen of tears, and the sight of them was like a semi running straight over top of me.

"No, you can stay," I said. "Just ... lock up when you leave. I just ... I can't be here right now."

Her eyes met mine. "You're not firing me?"

I swallowed. "I-I don't know what I'm doing."

My honesty clearly took her by surprise. Her nod was shaky. "Okay. I-I'll just ... finish those ads, I guess."

With jerky movements, I pulled my keys out of the front pocket of my jeans, and I was out the door before I could betray myself with another misspoken word.

CHAPTER 9

MAGNOLIA

*a*fter Grady left, all I could do was sit in the quiet and feel the absence of his energy in that drab gray space. Not that I wasn't working. No, I worked my ass off for the next two hours.

Until my phone rang and his voice came on the other end to tell me that I no longer had a job, I was going to accomplish everything we'd talked about that morning and then some.

In the two days I'd been gone at the Chamber office, Grady had compiled a document of login information for all the various accounts. I zipped through Facebook, adding a few posts about sights in Green Valley. Next came some graphics for social media use with hiking packages that included picnic lunches.

He had an ad account set up, but I set up a few small-budget ads in addition to what he already had running, using a picture of Grady hiking up a trail, probably something his sister had taken.

My eyes closed briefly as I thought about the mess I'd made. Why did I think it would be easy to tell him?

Firing was the least I deserved.

If Tucker was ever going to work with him, having me around the office would be awful for everyone. I thought about the time I ran into Grace at the Piggly Wiggly the day after Tucker broke up with me.

My chest felt tight, not because I missed Tucker—he'd been right to end our relationship—but Grace had been so kind to me. She wasn't a bad person even though everyone in my family had certainly vilified her for gliding off into the sunset with the man I'd shared all my firsts with.

When a piece of hair fell forward over my shoulder, and when I thought about the effort I'd put into it for the first time in so long, I laughed sadly. Tucker and I were a lot like my hair. We'd been together for so long that I saw no reason to change. And that was the problem. We'd gone years in a sad state of complacency, and we were the only ones who suffered its effects.

No matter how mad my family got at her—and I'd heard my Aunt Julianne call her some names that would make the pastor fling holy water—I never once blamed Grace for my single status.

I blamed myself.

Just as I was doing now.

Working, and working hard, allowed me to quiet that part of my mind that could easily keep me up at night if I let it.

It was what I'd done for years with my father, muting my own terrible, vicious inner critic with sheer competency.

Do this right, do this well, and you'll be just fine, Magnolia. No one will notice how terribly unhappy you are.

Pull this event off, earn that pat on the back, and no one will notice how embarrassed you are for how he treats people.

Find a new job, lie to your new boss, and prove your worth, and maybe you won't have to face the fact that no one else in this town would hire you anyway.

I sniffed, horrified by the burning sensation behind my eyes.

That was the truth I didn't want to see, and the voice I didn't want to hear.

No one else would dare hire me in this town because of my father. And I'd look a fool, going door to door, when everyone on the other side of those doors knew that my last name would get me in just fine at any of the places that my own family owned.

The MacIntyres would hire me.

So would the Boones and the Paytons.

They'd make room for me—they'd protect me—so that I wouldn't have to face reality.

I was living a life of someone else's creation, and I'd resorted to deceit in order to carve out a space somewhere for myself.

A tear slid down my cheek, and I dashed it away with my fingers. There was no time for that. Not today. If Grady was hiking his way through his confusion, trying to figure out a solution to the problem I presented, then I probably had a couple of hours to impress the hell out of him.

With dry eyes and a renewed sense of determination, I got up from the desk and lowered the shades on the windows. No one needed to see inside this office. Not today.

I made my way through all the social media to clean things up and finished shelving some of the stuff he'd been working on when Grace showed up.

My phone rang twice, but when I saw it was my father both times, I sighed and sent him to voicemail. Behind the last row of the shelves, around the corner from the bathroom, I found a few unopened boxes of things that Grady must have ordered as soon as I left my first day of work. Books about Tennessee history and wildlife filled one. Another had a large wrought-iron clock that was cut in the outline of the state.

Behind those, I saw a black card table and two chairs. Tapping my thumb rapidly along my thigh, I remembered the black and white plaid blanket I kept tucked away in the trunk of my car in case of emergency.

Ten minutes later, I had the table set up underneath the window, covered with the blanket as a makeshift tablecloth, and the books fanned out in the middle. Maybe no one would ever sit at it except the people who worked for Valley Adventures, but it made the room look a bit more inviting. And more than anything, I wanted Grady to come back from wherever he was and feel excited about this space.

I could rotate the decorations for the holidays, a nice touch right in front of that window. Something the Green Valley residents could smile at as they walked by. In my head, I'd already cataloged what Thanksgiving items I could bring from home.

As I was hanging the clock on the wall, standing back to make sure it was even, my phone buzzed with a notification. A message had come through to the VA Facebook page.

Hi! I tried to call the number on your website, and it went straight to voicemail. What kind of availability do you have for a group hike this afternoon or tomorrow?

She included her phone number, and with shaky fingers, I tried to call Grady. Straight to voicemail.

"Lord, Magnolia," I whispered. "Watch you cost him his first client because you sent him straight into the wilderness to think."

I waited two minutes, then tried his phone again. Nothing. Staring at the message, I made an executive decision. Booking something before we were ready wouldn't do Grady any favors. I dialed her number and took a seat at the desk, pulling out my notebook before she answered.

"Hi, this is Magnolia from Valley Adventures returning a call for Ginny."

"Oh! Great, that's me. Thanks for getting back to me so fast." I heard young boys whooping and hollering in the background.

"No problem. Grady, our owner, is out on a hike right now, so he's probably not getting any service, which is why you couldn't reach him."

"Makes sense." I heard a door close. "My husband and I are ready to venture out of Gatlinburg for a couple of days, and I swear, no sooner had I searched something did one of your ads pop up when I was scrolling Facebook. Do you have any of those family picnic hikes available today or tomorrow? That sounds perfect for the five of us."

I scrawled that down, then tapped the button for speakerphone and set the phone down on the desk. No sooner had I done that, but the office door swung open and a disheveled, sweaty Grady walked in.

His face, normally covered in a wide smile, was serious, and he gave me a nod. I pointed at the phone and mouthed, "They want a hike."

Those golden-brown eyes lit up.

"Ginny, we'd be happy to accommodate your family. You said you prefer today or tomorrow, right?"

"Yeah. We didn't have anything scheduled for those days, and honestly, we're just ready to see something a little different."

Grady pulled out his phone and snagged one of the chairs by the card table, a quick smile flashing across his face when he looked at the wall clock. "Let's do tomorrow at ten," he whispered. "If you could get food figured out."

I gave him a thumbs-up. Daisy's would have no trouble packing me some sack lunches.

Grady leaned in, and I caught a lungful of delicious man smell. Despite how hard he must have hiked while he was gone, Grady smelled like soap and skin and spice. The skin of his arm when it brushed mine was hot. It almost made me lightheaded, and I caught myself stammering over my words.

"A-and you wanted an easy or a moderate hike?"

She answered a few of my questions, and I wrote down her answers as fast as my normally neat handwriting could manage.

"We can't wait to meet y'all," I told her. "And if you can just get me your email address, I'll send you an invoice. We don't quite have our website ready to accommodate payments yet, but you'll be able to pay using debit or credit through the link I'll email you."

Grady was watching me carefully as he tapped a few things into his phone, and I had to fight not to stare right back.

This was a different side of him, quiet and watchful, with maybe a hint of sadness.

"We can't wait, Magnolia. Thank you so much for calling me back so soon!"

"It's my pleasure," I assured her. "Please don't hesitate to reach out before tomorrow if you have any other questions."

She hung up, and I sank back in the chair.

Grady didn't say anything, and neither did I. Our eyes held for a few moments longer, and a muscle ticked in his strong jaw.

That's the edge I saw, I realized. It wasn't sadness. Something about Grady looked dangerous. Not in a scary way, but enough that I knew maybe even he wasn't sure what to do with me just yet, and that drove him crazy.

I exhaled slowly. "Should I quit now and save you the trouble?"

"No," he said immediately. "I don't think I could handle you leaving me." He paused. "Uhh, leaving me on my own right now."

My face felt warm, and I glanced away.

"I think it's pretty clear that I wasn't doing a great job of getting this off the ground," he said, another one of those self-deprecating grins briefly crossing his face. "I don't think I should be left to my own devices, considering I just left for two hours, and you managed to get me my first customers."

"You'd have done just fine." I smiled. "Eventually."

Grady exhaled a soft laugh. He raked a hand through his hair, and it stuck out everywhere given it was still damp with sweat. There was a clear V on the front of his long-sleeve T-shirt from whatever exercise he'd done while he was gone. He must have noticed me staring because he stood and plucked the shirt away from his broad chest. "I probably stink, sorry."

"No, you're fine." I hooked a hand over my shoulder. "But we do have extras if you need something dry."

He stood and walked back to the shelf that held a neat stack of white T-shirts with the Valley Adventures logo on the chest. Maybe he thought I wasn't looking, because with his back to me, Grady yanked the sweat-soaked shirt off and tossed it to the floor. His back was layered in sleek muscles and so were his long arms. My mouth went a little dry at the way his broad shoulders curved into his biceps, at the flawless expanse of his bare skin, and the way his narrow hips looked in the dark jeans he was wearing.

I jerked my eyes back to the desk in front of me. Great. As if this situation wasn't complicated enough without me ogling the only man in town who already had every right to terminate my tenuous employment.

Grady sat down at the card table and rested one hand on the blanket. "This looks nice here."

"I hope it's okay that I didn't ask first. I just ..." I shook my head. "I just wanted it to feel welcoming in here."

His eyes were intense as he watched me speak, and the quiet descended between us, heavy and full.

"I don't want you to quit, Magnolia."

My chest relaxed incrementally. "Okay."

When he spoke again, he spoke slowly, like he was choosing his words very carefully. "I wish you hadn't kept who you are from me." His eyes never wavered from mine. "But I understand why you did."

I nodded. "Everything I told you in my interview was true." My shoulders lifted in a small shrug. "I know that probably doesn't help much right now. And I won't make excuses for why I did it. But I do want this job, Grady, I promise you that."

His lips finally softened from that hard, straight line into only the slightest hint of a smile. "I believe you."

"Do you want me to talk to Tucker?"

"No," he said immediately.

My eyebrows lifted at his hard tone.

"No, that's okay," he said, a bit more gently. "I'll take care of Tucker and Grace."

"I don't want to cause problems between the two of you."

"You won't."

I wanted to ask him how he was so sure, but instead, I decided to simply trust it. Because I felt like it might help our new agreement, I grabbed a butterscotch candy from the drawer and tossed it to him. He smiled, just a little, as I took one for myself.

For a moment, the only sound between us was the crinkling of the paper as we unwrapped our candy. I popped the hard disc of sugar into my mouth and felt a strong pang of nostalgia at the flavor. Grady's eyes closed for a moment while he did the same.

Tucking the candy into my cheek, I asked, "And now?"

Grady opened his eyes, pinned directly onto me, and I fought not to fidget under the intensity of what I saw there.

Finally, he glanced away and ran his hands down the tops of his thighs. "For now, let's get everything ready for Ginny and her family tomorrow."

CHAPTER 10

GRADY

The sound of a bell, happy and welcoming, heralded my entrance to Big Bob's Bait and Tackle. I glanced up at it because it seemed like you couldn't actually claim a legitimate business until you had one.

I'd visited my pops at work before, but I'd never walked in those doors looking for the "Bob" in Big Bob. Not in a creepy stalker way, but I found myself fascinated that the woman who birthed Magnolia—who got such a horrified look in her eye when I suggested she come on the hike with me and Ginny's family, that I laughed every time I remembered the way her eyebrows pinched in—owned a tackle shop.

Not that we had to be like our parents. But it was such a dichotomy, and I found myself wanting every stray piece of information on Magnolia, simply to feel like I might know her better.

The store was big and clean. And busy. Rows of fishing poles cut straight through the space, and bright lights hung from steel beams in the ceiling, making the whole space look bright and modern. Customers walked through, looking at the bait and spinners and hooks displayed on the walls.

The whole back corner was clothing. Vests and waders and hats all neatly displayed and organized.

This was no small-fry operation.

I remembered when I came the first time, and my dad had shown it off with pride, almost as though it was his own. Every employee seemed to feel that way. I'd met a couple of his coworkers that day but not Bobby Jo.

But what I did remember from my dad was that everyone loved working for her.

Which meant Magnolia's mom was probably a better person than her dad when you started grading strictly on their ability to interact with ... you know ... other humans. That was a part of what sent me running when she admitted who she was even though it hadn't taken me long to come to the decision that I'd go toe to toe with Tucker if he asked me to fire her. What had sent me away was a deep, visceral sense of embarrassment that I'd assumed J.T. MacIntyre would've had a white daughter because he was white.

Laying that at her feet to deal with was absolutely not going to happen, so I knew getting out some self-directed frustration was a better choice than staying and trying to talk it out with her.

I hadn't even taken a hike as she assumed. My non-running ass ran a 10K before I even realized what I was doing.

And if the way she handled Ginny's call was any indication, I'd made the right decision. When I met our first customers that morning with delicious lunches from Daisy's Nut House ready to go, everything was perfect, and the hike had gone off without a hitch. A happy family of five left me to head back to Gatlinburg and promised to spread the word. Because of Magnolia.

Even if I wasn't pining for her—which I was—she was a great fucking employee, and Tucker could kiss my ass if he wanted to let her go.

But now, going into this situation with clear, open eyes of what I was really dealing with, I wanted to know more about her before I could figure out how I was going to handle this with Grace and Tucker.

I'd hardly made it past the opening of the store when a woman approached me, and I swear, it took everything in me not to stare. Which, when you came from LA and saw celebrities regularly, was saying something.

Bobby Jo—the Bob in Big Bob's—was probably one of the most beautiful women I'd ever seen, outside of her daughter.

She was dressed casually in baggy jeans rolled up at the ankles and a gray shirt bearing the store's logo, her dark hair pulled back off her face.

"Can I help you find something?" she asked, a slight smile on her face.

It took me a second to find my voice because:

1- how had that horse's ass J.T. MacIntyre pulled this off

And

2- how

I met the dude once, and it was once more than I needed to to realize no one in Green Valley exaggerated when it came to what a douchebag he was. I mean, he wasn't an ugly douchebag, but Bobby Jo was on a different level. You weren't even sure you were looking at an actual human being.

When I didn't answer, she raised an eyebrow slightly, like I was amusing her with my absolutely horrifying people skills.

"My dad," I managed. "I'm, uh, I'm Grady Buchanan. He said he needed a ride home from work because his truck was acting up."

The "customer smile" melted into something a touch warmer, and she held out a hand. "Pleasure to meet you, Grady. I'm Bobby Jo."

I want to marry your daughter and she has no idea, I thought miserably.

Instead, I shook her hand. She and Magnolia looked so much alike, and I knew I was getting a glimpse at how magnificently she'd age. They had the same cheekbones, same jawline. Her eye color must have come from J.T., though, because Bobby Jo had big, dark eyes instead of the golden-green that Magnolia did. Her skin was darker than her daughter's but not by much. J.T. was hinted at in Magnolia's face. Everything else, from the bone structure, to her hair, to her height, to her skin, she got from her mom.

"Your daddy is finishing up with an order in the back," she explained. "He should be done shortly."

I tucked my hands in my jeans. "No problem. This is a pretty great place to kill some time."

She looked around, pride evident in her voice when she answered. "It is."

"How long have you owned it?"

I already knew. Pops had told me when I first moved into town, but it felt important to hear it from her, to take this opportunity to know her better.

"Long enough to betray my real age, young man," she said with a tiny smile, and I laughed. She studied my face for a minute, and I wondered if she knew Magnolia was working for me. "Your daddy has been telling everyone about the business you're starting."

"It's been quite an adventure already," I told her. "Bit more complicated than I thought, if I'm being honest, but I seem to be getting on the right track this week."

Her gaze was steady and knowing. "Getting good help makes all the difference, doesn't it?"

I exhaled a laugh. "Yes, ma'am. It does. How'd you know?"

The bell tinkled again as someone opened the door, and Bobby Jo lifted a hand at whoever walked in, but she made no move to leave our conversation.

"Can't hide much here," she said. "It's a blessing and a curse, depending on what people are trying to find out."

I thought about Tucker and Grace, how they felt like they needed to hide their relationship because of Tucker's history in the town, and nodded my head.

Bobby Jo glanced around the shop, then down at a simple band around her ring finger. "For myself, I've never cared much what people have to say about how I live my life."

"The rest of us should take notes."

When she smiled, clearly amused by me, I got the sense that she wasn't a woman who laughed often, but when she did, it was probably at something really, really funny.

"You seem to be doing just fine," she continued dryly, "as not many people would risk my husband bearing down on them by hiring her. I may not have much influence over my daughter's decisions, but I like the idea she'd work for someone brave enough to risk it."

I scratched the side of my face and decided not to tell her that her daughter chose not to disclose her last name when I hired her. Instead, I chose my words carefully and made sure to hold eye contact when I said them, so she might know how deeply I meant them. "Magnolia is a force to be reckoned with, ma'am. You should be very proud of her."

Only the slightest lift in her eyebrows betrayed her surprise in the gravity of my answer. My cheeks flushed at what I might have given away, and Bobby Jo narrowed her eyes slightly, then nodded, as if she'd come to a decision about me.

"I am," she said in return. It was full of subtext, though, and only the slightest edge of questioning.

I wanted to hide.

Forget military questioning or torture. If anyone wanted international secrets ferreted out, they should hire Bobby Jo MacIntyre to stare her way into whatever information they sought.

She glanced at a clock on the wall behind the sales counter. "Your daddy should be out any minute, and I've got a meeting with a supplier shortly." Her fingers tapped out a short rhythm on the endcap, those dark eyes appraising me. "Good luck, Grady."

When she walked away, I was about to heave a sigh of relief when I realized the full ramifications of the fact that Bobby Jo knew, which probably meant my pops knew.

We were headed to dinner at my uncle Robert and aunt Francine's place. Grace was meeting us there (Tucker had something already planned that he couldn't get out of), along with my cousin Connor and his wife, Sylvia.

Statistically, the odds were not in my favor to keep the lid on this for much longer. It was like a bottle of oil tipping over on its side. Once it was out, you were bound to have a leftover mess even if you did your very best to clean it up.

I hated lying to my sister—not just hated it, I was terrible at it.

And Tucker, he was the first friend I'd made in Green Valley. Bro Code was not a joke, it was not something to mess with, and Magnolia was his first *everything*. Beyond the issue of working together, I couldn't even conceive of how to deal with that just yet.

"What are you doing here?"

Grace.

I pinched my eyes shut for a second. She punched me.

"Ow." I gave her a warning look. "You need to learn healthier communication skills."

"You could've responded to the text and let me know you were picking up Dad. I hurried out of an engagement shoot because I figured you weren't by your phone." She looked frazzled, and the longer I stared at her, the bigger and bigger this problem became in my head.

There was no way to blurt out the truth. Or not the whole truth, at least.

It was ironic, of course, that all this had started with an omission. Magnolia didn't share her full first name or her last name, but everything else she'd told me was true.

"Pops not done yet?" she asked, trying to fix her crazy-ass hair. Grace's hair was always crazy when she worked.

Her question didn't require an answer, which is probably the only reason she didn't notice when I didn't give one. A pair of elderly guys wearing matching red trucker hats walked past, blatantly talking about us.

I heard Tucker's name whispered by the one on the right. Then Grace's. And I rubbed at the back of my neck because I was about ready to dig a hole in the ground to get out of this place unscathed. The only way it could get better was if J.T. and Magnolia joined us, followed by Tucker. And a photographer from the newspaper.

Grace simply rolled her eyes. "Maybe when Tucker and I are married someday, they'll stop talking about us." She tilted her head. "Actually ... no, they probably won't."

Pops came through a door that opened to the back of the store, smiling at the two guys.

My throat felt clogged with words, and I couldn't figure out what I wanted to say. How much I should say. But I felt like I'd puke if I didn't get something out.

"Grace," I started.

She waved. "It's fine. It really doesn't bother me. Once Magnolia finds her Southern prince and they can rule the town, everyone will move on."

Was my face green? It felt green.

My sister grimaced. "That was unfair because I don't actually have a problem with Magnolia. She seemed perfectly lovely the one time we met and I shoved wine in her hand. A little lost maybe, but nice enough."

A little girl stopped Pops as he approached and asked him about a bright pink fishing rod. He leaned over to answer her question, and I had to take a few deep breaths just so I wouldn't pass out.

"Grace," I repeated.

"I'm fine, seriously." She glanced over at me, then did a double-take. "Holy crap, what's wrong with you?"

One more breath in, then out.

"I hired Magnolia to run the office for me."

The guy in the trucker hat dropped the fishing rod in his hands. "Good Lord Almighty," he whispered.

Grace stared at me, color high in her face. "What did you just say?"

I shoved a hand in my hair. "I'm messing this up. Can we go stand outside?"

She grabbed the front of my shirt. "Did you just say what I thought you said?"

A few more people were staring, and I gently removed her death-grip on my shirt. "Let's go talk outside." I glanced at my dad and nodded to the door. He gave me a thumbs-up.

Grace only hesitated for a second, then followed me out onto the sidewalk. For as busy as it was in the store, the sidewalk outside of Big Bob's was quiet.

"Magnolia?" she repeated, facing me with crossed arms. "You hired Magnolia MacIntyre, my boyfriend's ex-girlfriend and first love, to run the office that you will be in every single day, and the office that he will hopefully be in every single day? Am I hearing you right?"

Okay, so the puking feeling hadn't gone away because Magnolia was Tucker's first love. And without any idea of what the future held for me here in Green Valley, I wanted her to be so much more than my love. I wanted her to be *my* future.

That came with complications. It came with a whole shit ton of awkward. Her dad would probably hate me. People would talk about us in a way that would probably erase Grace and Tucker from the gossip chain forever.

And I'd face all of it for her.

Staring at my twin sister, I knew—knew with a certainty that was unshakable—that I couldn't tell her the whole truth. At least, not yet. For some reason, this crazy, made-no-damn-sense, couldn't-shake-it family legend had turned out to be true for all of us, and as much as I'd wanted it to be BS, it wasn't. And I would respect Magnolia enough to allow her to be the first person I told. No one would know what was locked inside my heart until Magnolia had heard it from me. Heard all of it.

So I met my sister's confused gaze and nodded. "I did. At first, I didn't make the connection."

"How did you *not*?" She shook her head. "You are the one who made fun of her name when I first started dating Tucker. How is it possible you forgot it?"

"It doesn't matter, okay?" I set my hands on my hips. "I gave her the job, and Grace, she's exactly who I need."

My words hung awkwardly between us, and my sister blinked. "She's ..."

I held up a hand. "She's organized and efficient, and she has done borderline miraculous things in less than a week, and that's what this business, and what I, needed."

Grace's eyes were huge in her face as she listened to me talk, and for the first time I could remember, I'd rendered her speechless. Normally, I'd high-five myself or tease her about it, but this wasn't a joke. And our ability to move forward in this strange little tableau would set the scene for whatever came next for me and Magnolia.

Whatever that might be.

Grace opened her mouth. Closed it. Opened it. Then clenched her jaw and stared down the street, studying downtown Green Valley for a moment before her eyes pinched shut.

I found myself holding my breath as I waited for her to say something.

Her hands covered her face for one moment, then her shoulders relaxed. She dropped her hands and speared me with an unfathomable look.

"You're on your own when you tell Tucker."

"I—" My head tilted. "That's it?"

She pointed a finger at me. "I will keep my mouth shut for twenty-four hours, Grady. Twenty-four hours is all you'll get from me before I tell him myself, and the only reason I'm giving you that is because he can't come to dinner tonight. I will not lie to the man I love, not even for you."

Gratitude had my chest relaxing on a mountain-sized inhale. "Thank you."

Grace watched my face. She wanted to say something else, but she didn't.

"What is it?" I asked.

"I'm worried for you." She shook her head. "Her father almost ruined Tucker and his dad's business. He can't be happy that she's working for someone else, and if he comes after you, I'll be forced to like ... key his car or something."

I set my hands on her shoulders. "I'll be fine. He won't come after my business, so please don't key anything. I'm pretty sure they'd arrest you, and you look *awful* in orange."

There was no smile at my joke. She really was worried.

Squeezing my hands, I gave her my most reassuring, older than her by two minutes look. "Gracey B, you are an excellent sister."

"I know," she said dryly.

"You're really okay with this?"

"Okay is not the word I'd choose just yet," she said. "But ... I trust you. And if she's what you need"—she visibly swallowed—"then I trust you."

I wrapped my sister up in a tight hug. "Thank you. I know this is weird."

She laughed into my chest. "The weirdest, brother. But with you? I expect nothing else."

The door to the shop opened, and Pops shook his head. "We hugging on the street now?"

Grace pulled back and smiled. "Yeah. You guys ready for dinner?"

I put my arms around them both as we walked toward where Grace was parked next to me.

One down. One to go.

CHAPTER 11

GRADY

*D*owntown Green Valley was draped in lights heading into the holidays. As I walked from Donner Bakery, armed with coffee and tea and more pastries than I needed, it was the first day that felt like winter. I'd borrowed some winter gloves from Uncle Robert, and as I walked from the bakery to the law offices Tucker shared with his dad, I was thankful for them. It was still early, so the streets were fairly quiet. I was thankful for that too.

Tucker's absence at dinner the night before had been a small blessing because it allowed me to take the previous evening after we finished a family dinner with Uncle Robert and Aunt Fran to think over how I wanted to approach this.

When I moved to Green Valley, Tucker and I hit it off immediately. Stuck in a job he didn't love, he was one of the first people truly on board with the idea of Valley Adventures, and once he cleared some hurdles with his parents, we started planning for him to help on the side. Eventually, if the business grew to what I thought it could be, he'd slowly transition away from the law offices where he practiced with his dad and join me full-time.

But this ... it held the possibility of changing all that for him.

A truck rumbled down the quiet street, and I lifted my hand in greeting at whoever was driving. He waved back.

The change from LA to Green Valley hadn't been as jarring to me as it had been for Grace, but I also had to admit that a huge reason for that had been because of Tucker. And Magnolia. She came in with all the subtlety of a wrecking ball that was lit on fire, and not by choice.

For the first time since I'd crossed the city limits, I could empathize with my twin sister. The addition of Magnolia to my daily life changed the tenor of how people looked at me. Looked at us for how this would play out.

Even thinking her name had my chest aching. Had me wondering if she was at the office yet, what she'd eaten for breakfast, what her house looked like, what she was afraid of.

Had me wondering all sorts of other things too.

What her lips tasted like.

If she hogged the bed.

If she'd mind if I woke her up in the middle of the night with my hands and mouth.

I blew out a hard exhale because it was not the time for that train of thought, and it was cold enough that I saw my frustration manifest in the air in a small cloud. The California boy in me was thrilled, so I did it again and found myself laughing.

"You need to get out more."

Tucker was leaning up against his truck outside of the law offices, watching me with an amused expression.

"No argument there." I handed him a coffee. "No cream and one sugar on the advice of my sister."

He nodded his thanks and took a long sip. "Thank you." As he lowered the cup, he eyed me curiously. "What did you need to talk about this early?"

Using my coffee cup, I gestured at an empty park bench in front of the building adjacent to the Haywood and Haywood offices, which were still dark. "Should we sit?"

He grinned. "If you think that park bench can hold both of us, you go right ahead and try it. I'll wait here." Tucker walked around to the back of his truck and lowered the gate. "This'll work."

We were both tall enough to sit on the open bed and still brace our feet on the ground. But somehow, it felt more comfortable than facing off. I'd faced off with Tucker a few times since I moved here, and every time, it had been about my sister. He'd more than proven himself. I knew he loved Grace, almost to distraction sometimes, but now I'd be the one who might deserve the tongue-lashing. The warnings. The hard stares. And he wouldn't even know the half of how awkward this might get.

"What's going on, Grady?" He glanced sideways. "Am I right to assume this is related to why your sister was acting cagey as all hell this morning?"

That made me laugh. "Was she?"

"No matter how I tried to get her to talk, she held strong." He grinned. "Which is impressive, considering what I tried."

"Dude," I groaned.

He grinned. "Sorry."

"Yeah, she gave me twenty-four hours to talk to you about this," I admitted.

Tucker's smile melted away. Instantly, he was in lawyer mode, all even facial expressions and the proper amount of gravity. "Talk to me."

"You know I needed help at the office," I said. "I, uh, I wasn't doing the best job keeping myself focused on how to get VA off and running in the most efficient way."

Tucker grimaced. "I noticed. But starting a business is often slow, especially if you want to do it right. No harm in being a little unorganized at first." He jerked his chin over his shoulder toward the law office. "I wish I could help more, but ... we've rebounded our caseload since J.T. pitched his little fit a few months ago. We've got our eyes out for someone who can start taking on some cases, but we haven't found the right person just yet."

My gut tightened at the mention of Magnolia's dad. I'd yet to speak to the man face-to-face, and he loomed so large in my head, like he was a caricature rather than a flesh-and-blood human being.

"I found someone to run the office while you were in California," I told him. "And I'll give you the full story of how this all happened—"

He glanced over at me. "I sense a *but* coming."

"But," I said slowly, "she's perfect for the job. And I may have missed out on a great employee if I'd known who she was when she came in to interview."

Tucker set his coffee down and shifted sideways so he was facing me head-on. "Now why did I just get nervous?"

I followed his lead and set my own drink down next to the bag from the bakery, but then I stood instead of shifting my back up against the side of the truck. "I hired Magnolia as the office administrator."

Tucker's face went comically blank. "You ... wait, what? Not *my* Magnolia or"—he shook his head—"you know what I mean."

She's not your fucking anything, I wanted to growl. *If she's anyone's Magnolia, she is mine.*

Or she would be, if she wanted to be.

I had to swallow down that Neanderthal reaction like it was made of barbed wire, so it took me a few seconds to speak. In general, I was an easygoing guy. Laughing and smiling came as naturally to me as breathing. In my entire life, I'd only felt violent when I thought my sister might get hurt.

And that was nothing compared to what Tucker's innocently spoken words of confusion made me feel.

He was lucky he was still conscious.

Once. He was allowed that kind of misspeak about Magnolia once before I shoved the words back down his throat with my fist. I didn't care who his girlfriend was.

"Magnolia MacIntyre," I said evenly or as evenly as I could manage. "That's correct."

My mouth wouldn't form the words *your ex-girlfriend.* It couldn't.

Tucker gaped at me. "And you didn't think that'd be ... awkward?"

I set my hands on my hips. "I didn't realize that's who she was at first. She introduced herself as Lia. I hired her thinking that was her name."

"That doesn't sound like her." He rubbed his forehead, suddenly looking exhausted. "The lying or the nickname. She hates nicknames."

I didn't want to learn anything about her from him. I wanted to learn it from her.

Don't act like a crazy, possessive asshole, Grady, that is not an attractive trait in the male species.

I was able to let out a slow breath. "She was worried I wouldn't hire her if I knew who she was."

His eyebrows lifted meaningfully. "Yeah, because it'll be awkward."

"At first." I held his gaze. "I know you didn't part on bad terms."

"We didn't. But not parting on bad terms is a little bit different than seeing each other every day at the office." He sighed. "I'm a little shocked Grace sat on this information for even a single day."

"I think the only reason she did was because you couldn't make dinner last night." I shrugged. "And she was shocked, don't get me wrong, but she trusts me. She knows I don't get stubborn about stupid shit, so if I'm putting my foot down about keeping Magnolia on, it's because I know in my gut it's the right thing to do."

Tucker watched me carefully. "And that's what you're doing? Putting your foot down?"

"Yeah. I am." I softened my voice, but still, my tone brooked no arguments. "I look forward to you taking more responsibilities at Valley Adventures, Tucker, but I still own the majority of this business. I'm telling you now, like this, because you're my friend and I respect the hell out of you. I'm telling you like this because someday, you'll be my brother-in-law. But make no mistake, I am telling you. I'm not asking for your permission. And I hope you can respect that."

In the long, protracted pause that followed my little speech, Tucker studied me in a way he never had before. Suddenly, I felt exposed. Naked. More vulnerable than I liked. What had he heard between the words and letters? The subtext that I'd been trying to hide.

Because it was all there, if anyone had cared to dig deeper.

It wasn't about me owning the business. It wasn't even really about hiring her in the first place.

Left up to me, Magnolia would be around forever.

Left up to me, they'd have to get used to seeing her by my side.

Left up to me ... we'd live, and we'd be happy.

But it wasn't just up to me, no matter what insanity my family believed.

Tucker pulled his gaze from my face and carefully picked up his coffee again. He took a sip, and I could practically feel the weight of his deliberation.

It took him no more than a minute.

"I can respect that," he said quietly. His cup went back down onto the truck, and as he stood from the truck bed, he held out his hand. "She'll get no problems from me."

I took his hand easily. "Thank you."

Tucker grinned. "She must have had a helluva first week on the job."

"Haywood"—I sighed—"you have no idea."

When we finished some small talk, once the heavy conversation was over, I took my time walking back to the office. The coffee I got her was probably lukewarm at best. The tea no better. I'd dropped the baked goods once, and I was quite sure they didn't look as appealing as they had when I purchased them.

But I felt as good as I could remember in a long time as I walked the few blocks from Haywood and Haywood back over toward Valley Adventures.

When I approached, I couldn't help but smile at what I saw through the front window because she'd swapped out the card table and blanket from the other day, bringing in a beautiful oak piece that was stained a deep golden color. On top of it was a vase exploding with bright yellow and orange flowers, a bright sign of the Thanksgiving holiday just around the corner while the air chilled my skin.

Using my elbow, since my hands were full, I pushed the door open and almost dropped everything I was carrying when the sound of a bell heralded my entrance. I looked up slowly, smiling at the small silver object.

Magnolia had her back to me, phone pressed to her ear. A quick smile over her shoulder was all I got for a greeting, but I was oddly relieved because the phone call allowed me a greedy moment to study her.

I'd never paid much attention to what women wore because it had never felt like such an extension of their personality as Magnolia's clothes did. Always bright, always well-put-together, always classy, but with a twist that felt intentional.

I'm a proper Southern belle, but you can't dictate everything I do.

That was what came to my mind when I set the coffee and tea down and smiled at the high-waisted pink pants she was wearing, with a dark green sweater that—I squinted, then had to stifle a laugh—was trimmed with tiny feathered fishing lures. In her hair was a pink scarf holding her dark hair off her face.

"That sounds wonderful," she said, scribbling something onto a pad of paper in her hand. "And I know you've got all those students who need an internship, so you just send 'em on over to us, and we'll help each other out."

She smiled again when she saw the bag from Donner Bakery.

Magnolia clucked her tongue. "Todd, you know your momma was just my favorite at the Junior League. If she knew you were hassling me about this, she'd have your hide." A satisfied grin crossed her face. "Excellent. I'll wait for your email. You have a nice day too."

I hitched a hip onto the desk as she tossed her phone down, sinking into the chair and crossing her long legs.

"What was that?" I asked her.

She finished jotting a note and then looked up at me. "Todd Cooper over at the University of Knoxville. He's one of the professors in their environmental management department. I knew his momma from the Junior League. Their students need internships before they can look for jobs as park rangers, so I thought we could look into taking one on when we get busier. They get the hours, and we get someone who can help with some of the guided hikes for free."

"That is genius," I murmured. God, I wanted to grab her face and kiss the absolute hell out of her. I wanted to sink to my knees on the floor in front of her and wrap her up in my arms because something about this side of her—the driven, whip-smart personality—was absolutely driving me out of my mind.

"And you'll need that help sooner than you think, Grady." She slid a calendar in my direction.

I picked it up, my eyebrows hiking up on my forehead. "There are five bookings on here."

"I know."

"Five." I held up the calendar. "For the next ten days. *Five*."

She laughed. "I know. Ginny meant it when she said she was going to tell people when they got back to Gatlinburg."

"You are the best thing that has walked through these doors." Honestly, she was. That was no curse talking, or the fact I wanted to lay my head in her lap and stare up at her, or peel every inch of those clothes off her body and listen to her talk for hours. She just *was* the best damn thing that had walked through those doors.

Her face was pure amusement, but I could tell my praise made her happy.

"I wish I could take credit." She stood, taking the calendar back and laying it in the spot to the right of her laptop. "But that's all you, boss."

My face twisted up in a grimace. I didn't want her calling me that.

"What?" she said on a laugh.

"Don't call me boss." I shuddered. "I'm just ... Grady."

Magnolia set a hand on her hip. "Okay, just Grady."

117

"I met your mom yesterday."

Her face smoothed out, and the smile turned more polite, less natural. "Oh? And did you ..." She swallowed. "Did you tell her how we know each other?"

"She seemed to know."

Magnolia deflated a little. "That doesn't surprise me, I suppose. There are only so many—" She caught herself.

"So many people who would hire you, knowing your dad."

She nodded.

"She was nice," I told her. "She loves you a lot, you can tell."

When she adjusted the scarf around her head, it seemed like a nervous gesture she couldn't quite contain. "She does."

"What is it?" I asked gently.

Magnolia's eyes met mine, like she was searching for the words for something and didn't quite know what they were. "I know my momma loves me. But she's ... she's different. *She and I* are very different. My parents were almost forty when they got pregnant with me, and ... I don't think she ever gave much thought to being a mother. So, when I came along, she *loved* me. But her love, for a lot of people, means space. Freedom, in her mind."

"Well," I said carefully, "I think the important thing is that you know she does, right? I didn't see my pops a lot growing up because my mom hated Green Valley and never wanted to come back after they divorced. But not seeing him, I could still recognize where he loved and supported us. Where it counted, at least." I took a sip of my coffee. "I think that's where people fall into a trap. They can't recognize love if it's not shown in exactly the way they want it to be shown, and it's just not that simple, you know?"

There was something on her face, something in my words that struck a chord with her, but I also saw the moment she decided the conversation was just a little too much for her.

"I do know," she said, then straightened the hem of her perfectly straight sweater. "I got the email confirmations from the conference in Nashville next week. I wasn't sure you wanted me to come with you until I saw my name on the registration list."

"Is that okay?" Shit. I hadn't even thought she might want to stay back while I went. "I'm sorry, I should've asked first. You don't have to come if you'd rather not."

Magnolia waved that off. "It's fine, I promise. I just ..." She paused. "I wasn't sure how long you planned on being there. If it was a day trip sort of thing, or if you planned on staying overnight."

Right. Traveling with Magnolia, even for one day, made me dread the trip, as much as I looked forward to the possibility of it. But maybe she didn't want to be stuck in a car with me and forced to stick to my own timeline. Maybe she didn't want to stay overnight in Nashville with her boss.

Answer this one wisely, Grady.

"I wouldn't mind doing both days," I said slowly. "Might feel less rushed in talking to people."

She nodded, and I couldn't help but notice that she was avoiding eye contact.

"You are more than welcome to stay back if you don't want to come," I assured her. "I'd love to have you with me—" I paused, trying not to stammer over my words like a freaking dope. "Because you're obviously more well-spoken than I am."

She gave me a long-suffering look. "That's not true."

"You don't trip over things either. I make a horrible first impression, and you can't deny that."

Finally, she smiled, and I felt like I'd won something important. "You were charming," she admitted. "Clumsy, but charming."

I held my fist up in the air, and she laughed.

"Whatever you're comfortable with, Magnolia. All you have to do is tell me, and I'll be fine with it."

"Okay," she said on a loaded exhale. "I'd like to learn. I'd like to meet people too because I know how important that is. I-I'm fine with an overnight trip, if we have the budget for two rooms."

"We do." I held her gaze. "But only if that's what you want to do."

"Grady," she started, then stopped. "I'll just say it because if I were you, I know I wouldn't think about it, and I'd want to know if it was someone working for me."

I faced her straight on. "Tell me," I said gently.

"I think one day would be more than enough, and I'm not sure how I feel about being away from the office for two. But I don't feel comfortable driving by myself home from Nashville, especially after dark."

My eyebrows bent in confusion. "Okay. Yeah, that's ... fine. My mom doesn't like driving at night either. She can't see as well."

Magnolia smiled softly. For some reason, I knew I was off base. "It's probably a little different in LA. It's different here in Green Valley, too, I guess. But ... in the South, girls with my color skin don't drive at night. It's not safe."

My heart stopped, and I hated—*hated*—how long it took me to think of it from that angle. Because I didn't have to. Every inch of my skin felt tight and uncomfortable, and so many reactions warred to take first place.

Anger that she had to even think that way.

Frustration at my own reaction.

Helplessness when I thought it might've been hard for her to admit that to me.

And a needle-sharp sense of protectiveness, something powerful, something I was hardly aware of as it slid under my skin, which she wasn't asking for from me and probably didn't need.

At that moment, no more than a blink of an eye to her, I remembered a race-centered conversation I'd had with one of my coworkers back in California, a black man my age, who told me once, "Don't get mad for me, Grady. I don't need your anger. I just need you to listen."

I swallowed carefully. "Magnolia," I said when she looked down at the floor. Her eyes lifted to mine. "We'll make a day of it, okay? I'll drive, as long as you can handle my horrible singing."

She took a second before she answered. "I can stay back, Grady."

"You said you want to come, right?"

A short nod was what I got in answer.

"Then I'll drive us." All I could do was keep my answers simple. Because everything in my head was very *not* simple. And I couldn't unload that onto her. I couldn't unload it onto anyone.

Magnolia lifted her chin a notch. "Thank you, Grady."

I nodded. "I, uh, I brought you coffee that's probably cold now. And tea because I wasn't sure if you wanted that instead."

She approached the desk slowly and pulled open the bakery bag. Whatever mess she saw in there made her smile. "Those muffins look a little sad."

"I dropped them. Twice."

This time, her smile showed her straight, white teeth and a dent appeared in her cheek. Instead of pulling out the muffin, she carefully laid her hand on my forearm and squeezed.

It was such a simple touch. I couldn't even feel her skin on mine because I was wearing a long-sleeve shirt, but it didn't matter. With the way her fingers curled around my arm, I wasn't sure I'd ever treasured a single moment of my life more.

"Let's get back to work," she said quietly.

I notched two fingers to my temple in a salute. "Yes, ma'am."

CHAPTER 12

MAGNOLIA

*T*he day started poorly, when I rolled over and realized I was supposed to be awake about a half an hour earlier.

The screen on my useless phone showed that I'd set my alarm the night before for p.m. not a.m., and I had roughly twenty-two minutes before Grady picked me up for our day in Nashville.

Rushing around like a headless chicken was not my idea of fun, especially well before six o'clock in the morning, but I realized one small perk that I'd gained in the chaos of those twenty-two minutes.

I had no time to be nervous.

"Nervous," I muttered. I could hardly even look my reflection in the eye as I said it. Why should I be nervous?

No matter how much I reminded myself that I shouldn't be, I couldn't lie to that swirling pit in my belly when I found myself wondering what someone would think of my home. What they'd think of my manners or what I was wearing. What they'd think of me.

I hadn't been nervous to spend time with someone since ... I straightened at the bathroom counter and stared down at the container of liquid blush in my hand. Not since I first started dating Tucker.

Those nerves were different, of course, because seventeen-year-old Magnolia was an entirely different person than I was now. Plus, those were the nerves of first touches and first kisses, of a boy who gave me butterflies.

Grady was my boss, first of all. But he didn't give me butterflies, either.

Butterflies had whisper-thin wings and delicate feet. The way they pitter-pattered inside you when you were getting to know someone was exciting. But to me, butterflies were subtle and subdued.

Somewhere in the middle of lukewarm coffee, falling over boxes, and broken muffins inside a crumpled Donner Bakery bag, Grady Buchanan jumped with those long legs straight over butterflies and into territory I didn't quite know how to name.

I dipped my finger into the blush and spread a small amount over my cheekbones. That and mascara was all I had time for with my twenty-two minutes. Winding another scarf—pink plaid today—around my head and tying it at the base of my skull, I wished I could pinpoint when he'd done it.

And how.

That was when I finally met my own gaze and had to be truthful with myself.

The moment I heard myself explaining my mother to him, it hit me over the head like a truth dropped straight from the heavens.

I felt safe with him. And safety meant all sorts of different things to different people.

To me, I'd found safety in my family, something most of Green Valley didn't understand because they didn't always understand us.

For a very long time, I'd felt secure in my job at the Chamber. Until I didn't.

Grady, without even realizing it at the time, had made me feel safe enough to jump from one place to the next. What had always been my safe place became a launching pad. And in a short amount of time, he'd shown me time and time again that he had my back.

With a glance at my watch, I knew there'd be a knock on my front door at any moment. Dressed for a long day, I'd opted for a comfortable pair of dark pants, a soft chambray shirt, and bright pink flats. Looking at the shoes, I smiled, because without heels, Grady would tower over me.

I tidied up my bathroom counter and went into my kitchen. The window over the sink had a view of my driveway, so I'd be able to see him approach. Because the air was cold, but I knew his car wouldn't be, I'd set my coat in the bag I'd packed with some snacks and two large travel carafes of coffee. At least the alarm on my coffee pot worked just fine because missing that would've had disastrous effects on the day.

Despite how it started, the rest of the day held promise. We'd spend hours in the car, hours at the conference together. Away from prying eyes of the town. Away from everything, and I found myself far more excited about that than I should have been.

The sun was barely making its way into the sky, just the tiniest hint that a new day was starting.

Headlights sliced through the soft bluish-gray light in my driveway, and I took a deep breath.

There could be an entire zoo of animals marching through my body because of Grady, but he was still my boss, and he was still Tucker's friend.

"Calm yourself down right now, Magnolia Marie," I whispered.

Instead of waiting for him to come to the door like I might normally have, I grabbed my purse, the bag of snacks, and locked up the front behind me before he could take more than one step out of his car.

"Morning," he said, arms braced in the opening of his door and the top of the vehicle. From the way it traveled up his throat, out of his mouth, and made its way to me, that was the first word he'd spoken since he rolled over in his own bed. Because that normally deep voice was deeper, huskier, and *Jesus be a hedge around me*, it pulled up goose-bumps over my entire body.

No, no, indeed, there were no butterflies in the vicinity.

I had elephants trampling all over my poor body.

"Good morning." I returned his greeting and was quite proud of myself when my voice came out even and polite.

"If you have coffee in that bag, I will double your salary."

As I sat in the passenger seat and braced the bag between my feet on the floor, I gave him a tiny smile. "I should get that in writing before I open it."

The dome light in his car sent harsh shadows on his handsome face, and I found myself studying him a bit longer than I normally might've. He hadn't shaved, and the golden-brown stubble lining his strong jaw looked like it would feel prickly against my palm. His hair was slightly disheveled, and my fingers itched to smooth it into place. All in all, Grady Buchanan looked rumpled and tired, and it did crazy, stomping-elephant, thinking-immoral things to my insides.

It made me think about the muscles in his back and arms when I saw him change his shirt, and the way his hips moved when he paced the office.

And none of those thoughts were a good idea.

With a flourish, I handed him the first travel cup. "Black with a little bit of sugar."

He groaned as he took his first sip. "Oh, you are my favorite person in the entire world, Magnolia."

"And you are entirely too easy to please, Grady," I teased.

His eyes met mine over the rim of the coffee, and goodness, did they glow something unholy as he looked at me. Or maybe that was the way the light hit his face.

That must have been it because when he put the coffee in the cupholder and hooked his seat belt, that glow was gone from his eyes and replaced with his typical happy smile. "I figured we could stop about halfway for some breakfast if that sounds good to you."

My coffee went into the cupholder next to his. "Perfect."

His grin was infectious when he looked over at me. "Glad to hear it because you're gonna have to tell me where we should stop."

"There are some good restaurants in Cookeville," I told him. "I have a few marked in my Yelp app."

Grady backed the car out of my driveway and pulled out onto the road that would lead out of town. "Yeah, I assumed there'd be something right off the highway, and we could wing it."

"Absolutely not," I said. "We do not *wing it* when it comes to restaurant choices. God made review systems for a reason."

For a moment, I was sucked under a tidal wave of embarrassment at how that sounded. It was the sort of thing that my cousins might have rolled their eyes over or called me prissy. But his answering laugh was so delighted, so thoroughly amused by me, that I relaxed into the seat.

"My trust in you is endless, Miss MacIntyre," he said, casually hooking his wrist over the top of the steering wheel as he drove.

Could he have known what those words might do to me?

I'd found a holding pattern in the past few years of my life, where it felt more like everyone in my life simply tolerated the way I operated. Yes,

I was particular, and yes, I liked to know how things would work ahead of time, and yes ... my father was a touch overprotective.

Tolerance was different than trust, though. They weren't even in the same universe. I was sick of living in one while desperately wishing for the other.

With the music playing softly in the background, Grady and I fell into companionable silence as we sipped our coffee and drove with the rising sun behind us. Despite the fact we'd waded into surprisingly deep conversations in a fairly short period of time, the first hour or so of the drive stayed in that quiet state. As we approached Cookeville, somewhere in the middle of Green Valley and Nashville, I'd closed my eyes for a few minutes, lulled by the swaying of the car, the rumble of the tires, and the sound of Grady humming quietly along to the music.

He didn't have a terrible voice. It was really quite nice, I thought as I dozed.

"Well, thank you," he said.

My eyes snapped open. "Did I say that out loud?"

Grady chuckled. "Yes."

Every cell in my body wanted me to cover my face with my hands. Mortification was not a good look for me, and I just knew it was covering me like a big ole blanket. So, I kept my face even, staring out of the front of the windshield as he took an exit for Cookeville.

How did one corral such feelings? The kind that made me blurt things out loud without a second thought. Or ponder his singing voice in the first place.

Maybe the problem was that this didn't feel like a day out with a coworker. He pulled the car into a parking lot for a café that I'd been to before. It felt like a date, and that was definitely an issue because I was quite sure that Grady didn't look at it like that. Everything he'd done was perfectly professional. Perfectly polite.

He held the door open for me, but he would've done the same for anyone.

As we spoke to the server, he gestured for me to order first. The fact that a few elderly couples inside the building stared openly at us, the colored woman and the white man—something I was used to after being with Tucker for so long—simply served to reinforce that fact.

We were there together, together together, even if that wasn't his intention. Judging by his reaction to my admission about driving at night by myself, maybe Grady didn't even notice those things. Or maybe he didn't notice because to him ... this was nothing more than just breakfast with the woman who worked for him.

Our conversation at that table helped temper the foundation-shaking stomps inside me.

"Tell me what you liked about working for the Chamber," he said.

He gained so many points with me by not making it about Daddy, or my family, or anything like that. Which was why it was easy to tell him. Our breakfast break was longer than it probably should have been, but as he inhaled his pancakes in about half the time it took me to eat my omelet, we talked a lot about the state of business in Green Valley. About what worked and what didn't for the people who were trying to make their living in a place still fairly tucked away from the rest of the bigger cities in the state.

"You love that town a lot," he said as we left the restaurant.

As he slowed his long-legged stride to match mine, I took notice of the fact that my head cleared somewhere around his bicep.

"I do," I told him. "It's not perfect, but it's home, you know?"

Grady smiled at me over top of the car as we both opened our doors to climb back in. "Not yet, but I'm getting there."

"What made you decide to move?" I asked as he took off again, starting the last hour to hour and a half of our drive.

He thought for a second before answering. "Do you ever look around and think, if I stay in this place for a second longer and don't find something new and exciting, I might go insane?"

"Never," I answered with utmost sincerity.

Grady laughed. "Insane might be a strong word. But I just hit the point when I realized just because I was good at my job didn't mean it was the right thing for me to do. I needed something that got me excited when I woke up in the morning. Somewhere I wanted to go every day, where I might not know how the day was going to end, or where it might take me." He glanced over at me. "This is the only life I have, you know? I don't want to waste it doing something that only pays the bills."

I sighed. "You're very brave, Grady. If I don't plan every possible outcome for my day, I feel like a top that's about to spin off a cliff."

He kept his eyes on the road, quiet for a few moments after I said that. "Bravery comes in all sorts of shapes and sizes, though. You left a job you were good at *and* that you loved because you knew it was the right thing to do. Don't tell me that's not brave." He grinned. "Because while I know it's not good Southern manners to argue with a lady, I'll tell you you're wrong every day of the week."

I bit down on my pleased smile and turned toward the window as the scenery flew by. "You're right, it's not good manners."

In response, he laughed quietly. "Well, you've got all day to fix what's wrong with me, Magnolia. That should be a good start."

Elephants. Big, fat, graceless elephants. I could hear them trumpeting in my ear now.

As soon as he said what he said, and I thought what I thought, I now was dreading the day's end.

CHAPTER 13

MAGNOLIA

*B*eing inside a convention center for outdoor enthusiasts with someone like Grady was like visiting a candy shop as someone who hated sugar.

His joy, his excitement was so effusive that I almost felt the stirrings of it myself, just from being near him. Within limits.

"That's incredible," he breathed. "Wouldn't that be awesome?"

"Oh, my Lord," I muttered, "that looks like my nightmare."

His laughter filled the space around us, drawing the attention of convention-goers looking at the same weird tent/car attachment that had Grady drooling.

He tried to explain it to me, God bless him. With passionate language and grandiose motions with those big hands of his, he told me how efficient it was to be able to *attach a tent to the top of a vehicle* so that you had a place to sleep, and all I could feel was abject horror that anyone would choose to do so.

Grady laughed again at my grim facial expression. Gently, he nudged my shoulder with his. "I think you'd love it if you gave it a try."

"I think if my employment was conditional upon that contraption, you'd find yourself without an office administrator."

"Well, we can't have that," he murmured around his grin. "Just think of how boring the office would be if the decorations were left up to me."

Happiness fairly burst out of me at his easily spoken words, because instead of shaming me or guilting me for not loving something that he so clearly did, he found a way to make me feel at ease with who I was.

We wandered through a couple more booths, and I took down information on my phone when he pointed out things he liked, such as gear or marketing items.

He stopped to admire a bright hammock strung between two fake trees in the middle of a massive corner booth. The orange and blue fabric was eye-catching, and I had a moment when I imagined it hanging over the green grass of my backyard, a wonderful place to lay in the shade of a tree and read on a summer afternoon.

"I could nap in that thing right now," he said, testing the way it was connected to one end.

"Don't you dare try to crawl inside, Grady Buchanan."

His smile was wide on that handsome face of his. "What's the worst that could happen?"

"You'd like a list?" I started ticking off items on my fingers. "You fall and break a bone. You rip the hammock, and they chase us out of here. The trees fall on top of us, and at best, you destroy their booth, and at worst, someone gets a concussion and/or a brain bleed from one of these landing on their head."

Grady didn't look at me, but he chuckled, low and quiet. "You're like my own personal warning label. I need to tuck you into my pocket so you can warn me of any impending doom lurking around the corner."

"I'd exhaust myself keeping up with you," I teased. "Though it'd be fun to try, I suppose."

Even to my own ears, I heard the flirty note in my voice. Grady's movements slowed, but he never moved his gaze off the hammock. A good thing too because I felt my face grow warm from how easily that had come out. It was one thing to think elephant-feeling thoughts and notice muscles and smiles, but to outright flirt with my boss ...? That was a horse of a different color.

Grady set his bags on the floor, and I groaned when I realized he meant to climb in.

"Grady," I hissed. "You're too tall."

"If a camping hammock can't hold a guy who's six-three, they're making it wrong," he said. With a quick glance at the booth workers, engaged in conversation elsewhere, he turned to slide inside. From the booth next door, someone shouted when they won a game. Grady sat too quickly, and the entire hammock spun, dumping him unceremoniously onto the concrete floor.

I laughed behind my hand at how he sprawled out on the floor, his hands clutched to his chest.

He grinned up at me. So completely non-self-conscious he was, lying there after his spill. How did anyone spend time with this man and not walk away completely and thoroughly charmed? "That didn't work out how I planned."

"I'd wager not." I held out my hand to his, and for a second, all he did was stare at it.

His palm was rough and warm when it clasped mine, and for just a moment, a tingle raced stealthily up my arm at the way his long fingers curled around my skin. I braced my feet and helped him stand. And maybe I imagined it, but color crept up his neck now that hadn't been there when he'd fallen.

"Do you enjoy being right about that kind of stuff?" he asked, gathering his bags off the floor.

"Immensely."

His answering laughter warmed me to my core.

We wandered through a few more booths, and I had to remind myself often that this was work. That I should be paying attention to other things besides him.

Grady nudged me, pointing at a massive fifth-wheel trailer parked along the back. It was sleek and beautiful, black with tan trim and glossy wheels. "Let me guess, you'd camp in that."

"I most definitely would," I told him. "Though I'm not sure you could qualify that as camping."

"On that, we agree." He poked his head in through the door to glance at the inside. "It's bigger than where I'm living right now."

The next booth had me stopping with a smile. "I'd camp in that too. It's adorable."

He grimaced. "Camping isn't supposed to be adorable. It's camping."

The silver egg-shaped trailer caught the reflection of the bright lights overhead. I opened the door and stepped inside. "See, it's perfect. A bed, a toilet, air conditioning, and enough cabinet space for me to actually cook some meals in that perfectly adorable little kitchen." My hands trailed along the edge of a small blue and white pillow. "And if there's room for décor, then I can handle it for my sleeping arrangements."

Grady had to duck his head to stand inside, and for a moment before I moved, I almost sank backward into the warmth of his broad chest against my back. "The Airstream is a classic, for sure." He leaned in, whispering by my ear. "But it's still not camping."

I fought against the urge to shiver.

What was he doing to me? We'd moved from elephants to back-leaning to shivering.

I blinked, trying desperately to find something to pull my brain from each one of those things. A small white pad of paper was sitting on the butcher block counter. "Should we try to win it?"

Grady laughed. "Win the Airstream Bambi? Why not."

We both filled out a card, tucking it into the box for entries on our way out. Like I had when he got up off the ground, Grady held out his hand for me when I reached the exit to the camper. I could've made my way down the steps perfectly fine, and I think he knew it.

But all the same, I slid my palm against his and gripped tightly while I took the two stairs down.

I glanced up at him. "Thank you."

Again, I noticed a slight flush to his cheeks and wondered at it. "My pleasure."

We kept walking, and for just a few moments longer, I curled my fingers in, trying to capture the warmth that his hand had left behind.

CHAPTER 14

GRADY

*T*hirteen hours after I picked her up, we were back in the car, exhausted, overwhelmed, excited, loaded down with useless swag and a billion business cards, and it was—without a freaking doubt—the best day I'd ever spent with another human being of the female variety.

After those thirteen hours, I was certain that Magnolia MacIntyre could take over the world if she wanted to. There hadn't been much time for us to talk in-depth at the convention because the space was big and loud and packed to the gills. More than once, I found myself leaning down so that I could hear her more clearly, and she'd look up at me with those eyes, and I could've sworn I saw something there. Something ... something new that hadn't been in her eyes before.

Curiosity, maybe.

Interest, possibly.

As we walked back to where the car was parked, a large group passed us, the lanyards around their necks proclaimed them as convention-goers. The men were either oblivious or assholes because they didn't move aside to make room for Magnolia and me to pass. I set my hand on her shoulder and gently guided her in front of me so the guy on the end didn't knock her over.

He held my stare as he passed, and it took every-fucking-thing in me not to shoulder check him when he did.

I was easily four inches taller, but on the flip side, I wasn't stupid, given he was walking with six of his buddies.

"Dick," I muttered, once they were out of earshot. Magnolia gave me a tiny smile as she moved back next to me.

"The world is full of them, unfortunately," she said.

I unlocked the car and then opened the back so we could set our bags inside.

"Doesn't make it right, though." I turned the key in the ignition once we both had our seat belts on. A bit over three hours in the car with her was all I had left. No interruptions from townspeople or twin sisters or ex-boyfriends.

"No," she agreed slowly. "But I'd rather be someone who knows how to pick their battles instead of just taking a baseball bat to the entire world. Because I'd exhaust myself if all I did was spend my time taking on each one."

I thought about that as I drove the car through Nashville and brought us a little bit closer to home.

"Sounds like you're speaking from experience there."

She smiled. It was a tired smile. "If I'd been walking with my daddy, he would've stopped the entire group and demanded that man apologize to me."

My eyebrows lifted briefly, but I couldn't even really pretend I was surprised. From what I knew of J.T., that was pretty on par.

"Should I have done that?" I looked over at her. "Just now."

"No." Her answer was firm and quick. "My daddy is a hothead of the worst order, so absolutely never take lessons from him on how to interact with ... anyone."

I couldn't help but smile. "He must do some stuff right."

She turned in her seat so she could face me. "What makes you say that? You don't really know him."

"He's successful and not just in business, right? From everything I've heard, he might be a bit ... abrasive, but he's got a wife who's smart and successful in her own right, whom he supports, and they have a marriage that's as solid as all those mountains that I look at every day." I kept my eyes forward on the road and decided to just ... not overthink what I was going to say or how I was going to say it. If this was the best thirteen hours I'd ever spent with a woman, and I'd hardly touched her, how badly could I screw this up? "He's got a daughter who's also smart and successful. I mean, I just watched you charm the hell out of every person we spoke to, and half of 'em didn't even realize what you were doing. If he can end each day knowing he's got a wife who loves him and a daughter who he's got to be proud as hell of, then that's a man who's done something right in his life." I smiled a little. "Even if he needs anger management therapy."

When Magnolia didn't respond right away, I risked a glance at her. She was staring out the windshield with a thoughtful look on her face.

"You know," she said quietly, "I've never really thought about it that way before."

"I am incredibly intuitive."

My gravely spoken answer had her cracking a smile.

"When Tucker broke up with me, I was so embarrassed," she admitted quietly. So quietly, that my heart sank like a rock.

Not because I couldn't handle hearing her say his name because I knew she didn't have feelings for him anymore. But I wanted to soak up all her hurt, absorb it into my skin so that she didn't have to feel it.

"How come?" I asked.

I'd never met anyone who'd ever made me want to do that before. Every relationship I'd had prior to laying eyes on Magnolia was light and easy and fun. Not frequent but about as deep as a cookie sheet. And in that car, knowing she was willing to confide this side of herself with me, I wanted nothing more than to pull those feelings away from her, even if it meant sitting in them alone.

She closed her eyes for a moment, just breathing. When they opened, I tightened my hand on the steering wheel so that I didn't reach for hers.

"When you have parents like mine, it's hard to face the fact that you were wrong about such an important thing." She glanced at me. "Love. Who you're supposed to be with. What your life is supposed to look like. And because I never saw it coming, my pride wasn't even bruised. I was just ... mortified."

My thumb tapped on the steering wheel as I tried to follow how we'd switched to this gear. What it meant for me and for her. For us. I wasn't blind to the change in her eyes during the previous thirteen hours.

"My parents broke every rule, every convention that they'd been raised in, by being together. Not even just when they got married, but they were in a relationship for years in a time when that was not accepted in polite society. And when you're wealthy"—she exhaled loudly—"po-lite society is where you find yourself."

She turned again, like she had earlier that morning, so her shoulder was braced against the seat, and I could see her face better.

"They weren't cowed by anyone, Grady. They refused to bow to pres-sure from their families who wanted them to be with someone else. They created a life outside of what anyone would dictate for them, and just like you've said, that's doing something right in life. It's building a foundation on the things that really matter. And then there's me." Her voice trailed off. "The product of that union, who only thrived in the structure that someone else built, who couldn't see just how much I was limiting myself, and limiting this man who I used to love, because I valued the safety of that structure over honesty."

I rubbed the back of my neck as I struggled to find the right words to say. There was no self-pity in her words, just naked vulnerability. The weight of that gift from this woman was not lost on me. It wasn't the time for a joke, which would be my default with just about anyone else.

"I think it's amazing, what your parents did," I said. "But everyone has a different path. And you're still on yours. Just because you're building your foundation in a different way doesn't mean it's wrong."

"No." She sighed. "But every time I see Tucker and see how happy he and your sister are, how perfect they are for each other ... it's a reminder of just how badly I could have messed up my life, and his, had she not shown up. My dad might be a hothead ..." Her voice wavered, and so help me, if she started crying, I'd have to stop the car and pull her into my arms and that was all there was to it. "He might piss off half the people who've met him, but he can look back at the choices he made and know he got this one big thing exactly right. All I see is how wrong, how miserable Tucker and I would've been."

It was a good thing that I had the task of driving. It was a good thing that for the next three hours, I had something to do. Because the truth of what she was saying hit me like the entire city of Nashville just got dumped on my head.

How was I *ever* supposed to expect Magnolia to be happy if she was with me?

Being with me—no matter how right I felt we were for each other— was asking her to face her greatest failure, her greatest embarrassment, day after day. It was asking her to sit in a room over holidays and birthdays with the first man she loved. With the woman he'd moved on with.

Occasional run-ins at work were one thing.

Living her life, asking her to place that relationship front and center, was entirely different.

And I couldn't ask that of her.

Maybe that was the worst part of this stupid curse. The part no one wanted to talk about. I was hammered over the head—almost instantly —with my feelings for Magnolia. Someone might dismiss it as lust at first sight, something shallow and unbelievable, but it wasn't shallow. It was—simply put—certainty.

A sense of rightness that I'd never experienced.

But along with that came an unwavering instinct to put her happiness before mine.

It was why my cousin Levi had been able to set aside his feeling for Joss for five years.

It was why Grace did her best to stay away from Tucker when she knew he had a girlfriend.

And it was why, as I drove us back to Green Valley, I knew that unless Magnolia told me that I was the man she wanted, I had to step back.

Rightness and certainty only went so far, because if you didn't factor in the other person—their fears and doubts and whatever they were dealing with—it turned into something selfish and ugly.

The desire to wrap her in my arms and hold her, hold this person who I thought was precious and rare and incredible, who I thought was sexy as hell and beautiful and sweet and smart and funny, should never overpower my ability to place her wants and desires first.

If she noticed my silence, she didn't say anything. Which was good because I had to take a minute to mourn how good I'd felt with her for the previous thirteen hours. The first handful of days of working together.

It wasn't about being a martyr for my feelings for Magnolia, it was that certainty again. The certainty that she was *more* important than what I was feeling.

"I'm sorry," she said. "Listen to me, dumping my problems on you."

"Don't apologize," I assured her. I cleared my throat. "I'm not ... I don't always feel equipped to give relationship advice. Just making sure whatever I say doesn't make things worse."

She watched me carefully.

"You and Tucker were together for a very long time." I shook my head. "And I can't imagine how hard it must be ... to try to move on from that kind of relationship. Especially when you live in a small town."

"He seemed to do all right," she said wryly. Then her eyes widened. "Oh, that was insensitive, I'm sorry. Your sister really does seem like a kind woman. I"—she shrugged her shoulders—"I actually liked her when we met. She was nice when she didn't have to be. And I don't mean to sound disrespectful."

"It's okay, really. I know what you meant."

She nodded. "Good."

Magnolia had no idea that what I said next felt like broken glass coming up my throat. That I could practically feel the damage done to my insides as I said them. "Maybe ... maybe that healing just takes time, you know? To realize that coming to the end of a relationship like that will look different for you than it did for him, and that's okay. Eventually, you'll know why it all happened the way it did, but you can trust that the embarrassment you feel now won't always be there."

Her eyes were serious when I glanced over. "You think so?"

I nodded. And as I did, I wondered if she could see what it cost me. "Yeah. Don't rush trying to feel okay with it. You don't need to compare yourself to your parents or Tucker and Grace, or anyone else."

"Just be myself," she said carefully. Still watching. Still studying.

This time, it was easy to give her a smile. "Yeah. Because you're Magnolia fucking MacIntyre, and that's more than enough."

"Such language," she tsked. But she couldn't hide her smile, slow and sweet and beautiful. "We've still got work to do with you, Grady. Good thing I'm a determined woman."

Certainty.

I felt it again, at the back of my head, that she was it for me.

I'd never been good at being patient. Never been great at sitting back and allowing life to unfold at its own pace. Setting the pace was more my style.

This, though, was different. She was different.

"Good thing," I murmured.

CHAPTER 15

MAGNOLIA

he farther we drove, and the closer we got to home, the conversation turned back to "normal" stuff. As much as I valued everything we'd discussed, everything I felt safe enough to discuss with him, it was a relief. The elephants receded, and for a while, I felt like me. The Magnolia that didn't get to come out very often.

"What are you going to do with all that junk?" I teased.

"Marketing swag has a valuable place in this universe." He stuck his hand behind my seat and pulled out one of the fifteen travel mugs he was given. "Did you see this? I almost cried."

I laughed. "It better not find a place at the office because I have dreams about how well that place is organized right now."

Grady sped around a slow-moving vehicle, and the headlights briefly highlighted the strong bone structure in his face and the casual strength in his frame he carried with ease.

The longer I was around him, the more he reminded me of a mountain lion.

Not a regular lion, with a big roar and a solid block of muscle on a large frame. Grady was graceful in his strength. Underneath his unassuming clothes, underneath that charming exterior, he kept his strength contained until the right moment. One moment when you couldn't not see it.

With a smirk on his face, he leaned back again to set the cup back into the bag behind my seat, and I caught a whiff of him.

Even after the entire day walking around that massive convention center, he smelled good.

I tried to channel his very good advice and think about how I should just be myself for a while. But in the dark interior of the car, I wanted to do all sorts of things when that smell crossed whatever invisible barrier was between our seats.

None of them were proper.

None of them were polite.

I could feel my Southern ancestors blushing in the grave because of my thoughts, yet I couldn't bring myself to stop them. They rolled around in my head, gaining momentum. Thoughts of his teeth on my collarbone. My fingernails raking along his muscled abs and around to his back. Thoughts of him over me, thoughts of pulling, pushing, sweating, thrusting.

I waved a hand in front of my face, because if my hairline wasn't glistening with sweat, then I didn't know my own name. It was insanity.

Closing my eyes, I let out a slow, quiet exhale and brought up the one thing guaranteed to derail such a line of thinking.

"Speaking of Tucker and Grace," I said.

He glanced over at me. "Were we?"

"No."

Grady smiled.

"Do they know?" I hadn't wanted to ask. Because it was a reminder of how I'd started in this job in the first place. He had to smooth things over with them because of my choices.

His smile disappeared as he nodded. "They do."

"Do I want to know how it went?"

"They're both okay, I promise." Grady sighed. "Grace was fine. She kinda feels the same as you do. She liked you," he said with a tiny smile.

"Your sister is the instigator of one of the worst hangovers of my entire life."

He laughed. "She's horrible like that."

His voice was so warm, so full of love, that I forgot for a moment to think about Grace as Tucker's love and simply viewed her as Grady's twin sister.

"I don't believe you think she's horrible at all."

"You don't have any siblings, right?"

I shook my head. "It was one of the things Tucker and I had in common. All the parental aspirations fell squarely on our shoulders."

"Seems like you're both doing a pretty good job of not letting that tie you down anywhere."

"I suppose we are." Resting my head back against the seat, I stared at the dark, winding road and mentally calculated how long we had in the car. Less than ten minutes, probably. My thoughts weren't obscene anymore. They were sad. I felt like the best first date of my life was almost over, and instead of knowing I'd get a kiss at my front door at the end, I was going to wake up in my bed to the realization that it wasn't real.

"Tucker was surprised, but he trusts me. And he knows what kind of person you are," Grady said slowly. "The good thing for you is that they know how terribly I would've screwed this up on my own. If I didn't have someone like you to whip me into shape, Valley Adventures would've been nothing but a pipe dream."

"I'm going to ignore that because there's a time and a place for you to be unkind to yourself, and this isn't it."

He laughed.

"Tucker was really okay with this?" I asked. He hadn't really answered my question. Not in a way that felt dishonest but more like ... evasive. Like he didn't want to talk about it.

A muscle in Grady's jaw clenched. "He was."

"Good."

"I'm sorry I didn't tell you earlier." He looked over at me. "That I'd talked to them."

"Grady," I said on a laugh, "you don't have to apologize for anything."

The headlights from his car swept over the green and white sign that proclaimed the Green Valley city limits.

"Oh, I don't know about that," he murmured.

He slowed down a bit when a line of bikers roared past us. The line of Iron Wraiths was obnoxiously loud, and I sighed at the way they zipped around the yellow lines in the road. Every once in a while, I heard them go down the street just past my house.

Grady was thinking the same thing. "They come past your house often?" he asked. His face was hard lines, lending him an unforgiving look that I hadn't yet seen on him.

"Every once in a while, I'll hear a group like that go by, yes."

He turned the car onto my street, passing my neighbors slowly. There were only four houses on our road, but my street was adjacent to another, so I had a couple of neighbors behind me as well. It was one of my daddy's caveats. Private, but not too private. Enough people around that if I needed help with something, I had someone nearby to call.

I grimaced when he pulled into the driveway, and I saw that the light above my garage was burned out.

"No outside lights?" he asked.

"I think the one above the garage burned out. It's supposed to be on right now."

He slid the car in park, already taking off his seat belt before another word came out of his mouth. "I can replace that for you."

There'd be no token protestation from me. I breathed a sigh of relief when he got out of the car. I'd lived on my own in the few years since I graduated college, but for all those years, I'd had Tucker to come over and do those small things for me. Now, some women might get up in arms because couldn't I change the light bulb my damn self?

Sure.

Just like I could skydive. I could bungee jump. I could get a giant tattoo on my ass and drink whiskey all day, every day, but that didn't mean any of those things sounded particularly fun. Climbing up a ladder to reach floodlights perched over my garage with no one to brace said ladder for me sounded like a perfectly delightful way to end up with a broken leg.

If Grady wanted to make his tall self useful while he was here, then it would be downright rude of me to take that away from him.

My Grandma MacIntyre used to tell me that she could fix every single thing in their house just as well as Grandpa could, but if she started, then all he'd do was bug her incessantly with how bored he was.

Compromise, she'd said, was about more than just making decisions. For a second, I missed her, missed them both so much that it knocked the breath from my lungs.

Using the flashlight on my phone, I unlocked the door, going into my single stall garage, and then pushed the button to open the door. As it slowly creaked open, shedding light onto the driveway, I realized just how strange it was to have another man here doing something like this for me.

Maybe Grady was right. If I couldn't have him change a light bulb without it triggering some odd sense of unease, how on earth could I expect to go on a date with someone? Kiss someone? Sleep with someone?

As Grady moved around my garage, his eyes tracking the perfectly clean shelves lining the back with amusement, my cell phone buzzed in my purse.

I didn't even glance at the screen before I answered it.

"Hello?"

"Robert across the street just called me to say that there was a strange man in your garage with you."

I rubbed my forehead. "Nice to talk to you too, Daddy."

"Who is it? And is that where you've been all day? I drove by on my way home, and everything was dark."

Grady must have heard my father's voice because I caught him grinning as he pulled the ladder off the hook on the wall.

"I was at a convention in Nashville for work. We just got home."

He was quiet on the other end of the phone. "You didn't drive, did you?"

"No." I stared at the man I worked for while he climbed up that ladder with ease, light bulb tucked safely in one hand. "Grady drove us, and I know I don't have to explain who that is because I reckon you know already."

Daddy sighed. "Marcia already screwed something up today."

150

"I highly doubt that."

"Fine," he said begrudgingly. "She didn't. But she jumps around like a cricket every time I come out of my office, and it drives me crazy."

That made me smile. "Marcia's always had me as the buffer. But she'll learn, they all will, that your bark is much, much worse than your bite."

"Are you happy?" He went silent for a second, and as bright, beautiful light flooded the driveway, Grady climbed down the ladder, his eyes pinned on me. "Doing what you're doing, are you actually happy, or is this just about proving a point?"

"Does it matter?" I asked quietly. "To you, I mean."

"Yeah." His voice was gruff. "I may not like it, but if you're happy, that's the only thing that matters to me, Magnolia."

My eyes closed, and I hated the way the bridge of my nose burned with unshed tears. This was the side of my daddy that no one saw except me and Momma.

When I opened them again, Grady had his arms braced on the top of the ladder, just watching me. There was no way he could've heard what my father asked me.

I held Grady's gaze as I answered. "Yeah, Daddy, I am."

Grady dropped his head and tucked the legs of the ladder together, moving past me quietly so he could hang it back up.

My father cleared his throat, and oh Lord, for some reason, I just knew he was trying to keep himself together. I thought about what Grady had said on the drive, how he must have done some things right for all the things he did wrong.

"I love you," I told him. "And I know this is hard because of how much you love me."

"Uh-huh," he replied, voice thick and full. "You know I do. I, uh, I gotta go, Magnolia. We'll see you next week for Thanksgiving, right?"

"Yes, Daddy. I'll be there."

He hung up before I could say anything else, and I kept the phone up to my ear for a second longer.

As I tucked it into my purse, Grady spoke from behind me. "Everything okay?"

I turned, bracing my back against my car. "Yeah," I answered slowly. "I think so."

Grady sucked in a slow breath, and it made his chest expand underneath his dark shirt. He'd pushed the sleeves up while he drove, and even though the air was brisk, it felt nice inside my garage where we were protected from the wind. When he tucked his hands into his front pockets, the muscles in his forearms flexed, veins popping under his skin.

My thoughts strayed again as I noticed those veins for the first time.

Elephants weren't just in my brain again, making their big, cumbersome presence known, they were pirouetting in tutus through my whole body.

Grady let out that breath, and for a moment, I saw something flash in his eyes that made me wonder if he had the same kind of thoughts. His eyes, warm and beautiful, landed for just a split second on my mouth, and when they did, my entire body went hot.

"It was a good day today," I said.

He nodded, his gaze leaving my lips and dropping to the floor. "It was. Thank you for coming with me. I think we made some good contacts."

What I'd said and how he'd answered were on two separate wavelengths. Mine served as a segue, one where I was weighing the intelligence of inviting him in simply to continue that good day with no expectations and no ulterior motives.

His was the establishing of boundaries. Professional boundaries.

I wasn't embarrassed because I saw the way he looked at my lips in that one moment he'd allowed himself to. But given the respect Grady had shown me in such a short amount of time, I could respect him in the same way.

"Thank you for driving," I told him.

He nodded.

"And for the light."

Grady smiled, a subdued, sweet smile, and it curled up my insides, a delicious kind of curl too. The kind your toes made when you were kissed and kissed thoroughly. "You're welcome." He jerked his chin to the house. "Go on in. I'll wait to leave until you lock up."

If this was the kind of man who still existed out in the world, the kind who could allow me to walk past without so much as a single touch, then I would be okay waiting.

CHAPTER 16

GRADY

*I*f someone had asked me to list the top ten traits that defined me, patience would never have been one of them. But I learned over that holiday season that I'd pegged myself wrong my whole life.

I was

So

Freaking

Patient.

Miserable? Yes.

But also, patient.

Thanksgiving

We gathered at Uncle Robert and Aunt Fran's house. People spilled from room to room, two long tables filled with delicious-smelling foods, and it was all I could do not to stare like a creeper at all the blissfully happy couples that the house contained.

My cousin Cooper and his wife, Sylvia, were still newlyweds as they hadn't yet celebrated their first anniversary. They met and started dating when they were fifteen. She sat on his lap, stealing bites of food off his plate, and they finished each other's sentences.

Assholes.

My cousin Levi, visiting from Seattle with his girlfriend, Joss. They were at the end of the table, though Joss wasn't in Levi's lap. She got the seat at the head of that table because it was easier for her to maneuver in her wheelchair. Watching them was like watching Cooper and Sylvia because they'd known each other for so many years, and there was an ease and comfort in their interactions. Joss rolled her eyes when Levi stood on his chair to whistle for everyone before Uncle Robert said grace over the meal. He messed up her hair when she turned to talk to someone on her other side. Instead of glaring at him, I saw her hand sneak over and pinch the inner skin on his thigh, which made him yelp loudly.

They'd been best friends for five years before Levi's very unrequited love had finally been ... requited.

And then there was Grace and Tucker. Their relationship was still new. They still traded long glances that made me want to puke. They leaned in and whispered things in each other's ears, snuggling on the couch and talking while football played on the TV.

The whole day was a glimpse into what this Buchanan curse meant. The bigness of it. The immense happiness on display was wonderful. It was terrible too.

Because trying to insert Magnolia and me into what I was seeing was hard to do with Tucker and Grace cuddling and whispering and looking. In my head, no matter how I turned it around and around, I couldn't make the puzzle piece fit.

No one noticed how quiet I was except Grace, who threw a wadded-up napkin at my face as I finished my second plate of food.

"You okay?" she mouthed.

I winked, which had her shoulders relaxing.

Some twins I knew could genuinely read each other's minds, but not Grace and me. We didn't always mirror each other's feelings, but every once in a while, I could be in the room with her and know that she needed a hug from her brother without her saying a single word.

That must have been what she was feeling too because after plates were cleared, bellies were full, and music played over the chatter of happy voices, she found me in the kitchen and wrapped her arms around my middle.

I hugged my sister back, kissed the top of her head, and then went to find a quiet place to sit where I wouldn't have to watch everyone around me live out their loves on display. As I left the room, I felt her eyes heavy on my back, but I didn't turn around.

December

The office was quiet for the weeks leading up to Christmas, but our spring calendar was booking up nicely. Between seeking out some corporate partnerships and the lull in immediate business, Magnolia had started doing some of her work at home with my permission.

But the times we saw each other was like tearing at a freshly healed wound. For a few days, the bleeding would stop, it would start closing, and I would reaffirm that I was capable of being around her without being with her.

Then I'd see her.

See her smile.

See her laugh.

See her pretend she wasn't rolling her eyes at something I did.

And just like that, the pain was fresh, and the scar reopened. She hung Christmas lights through the office, humming to music in the background, and I'd discover something new—like she couldn't sing for shit —and it got even worse.

I loved that Magnolia couldn't sing.

Everything else about her seemed so perfect or perfect for me, at least, that this one imperfection somehow made her even more endearing to me.

She brought in poinsettias for the table in the front window and a small Christmas tree that she set next to the desk, decorated in red and white lights.

A red wreath for the door.

"Do our decorations coordinate?" I asked one day, looking between the flowers and the tree and the miniature ornaments on the tiny branches.

She tsked. "I'm not an amateur."

"I never would have suggested such a thing."

Eyeing the lights carefully, she stood on a stepladder and moved the left side until everything was even. "My momma told me that her mom, my Mawmaw Boone, loved to decorate for the holidays. I didn't know her, she died just after I was born, so I always feel like I'm doing something she'd love when I make everything look nice for special occasions."

Would she think it was weird if I just sat and watched her all day? She probably would.

"My mom decks out her place too," I said. "The only thing that freaks me out is the giant bunny in the front yard for Easter."

Magnolia laughed. "Just wait until Halloween, Grady. I'll blow your mind."

I smiled for hours after that one exchange. It tided me over for days when she worked from home.

The next day, I arrived at the darkened office and immediately plugged in the small tree and the lights along the shelving. It made everything warm and bright. When I turned, I noticed a small, neatly wrapped box on the corner of the desk.

Sitting at the desk chair, I took a second before I pulled it toward me.

The tag on the box was handwritten.

Merry Christmas, Grady

Obviously, she didn't need to say who it was from. No one else would be leaving me a present. Each corner was folded with ruthless precision, and I thought about her taping down the immaculate edges.

Magnolia should go into business as a gift wrapper because I'd never seen anything as perfect as that small box. I opened it as delicately as my big, oafish fingers could manage, trying to preserve the gold-embossed wrapping.

I lifted the lid, and on top of something wrapped in white tissue was another small notecard.

I hope you never need this, but if you do, you'll be able to find where you need to go.

Magnolia

My heart was drumming uncomfortably, skipping over some beats while spending extra time on others. Underneath the white tissue paper was a beautiful vintage-looking compass.

It was gold and heavy in my hand. The lid lifted to reveal a beautiful black and white face, the arrow moving unerringly as I spun in the chair.

The sight of it rendered me mute because she'd seen this piece of art and thought of me.

Why did that feel like a sign?

And why was I such a jackass that I hadn't gotten her a Christmas present?

Probably because I was afraid that I'd pick out something too obvious. That would make my feelings too apparent.

Like an engagement ring.

Look, Magnolia, I got your name tattooed over my heart. Merry Christmas!

I laughed under my breath. Probably not.

I sent her a text even though I didn't really want to set the compass down.

Me: The compass is beautiful, thank you very much.

Magnolia: You're very welcome. I know it's a bit much for a Christmas present for your boss, but I saw it at a vintage store in Merryville and thought of you. Enjoy your days off, Grady.

Obviously, I didn't see her after that since we closed down the office for a few days before and after the holiday. But when I got home that day, I kept my gift out on my kitchen counter where it absolutely tore my heart out every single time I saw it.

I found myself going on longer and harder hikes, probably things I shouldn't have been doing by myself.

Inside the converted garage apartment where I lived, I worked out every evening, just so that my body would hit the point of exhaustion before I flopped face-first onto my bed.

Christmas morning, while we opened presents at Pop's small apartment downtown, I caught Grace watching me carefully a few times, but since Thanksgiving, she'd stopped asking me if I was okay. We ate cinnamon rolls from Donner Bakery in our pajamas around my dad's Charlie Brown-esque tree and traded white elephant gifts with each other.

I ended up with a beat-up tackle box from Tucker, and I stared at it for a while, wondering if it had come from Big Bob's Bait and Tackle, a remnant of his time with Magnolia.

The tackle box did not sit out on my counter.

Before I went to bed that night, I stared at my phone and allowed myself one text to Magnolia. Just one.

Merry Christmas, Magnolia. I'm trying to figure out how the person who's known me the shortest amount of time ended up buying me the most perfect gift I've ever gotten.

My fingers deleted that second sentence before I could hit send. I closed my eyes, laid an arm over my face, and tried again.

Merry Christmas, Magnolia. I hope you got everything on your list this year.

"Stupid," I whispered, punching the backspace button like it had personally injured me.

Merry Christmas, Magnolia. I wish I could've given you the present I really wanted to give you. Maybe next year.

Backspace, until it was all gone. "Because that's not creepy."

Merry Christmas, Magnolia. I miss you when I don't get to see you. You're the most fascinating woman I've ever met in my entire life. I am in love with you.

Backspace.

Merry Christmas, Magnolia.

I hit send.

Immediately, she started typing, and I found myself stupidly, idiotically, breathless with anticipation.

Magnolia: Merry Christmas, Grady. Was Santa good to you this year?

I rolled over onto my side and took a deep breath before I answered.

Me: Got almost everything I wanted.

Me: You?

Magnolia: Pretty much the same.

I let out a slow breath. I felt like we were dangling on a dangerous precipice.

Magnolia: What are you up to?

Without thinking, I snapped a quick picture and sent it. Nothing about it was risky. Half my face, my shoulder, and in the background was the TV mounted on the wall, which was playing *Home Alone*. Also known as the greatest Christmas movie of all time.

My phone dinged, and all she sent was a picture back.

There might have been a TV, and I think it might have shown *Home Alone*, but all I could do was stare at that half of her face. My thumb traced the line of her bottom lip, and I felt my body react. Her hair was down—wonderfully curly, like it had been for the past couple of weeks—and underneath it, I could see a thin strap of white over the graceful curve of her shoulder.

A tank top maybe.

Somehow, I managed a response, but my hands were shaking.

Me: Great minds.

Me: Have a good night, Magnolia.

Magnolia: You too.

Magnolia: I think I'm going to work from home this week if you're okay with that.

Maybe the week would be good. Maybe I needed that to completely reset after the holidays. I sent her a thumbs-up.

Magnolia: See you after the New Year.

I sent another thumbs-up, like a jackass, because it's all I was capable of. I shoved my phone away from me, rolled on my back, and struggled to breathe evenly. One picture. One picture of half her face, and the line of her neck and shoulder, and I was acting like a kid who just saw his first nudie pic.

Boundaries existed for these exact reasons, and I knew just how careful I had to be. My hands ached to reach for the phone. My hands also ached to push my shorts down my hips and ease the ache that I felt when I thought about her for too long.

Instead, I turned off the TV, reached up and turned off the lamp next to my bed, and rolled over for a night of fitful sleep, plagued by dreams of her.

Almost January

The dream that woke me on New Year's Eve was the same one I'd had all week. The picture was long deleted off my phone because I didn't trust myself.

A week without one glimpse of her at the office, and I felt like I was dying.

I'd worked out more that week than I ever had before, and instead of it helping me sleep, it only served to take the slightest edge off any tension I felt when I thought of Magnolia.

But that tension came right back whenever I dreamed of her. It always started the same.

I was facing her in the office. In my dream, when my eyes landed on her mouth, full and soft-looking, I strode toward her and slanted my mouth over hers.

In my dream, Magnolia boosted herself up against the desk, wrapped her legs around my waist, and slid her hands around the back of my head while she slipped her tongue against my own.

In my dream, I found out how soft her skin was and how she moved against me restlessly.

In my dream, the surface of the desk was violently wiped clean and we fell against it, which was when it turned into a bed.

In my dream, she ripped at my shirt and I ripped at hers until they were gone.

In my dream, I tugged on her bottom lip with my teeth, soothed that spot with my tongue when she whimpered, then rolled my hips against her where we both needed satisfaction the most.

And just as I was pulling off her pants, and as she rushed to push off mine as well, sliding her hand underneath my boxer briefs, I woke up gasping. Woke up gasping and hard and in pain and frustrated.

Every. Single. Day. That week.

Cursed was an appropriate word.

I felt cursed. Plagued. Haunted.

And to punish myself, I'd decided to let that frustration build. Not to use my own hand to find the satisfaction that I wanted with Magnolia.

I didn't know what drove that self-flagellation, exactly.

But I did know that when I let Grace and Tucker drag me to a New Year's Eve party at the community center, I was in a terrible mood.

The parking lot was full, light and laughter and music spilling out from the open doors.

All I wanted to do was turn around and go back home and go to bed, and maybe, just maybe, tonight, both Magnolia and I would get a screaming, back-bending, long-awaited release in my dream. I kicked at a rock in the parking lot, then winced when it ricocheted off a truck's tire.

Grace tugged on my arm before we walked in. "Seriously, should I be worried about you?"

I sighed, tilting my head up at the dark winter sky. "No, don't be worried."

"You're a terrible liar." She waved Tucker inside the building, leaving me alone with my sister.

"I'm not lying." I finally met her gaze, and I could only imagine what she saw in my face. I'm sure my eyes had some shadows under them, and I definitely needed a shave. "I'll be fine. Just not sleeping great this week."

Grace opened her mouth, then closed it. She shook her head a little and then exhaled. "Someday, you'll tell me, brother." She squeezed my arm and then jogged into the building after Tucker.

From the darkness of the parking lot, I watched everyone inside dancing and talking and laughing. I recognized a lot of faces and didn't recognize just as many. But as a group of people moved aside, I saw the one I was looking for.

How did Levi do what he did for five years?

After eight days of not seeing her, I felt like a wilted plant that just got a cool drink of water.

Magnolia was wearing the same bright yellow dress that she'd worn at her interview, and I couldn't help but smile at it. It was so perfectly audacious, so perfectly her, to do something like that. But tonight, in her dark, curly hair—there was a bright yellow flower pinned next to her ear.

An elderly gentleman spun her around in a quick turn, and she tilted her head back to laugh.

This was Magnolia being herself.

I watched as Tucker nodded at her with his arm around Grace, and Magnolia smiled back. No one was watching them, no one was whispering, and she went back to dancing as if nothing had happened.

She was happy.

And I felt certain that I was doing the right thing.

Someday, I'd be able to tell her the truth when she was ready.

But it wasn't today.

Maybe I was a coward, to remove myself from situations where I'd be tempted by her mere presence, but I wasn't sure exactly how else to do it.

Maxine Barton pushed her walker out of the community center door and did a double-take when she saw me.

"Good God Almighty, Grady, you're gonna give me a heart attack, and believe me, that is not the way I plan on leaving this earth."

Maxine was a welcome distraction, and I smiled. "You've got a plan?"

"I will either be sleeping peacefully in my bed, or I will go out while some sixty-year-old silver fox makes me feel young again ... There'll be no other options."

"Can I walk you to your car?" I asked as I tried to stem my laughter.

"Might as well make yourself useful." She eyed me as she walked over the uneven ground. "Why aren't you going in?"

"Not feeling much like partying tonight, Miss Barton."

"Me neither. The older I get, the less I can handle crowds for too long."

She clicked the button on her key fob, and some headlights lit up on a sedan in front of us.

Maxine got in the driver's seat, and I folded up the walker for her, setting it carefully in the back seat. I tapped my fingers on the roof of her car and looked back at the community center. I thought about Magnolia in her lemon-yellow dress and how happy she was dancing.

I wanted to dance with her.

I wanted to kiss her at midnight.

Ringing in a new year on the calendar with her in my arms and her lips on mine sounded just about perfect.

And I knew I couldn't have that just yet.

"Maxine? Would you mind dropping me off at home? I don't want to make Grace and Tucker leave."

Through her open window, she eyed me curiously. Those eyes narrowed, but she didn't say anything and simply nodded.

Someday, I'd get a chance to do all those things.

But not today.

CHAPTER 17

MAGNOLIA

I should've stayed home.

It was my first thought when I got to my parents' house on New Year's Day. Every year, members of our extended family gathered to eat too much food and watch too much football. As I was growing up, it was one of my favorite days of the year. No one was working, it wasn't a work function (which caused a lot of unintentional family run-ins in a family like mine, whose reach was long in Green Valley) or anything, except enjoying each other's company.

It was also one of the only times on the calendar when the MacIntyres and the Boones frequented the same party. Oh, they got along fine because my parents had been together long enough now. While they were still alive, I knew my Mawmaw Boone and my Grandma MacIntyre used to share a weekly cup of coffee at Daisy's, but the New Year's Day party was a different sort of gathering.

Normally, it was a day for me to shine. I took the hostess mantle easily because hosting a large group like this was the quickest way to get my momma to perch herself on the lake with a cooler and a fishing rod.

My cousin Maya Boone poked her head around the corner into the kitchen. "Is the food ready yet, Magnolia?"

I herded her out of the kitchen. "The more you hassle me about it, the longer it'll take. Go bug your brothers."

"But they're all watching football, and it's so *boring*."

Aunt Julianne, Daddy's sister, snuck Maya a deviled egg off to the side. "You could always go outside and help your aunt bait some hooks. Maybe catch us our dinner."

Maya's face twisted up in a disgusted grimace, but she knew better than to verbalize how horrified she was by that idea. Wisely, she ate the egg instead. "Thank you, Miss Julianne," she said.

"Welcome, honey." Aunt Julianne smiled at her, then pinned me with her knowing gaze. "Out with it. Don't think you can pout around this kitchen and no one will notice."

With clenched teeth, I set myself to mixing up the dip just a bit more vigorously. "I'm not pouting."

"Please. You're about to start a fresh set of wrinkles on your forehead, and if you do that, then Lord help you find a new man, Magnolia."

The eye roll was internal, but when that gaze narrowed at me, she must have sensed it.

"If a man is deterred by some forehead wrinkles, then he's probably not worth tying myself to anyway."

She harrumphed. "Fine. But you're only twenty-six, honey, avoid speeding the process along, if you can." Then she glanced outside, through the wall of windows, where her brother's wife sat at the edge of the dock with two poles in the water. "Though, if you age anything like your momma, you'll be just fine, I suppose."

That made me smile. "True. The wrinkles all come from the white side of my family."

She clucked her tongue disapprovingly, but I caught a hint of a smile.

Grabbing a spoon from the drawer, I slipped her a taste of the dip. "More dill?"

At her nod, I shook the spice jar over the bowl and continued mixing.

"Is that brother of mine causing you more grief, honey?" Aunt Julianne asked quietly. She always referred to Daddy that way. *That brother of mine.*

I glanced into the living room, packed with my people, and shook my head. "No, he's ... he's been doing okay, actually."

"Miracles never cease."

"Aunt Julianne," I chided. "Are you so ungracious toward your own brother?"

She gave me a knowing look over the rim of her glasses. "I'm old, Magnolia. You don't earn the label of old lady without gaining the right to call a jackass a jackass, especially if you're related to him."

When I handed her another spoonful of dip, she nodded in approval. I slid the heavy crystal bowl toward the rest of the food lining the long kitchen island.

"The holidays were fine," I told her. "They had their first big Chamber event since I left, and I think he realized that everything would be okay without me."

"And that's why you're pouting?"

Shaking my head, I said, "I don't miss my job. At all."

I could feel those wrinkles she talked about appearing on my forehead. I'd felt off since Christmas, and I couldn't quite place why.

"Jackass or not, I love my brother," she said, putting the finishing flourish of paprika on the deviled eggs, "but it was far past time for you to spread your wings, honey. I'm glad you're not thinking about going back."

"Definitely not."

The strength of my reaction had her silvery-white eyebrows lifting on that heavily wrinkled brow. "Goodness, who're you trying to convince?"

My face flushed warm, and I turned to the fridge to make sure enough ice was in the bucket for drinks. "No one. I just ... I love what I'm doing now. It's a good place to work."

She chuckled. "You and hiking and outdoor anything. Boggles the mind, but I'm happy to hear it."

"*I* don't have to hike or do outdoor anything," I pointed out.

Aunt Julianne eyed my pink cashmere sweater. "Good thing."

Junior, Aunt Julianne's oldest son, swooped in and stole the basket filled with chips before I could stop him. "Thank you, Magnolia," he yelled over his shoulder. "Come on, stop 'em on this down, boys." That was directed at whatever bowl game was happening on the television.

"That boy you working for—the Buchanan—he good people?"

Her gaze was shrewd when she asked it, and I couldn't blame her. Since the day I got my first job, I'd always been employed by someone I was related to.

The thought of Grady brought a smile to my face and an uncomfortable pang in my chest. Why did I feel like this? Like something was missing. I'd hardly seen him the past couple of weeks, but I'd also been using my current tube of mascara for longer than I'd known Grady, so it was ridiculous to presume that what I might be missing was him.

"Very good people," I assured her. "And he's not a boy. He's my age."

"Good-looking?"

I raised an eyebrow.

"No harm in asking. Calm down."

Was Grady good-looking?

Only if you found tall, strong men with chiseled features, bright eyes, and glorious smiles attractive. Only if you found kindness and respect and loyalty and a good sense of humor attractive.

She hummed. "Taking you a long time to answer, honey."

"I'm thinking about what food I'm missing." Lying to your aunt was a sin, to be sure, but I didn't particularly want to answer her question.

"So, he's good-looking."

"Who's good-looking?" my dad asked. He kissed his sister on the cheek, then walked around the island and grabbed a beer out of the fridge.

I smiled at Aunt Julianne. It was the kind of smile in the South that was akin to hollering at the top of your lungs at a wayward child.

You keep your mouth shut and move along.

That kind.

She smiled right back.

I will do whatever I want, young lady.

I narrowed my eyes at her in warning.

She narrowed hers right back.

I sighed because I'd lost.

"Grady Buchanan," Aunt Julianne answered smoothly.

Daddy froze with the beer halfway to his mouth. "Why are we talking about that?"

"We *weren't*. Aunt Julianne was just asking if he was or wasn't, and I didn't answer." I handed Daddy a plate, hoping the promise of food would distract him.

For a moment, I thought it did. He set the beer down on the counter and slowly filled a plate. Aunt Julianne and I watched him fill it with all of Momma's favorite things.

"Be right back." He walked out the slider doors, through the sloping yard toward the lake, down the long, wooden dock, where he set the plate down next to her and whispered something in her ear. She looked up at him, and they traded a soft, quick kiss.

I had to look away.

The feeling I'd told Grady about on our drive home from Nashville, that embarrassment, it was lessening. Bit by bit and day by day, it was fading.

Daddy came back in the house, and without a word, he started filling a plate for himself. "That boy is doing better than I thought he would," he said casually. "Heard he's gonna be busy come spring."

"That boy has a name."

He raised an eyebrow but didn't look at me.

"Doesn't seem like you've been at the office much, though. Tucker still causing you problems? Because I can—"

"You can nothing," I interrupted. "I'm working from home because there's not much need for me in the office right now. Grady was fine with it when I asked. But as the weather warms up, I'll be back in there." Pride swelled in my chest. "He's been working hard, and it shows."

"And he's good-looking," Aunt Julianne pointed out.

Our gazes clashed, and she smiled again. *What are you going to do about it? He's my brother, and I'll bait him if I want to.*

This. This was why I should've stayed home. Because my family was certifiably insane.

"Why do we keep talking about his looks?" Daddy barked. "I didn't even think you knew him, Julianne."

"I don't." She peered down her nose at me. "But my very beautiful, very *single* niece might."

Daddy set his plate down, folded his arms, and glared at his older sister. "Why are you like this?"

"I don't know what you mean," she said innocently.

"Magnolia doesn't care what he looks like because he's her boss. She's his employee, and if he tries anything with her, that's a gross misuse of his power."

I gave him a long, level look, because honestly, the hypocrisy of those words coming out of his mouth was almost too much to handle.

My aunt rolled her eyes.

Daddy's face flushed pink because I'd learned the skill of containing an eye roll from her, and if she let one fly, it was pretty damn bad.

"Magnolia is standing right here," I reminded them both.

A celebratory roar came from the family room, saving us from that conversation going any further. Daddy grabbed his plate to go see what had happened, and Aunt Julianne smiled beatifically at me.

I clucked my tongue. She laughed.

"I'll get you a plate," I told her.

"You're a good girl, Magnolia."

A good girl who should've stayed home. It was amazing how people's attention toward you changed when you'd gone your whole span of early adulthood as a part of a couple. Like her sole purpose was to remind me that any eligible man was, well, eligible.

Carefully spooning some potato salad onto her plate, I kept my voice low so no one else could hear me besides her. "Him being good-looking is beside the point. You know as well as I do that some of God's most beautiful creations can still be rotten on the inside."

"But he's not rotten, is he?"

"No," I said immediately. "Not even close."

Her eyes were knowing.

"You stop that." I pointed the serving spoon at her. "I took this job because I was sick of having my family run my life."

"You took that job because my brother is an overbearing pain in the ass. You took that job because it was high time for you to step out into something bigger and better, Magnolia Marie."

"Want anything else?" I asked.

"One of those rolls, if you please."

I did as she asked, then handed her the plate. "I know why you're pushing me, Aunt Julianne."

"Because I love you and want you to be happy and would desperately like some little ones to love on before I die, which just might be any day now."

I smiled sweetly. "I'm so glad we haven't resorted to guilt trips at this point in our life."

"I don't have anyone else to spoil, Magnolia. You are it. My sons haven't found women to put up with them, and your daddy found the *only* woman in existence who would." At my laughter, her face softened. Her eyes went bright with unshed tears. "Someday, you'll have a family, honey, and you'll know the special kind of love that children bring into your life. Your parents being of the age they were when they had you … you're as good as my own granddaughter, the way I look at it. I've always felt that way about you, since our momma and daddy passed away. Seeing you find happiness in whatever you do brings a different joy than anything else I know. And I want to see you loved, really loved, while I'm still here to experience it."

Coming around the island, I wrapped my arm around her and gave her a squeeze. "I know."

"I'll stop, I promise." She cupped the side of my face. "But just know, all our crazy, and we have a lot of it, comes from such deep love. We want the world for you. Your daddy and my parents did. Your momma's parents did too, God rest their souls."

The conversation was over when she started on her food, and that was fine by me.

Nothing Aunt Julianne told me was new. Nothing I didn't know.

I knew they wanted to see me happy and loved. Tucker breaking up with me was hard on my family too because they absorbed my hurt like it had happened to them.

I knew what Grady was. Not just to me but in general.

And even though all our interactions through the holidays, save the texts on Christmas Day, had been completely professional in nature, it was all I could do to tamp down my excitement at being back in the office with him.

Maybe that was the strange ache behind my chest.

I missed all those things about him that made him attractive, the things that had nothing to do with the chiseled features or bright eyes or wide smile.

That he watched *Home Alone* by himself on Christmas Day, just like I had.

That every day that dawned with dry, sunny weather made me wonder what piece of nature he was out discovering.

That when the clock struck midnight the night before, I found myself glancing around the room for that tall head full of golden-colored hair, elephants and butterflies and all sorts of animals fighting for the number one spot. And when I didn't see him, that ache I was now feeling took root.

Kissing him at midnight in front of the entire town was a horrible idea, but it was all I could think about. For the first time in my life, I'd found myself thinking simply about what I wanted down to my marrow instead of what was the safest course of action.

It was a new year. Starting fresh.

And maybe simply being single at the same time wasn't a reason to see if Grady might be thinking about me in the same way I was thinking about him, but all those other things might be.

I saw my momma eating from her plate out on the dock and thought about how all the ways my parents were different. How those differences were what made them fit together so well.

Fire and water, I'd always thought of them. Nobody chose for them, based on the things that made them similar.

Maybe that was where I'd gotten it wrong with Tucker. He was so like me that we hadn't worked. And instead of feeling embarrassed, all I could do now was think about what that held for my future.

How some nameless, faceless man might complement me, simply by being himself. How I'd complement him, by being me.

I was done having people choose what was right for me.

Maybe all along, the key to my happiness wasn't in the safest choice, or the one that made the most sense, or in the path of least resistance.

Maybe my happiness was in knowing that I could take whatever leap I wanted to, and no one would have to push me from behind.

Because I was Magnolia fucking MacIntyre, and I was ready to take the choices in my own hands.

Starting with Grady.

CHAPTER 18

GRADY

*a*t the time, it had felt like a good idea to get out of bed at six and do a twelve-mile hike for research purposes before going into the office.

The effect that a couple of hours of physical activity had on my mood was undeniable, especially as the days had passed over the holidays without seeing Magnolia. I'd see her at the office when I arrived, and I tried not to care that I'd be looking like I'd just hiked twelve miles after barely sleeping.

When I made it back to my car in the empty parking lot by the Abrams West trail, I realized that it was no longer a novelty to see puffs of white when I breathed out. The California boy liked hiking in the high-thirty temps that those Tennessee winter mornings started in.

I liked seeing a waterfall go over the dark rocks, knowing that if I stuck my hands under the water, they would feel ice cold in a matter of minutes.

It would be a great hike for a family who could handle intermediate trails but didn't need a lot of elevation gain.

I got in the driver's seat and peeled the banana that I'd grabbed off my kitchen counter, taking notes on my phone while I shoved the fruit in my mouth. When I got back to the office, I'd have Magnolia type up another package.

As I tapped out another bullet point, a message banner scrolled down on the top of my phone.

Tucker: Are you at the office? I wanted to swing by to grab that VA shirt for the hike you've got me scheduled for next Tuesday.

Immediately, my mind raced. Was Magnolia at the office yet? Was I supposed to give her a heads-up that he was coming? It was hard to set aside the protective instincts when it came to her, but I let my head fall back against the headrest. Even if she was there, she didn't need my help in dealing with Tucker. They got along just fine.

In fact, everyone seemed fine except me.

I was the one freaking out.

Me: Not yet, but I will be in about twenty if you can wait. Not sure if M is there yet or not.

There. That looked like a completely professional answer. Like I didn't just shove the keys into the ignition and practically burn out my engine while peeling out of the parking lot. It was one of the first times leaving a hike, a good one too, when I wasn't basking in the scenery, when I wasn't thinking about how freaking amazing it was that I was finally making this happen.

All I could think about was her.

As I drove, I forced my attention to the roads. To the mountains. The trees.

These were the things that had made me uproot my life and move across the country.

So as best I could, I tried to slow the stress building like a slow thunderstorm under my skin. Even if Magnolia was there, she'd be fine. She'd more than proven that she didn't need me fighting her battles for her.

My phone rang, and I smiled when I saw her name.

"Hey," I said.

"Grady," she said, smile clear in the sound of her voice. "I just got to the office, and you are in so much trouble."

I winced. "Did I put something away wrong?"

"Nothing I can't fix, but there is a pile of boxes here that makes my soul weep a bit because I'm not sure we have room for ..." She paused. "Five tents?"

"Ohh, yeah, sorry about that. Remember the guy from the convention? He was showing us that tent with the separate screened-in room?"

She hummed. "Room is a very generous term, but yes. I remember the tent because I also remember him saying six people could sleep in it, and I think I could smell the sulfurs of hell when he uttered that egregious lie."

I laughed deeply. My life would be complete if I could get that woman camping and have her admit that it was freaking awesome.

"What do these giant boxes that I have no room for have to do with him?"

"He sent me a few samples. I told him about wanting to eventually build up to some overnight trips, if we could manage it."

Magnolia hummed again. "All right. I can work on finding some room today but no more big surprises, Grady Buchanan. Otherwise, you can rearrange all these shelves yourself."

"Yes, ma'am," I answered around a smile. "I'll be there shortly."

"I'm glad." She paused, and my smile widened at how happy she sounded. "I mean, that's good. You can do the heavy lifting."

Before she hung up, I said her name again. "Just a heads-up because I'm not sure how I'm supposed to manage this, but Tucker is going to stop by for something. He needs one of those long-sleeve shirts with the logo on the chest. The dark blue one."

She let out a deep breath. "Well, we might as well get this out of the way. Thanks for letting me know."

"I'll see you in a few minutes," I promised.

If I sounded like a worried husband, she didn't say anything, but I felt like one. By the time I turned down the street, my whole body was tense. Whatever relaxation I'd earned during that hike was long gone. The fact that Tucker's big truck wasn't parked in front of Valley Adventures meant nothing because he could have easily walked the few blocks from the law offices.

Throwing the gear shift up to park, I snagged my stuff from the passenger seat, jumped out of the car, and jogged to the front door, so eager to see her that I felt slight tremors over my entire frame.

When I pushed the door open, heard that bell, and saw her look up from the desk with a wide, sunny smile on her face, I fought not to lay my hand over my chest.

This was why I could hardly pay attention to the scenery on the drive over. Because nothing in God's greatest creation came close to rivaling Magnolia MacIntyre when she smiled.

"Hi."

I sounded like an idiot.

She gave me a peek of that dimple when her smile deepened. "Hi, yourself."

The door swung shut behind me, closing us off to the world. Since Thanksgiving, I'd hardly seen her at all and hadn't had any time alone with her. And I wanted nothing more than to grab her face between my hands and take her mouth in a deep kiss, which was exactly why I kept my feet planted right where they were.

"H-How was your New Year's?"

Her smile softened, and she took a seat behind the desk. "Just fine. Went to the party at the community center."

"I know," I said without thinking, then froze.

She did too.

"You were there?"

My hands tingled with inexplicable panic. "I ... no. Yes. Sort of."

"Sort of?"

File that under *Questions I could definitely not answer honestly.* "I got there and just ... didn't feel like being around people."

Like she had on the phone, Magnolia hummed. As she did, her eyes glowed a molten gold. "I looked for you."

"You did?"

Slowly, she nodded.

My mouth opened to ask her why she looked for me when the bell jingled, and the door swung open again.

I moved aside, noticing how her facial expression slipped from warm smile to something more polite, a bit more tense, at the arrival of Tucker.

He glanced between us. "Grady, Magnolia."

"Tucker," she greeted, sweet and polite, as she stood from the chair.

Awkward quiet descended into the space like a punch to the gut.

"Have a good time at your folks' yesterday?" I asked him.

He nodded, looking grateful for the harmless question. "Yeah, we did."

"Good."

Tucker glanced down at the boxes by my feet, all the tents. "Those are nice. You figure out some overnight packages?"

I nodded. "Working on it. Met the supplier at the convention in Nashville a couple months ago, and he said he'd send a couple for me to try after the first of the year. Thought I'd take one out to that campsite by Abrams West. I hiked it this morning, and if the group is fine with rustic camping, it would be perfect."

"It would." He knelt to look at the picture of the tent on the side of the box. "You could also go over to Beaverdam Creek over by Backbone Rock if you wanted something a bit more accessible."

"That's a good idea," I said, pulling out my phone to make a note.

As she shuffled through some papers, Magnolia piped up. "You could connect with the guys that run that rafting company too. Set up something for the group if they wanted to catch a little bit of everything. The easier you make it for people, the better."

"*Great* idea." My fingers flew over my screen.

Magnolia came around the desk, and my eyes were drawn to her, quite helplessly. My fingers froze when I was supposed to be typing. I wanted to catalog everything about her. She handed Tucker a manila file. "Here's for your hike on Tuesday. It's got the waivers they need to sign before you start and all the information about their family. Their son has a peanut allergy, which I noted on the order for lunches from Daisy's, but if they ask to verify anything, don't take it personally."

The file went under his arm, and he nodded again. "Thanks, Maggie." Her face took on the slightest edge, but he held up his hands immediately. "Sorry."

"It's okay." She turned around and walked to the shelf where we kept the shirts. "XL, right?" she asked.

"Yeah." His cheeks flushed just a little.

My hands curled into tight fists. At the nickname. At the fact she knew his shirt size. Not because of her past with him, not really, but because in the face of it, I felt like it was something we'd never be able to get over.

An impossible mountain to breach, full of peril and pitfalls, the kind that even seasoned hikers would warn you against.

"Looks great in here, Magnolia," Tucker said.

His warm smile in her direction made me want to punch him in the fucking face.

It was unfair. It was inexcusable.

He'd done nothing except meet her first, and for just one moment, I absolutely hated him for it.

As she handed him the shirt, she thanked him, her smile coming more easily.

I should've been happy to see them overcome this first moment working together. It should've heralded some breakthrough to be celebrated.

But the only thing I felt inside me was an awful, sinking realization.

Tucker said his goodbyes, and I must have managed something resembling a smile because he didn't look at me strangely or ask me what was wrong. But he wasn't my sister. He didn't know me well enough to feel the discomfort coming off me in waves.

The bell chimed at his departure, the door closing us in together again.

Magnolia sensed it. On at least some level, she sensed what had changed in me.

She leaned against the desk, primly crossed her legs, and pinned me in place with those eyes. "What just happened?"

I blinked. "What do you mean?"

"With Tucker." Her voice quieted, softened. "Something changed in you, like he flipped a dimmer switch just by walking in the door."

My face was hot, my hands tingling. This was not the way. This was not how I could talk to her about this. Not how I should talk to her about this.

Rubbing my forehead, I tried to focus on anything except her face. The tents she'd called me about were in boxes at my feet, and I pointed at one. "Do you need me to help you put these away?"

"Grady."

Not now. Not like this.

"We should get back to work," I begged.

Magnolia straightened from the desk. I'd never seen her look more confused.

Teeth clenched, resolve in place, I strode past her.

Her hand shot out and caught mine before I could.

I dropped my chin to my chest.

"Why did you look at him like that?" she whispered.

If I looked at her, I'd lose whatever shaky grip I had on my control.

But even not looking at her, I could smell her. Something sweet.

Not only could I smell her, but I could still feel her. Losing the sense of sight in no way diminished Magnolia's effect on me.

With her hand gripping mine, I knew how strong those long, graceful fingers were. I knew that her palms were soft.

Even if I pinched my eyes shut and cut off my sight, it wouldn't matter.

"Like what?" My voice was rough. Nothing about it sounded like me. It sounded like it came from a dangerous man, someone on the edge of his sanity. Someone backed into a corner, where even the slightest push would result in an explosion of action.

She tugged me closer. "Like ... like you were jealous."

My eyes snapped to hers. It wasn't hard because I was so much taller than her. I'd be able to curl myself fully around her. It would take no effort, if my body stretched on top of hers, to feel every inch of her.

"Magnolia," I said, my head shaking slightly.

"You're not denying it." Her other hand hovered over my chest, like a butterfly afraid to land.

She tilted her chin up, and my eyes landed unerringly on her mouth. The tip of her pink tongue darted out to moisten the full curve of her bottom lip.

I wouldn't lie to her, so instead, I kept the words stuffed down.

But in full view of that front window, I knew I didn't want this to be our first kiss either. I started pulling back.

"We shouldn't do this," I rasped.

Magnolia let me back away, but the disappointment was clear on her face. "Shouldn't isn't the same as not wanting to."

My head lifted, and it was my turn to pin her in place with my gaze. "I know that."

"Do you?" Her chin jutted out, stubborn and proud. "Because I know why I looked for you at midnight on New Year's Eve."

I held up my hand to stop her, my heart thrashing wildly behind my ribs. "Stop."

"Why? If you don't want this, then tell me, because—"

The slightest push. Explosive action. "Want has nothing to do with it," I interrupted hotly. I towered over her, and my hand cupped the back of her neck. "If I didn't want this, I wouldn't have been trapped in this hell the past two months."

Her eyes widened. "What?"

My hand dropped. I backed away. The words that had been crowding my mouth were gone now, and I couldn't take them back.

Magnolia watched me carefully, her mouth hanging open in shock. "Oh, Grady."

I had to get out. If I stayed here, I'd say or do something irreversible. And I couldn't ... wouldn't ... let this turn into a situation where she had no idea what she was stepping into.

The phone rang, and we both jumped.

When her gaze left mine, I didn't think. I just swooped down, grabbed one of the tents, and opened the door.

"I'm just ... I'll be back in tomorrow."

"What?"

"I need to test this." I held her incredulous gaze. "I'm sorry. I can't do this here. Not here, please."

And I left.

CHAPTER 19

MAGNOLIA

*B*y the time I pulled my car into a dense grove of trees just down from Grady's campsite and climbed out, I felt like Katniss freakin' Everdeen.

On my back was a real live camping backpack, full of real live camping gear that Google told me I needed.

On my feet were hiking boots, tucked into real live blue jeans, which I tried not to wear out in public as a general rule. They had their role in life, but so did beets and spiders and algebra. Didn't mean I had to like them.

On my head was a headband meant to keep my ears warm, because who in God's green earth thought it was a good idea to sleep outside when it was forty-seven degrees?

Grady Buchanan. That's who.

The man who looked like he was going to rip Tucker's head off for calling me Maggie.

The man who looked like he was going to grind his teeth to dust when I knew Tucker's shirt size.

The man who looked at me like he wanted nothing more out of his life than to kiss my past away.

The man who told me he'd been in hell from wanting me.

The man who ran.

Those were only a part of the list I'd compiled as to why I decided to run right after him to a place where he couldn't get away from me so quickly. Which is why I googled. Why I refused to give myself even one moment to reconsider this idea.

Following my gut when I saw him unloading boxes out of his car was what got us here, me and him. To almost kisses and whispered words that made me clench my thighs together to ease the unsettled, empty feeling he'd unleashed.

That feeling had me wearing a backpack, and I could almost die from the shame of it. My etiquette teacher would be horrified if she saw me now.

The backpack was my momma's, commandeered from their garage while she and Daddy worked. As was the lantern, the water bottles, and the bug spray. Everything else came from the shelves of Valley Adventures.

Finding that stuff was pretty easy.

Finding him was a different story.

He and Tucker had mentioned two campsites, and by the time I drove up to the first, I realized that I just might have to—Oh Lord, I could hardly think it—hike around to try to find it. But thank the heavens above, we'd decided to enable tracking on his phone so that I'd know where he was in case of an emergency if he was out with a group.

I'd approached slowly, my car bumping on the uneven road, and I recognized the tent right away, though I didn't see Grady. It was a tidy little spot, a nice flat opening on grass and dirt, the creek flowing alongside where he'd set up, and the pine trees towering clear overhead. You couldn't see much of the mountains, but the sky was clear and blue, and the air was clean and quiet.

That grove of trees behind his tent was exactly what I needed, so I pulled through an opening wide enough and turned my car off. For a moment, I stared in the rearview mirror, hardly able to recognize the bright-eyed woman staring back at me.

There was an excitement all over my face, one that I hadn't seen in years. That was how I knew that showing up here, a very un-Magnolia thing to do, was the right thing. Because I knew now that Grady wanted me, possibly for even longer than I'd wanted him.

Here we would have privacy, and here, he couldn't leave so easily.

The closing of my door echoed through the campsite, and I cringed. But there was no immediate sign of him. I walked through the grass and took a deep breath of that sweet mountain air, something I didn't do nearly enough.

On my shoulders, the unfamiliar weight of the backpack had me moving slowly as I came around the side of the tent. He had one chair set up in front of a small circle of rocks, no doubt to be used later for a fire. Next to that was a small blue cooler.

The camp chair I'd borrowed from my parents was clutched in my hand, and I carefully unfolded it so that it was sitting next to his.

A branch snapped loudly, and my breath caught in my throat. If that wasn't Grady, then I was probably about to get eaten by a bear, and I glanced at the flimsy shelter of the tent, trying to decide if that would help me at all, in case it was the latter about to emerge from the trees.

But it wasn't.

Grady appeared on the opposite side of the clearing, where a path disappeared into another grove of trees running parallel to the creek. He hadn't seen me yet because he was jotting down something into a spiral-bound notebook. He wandered over to the creek's edge and knelt, notebook tucked under his arm, so he could splash some water onto his face.

He was close enough that I heard him exhale sharply at the feel of that water.

I shifted in place, and he went still as a statue.

His head turned to me and he stared.

And stared.

"Hi," I said quietly.

Grady stood slowly and stared some more. "Magnolia?"

Under my breath, I laughed. He shook his head, exhaling his own sound of amusement.

As he moved toward me, his eyes tracked down the length of my body, landing on the hiking boots with a quick grin.

"What are you doing here?" he asked.

I'd practiced my speech in the car, and before I started it, I took off my backpack and set it on the ground by our feet. Clasping my hands in front of me, I locked my gaze onto his, practically daring him to argue with a single thing I was about to say.

"I know what it's like to be stuck somewhere that doesn't fit, Grady. And I know what it's like to take your first deep breath of freedom when you leave that place." I wanted to take his hand and slide myself into the space between his strong arms, but I could be patient. I could respect his struggle to keep boundaries in place because he'd done it for a reason. "I know that to you, that's what Green Valley is, what this company is. And the thought of you trapped in hell—in the midst of all that freedom—because of me ..." I sucked in a breath. "I can't stand it."

Grady had such a pained look on his face as he watched me talk. And all his feelings were stamped there, plain as day.

I saw a man who wanted to touch me.

I saw a man holding himself in check, no matter what it was costing him.

"I shouldn't have told you that," he murmured. "It's not fair to put that on you."

"Nothing about this is fair or unfair. It's just what you feel and what I feel, too." I glanced over his shoulder at the sheer splendor of our surroundings. "I came here because maybe what we need is to just ... spend some time together. Don't we do our best when it's just you and me? No interruptions. No watching eyes. No should or shouldn't."

A muscle in his jaw popped as he thought. Before he answered, he gave the slightest shake of his head. "I don't know how to say no to you," he said wryly.

"Then don't." I shrugged one shoulder. "I hate it when people say no to me anyway."

His smile lit every part of me that had gone cold and shadowed when Tucker broke up with me, and I had to face a town of people who judged me for someone else's decision.

"And you're going to sleep in a tent?" he asked, one eyebrow lifted.

Had someone shoved a watermelon down my throat? Because it felt like I was trying to swallow one at the thought of sleeping in a tent. My teeth clenched tight so that I didn't sound like a prima donna, I hummed in the affirmative.

"I didn't bring an air mattress."

A whimper escaped from my tightly closed lips. His smile spread even wider. "Th-That's fine," I managed. "I have a sleeping bag."

"You gonna go for a hike with me before we cook up some dinner over the fire?"

"Oh Lord," I groaned.

"Just a short one." His eyes traced the features of my face, and I couldn't remember the last time someone had looked at me like that, like each individual part of me was precious and wonderful.

"How short?"

"If I tell you, you won't come with me." He took a step closer, and that one step knocked the breath from my lungs. In the way he stood over me, I didn't feel threatened or small. I felt protected. Like he alone could be a barrier against whatever harsh elements came our way.

When he stood over me like that, I wanted a whole lot of things from Grady.

Touch me.

Hold me.

Kiss me.

Could he see those thoughts written on my face? Because I was thinking them. Grady closed his eyes and drew in a deep breath through his nose. When he opened them again, I saw his decision. He leaned down and pressed a lingering kiss on my forehead, brushing his nose against the top of my head when he pulled away.

Lightheaded from that touch of his lips, I swayed toward him.

"Come on, Miss MacIntyre," he murmured, holding out his hand as he stepped back. "Show me what you've got."

He might as well have been asking me to jump off a mountain with him.

With another hard swallow, I looked back at the campsite. "Do we need more supplies?"

"Nope. We won't be going that far, I promise."

I nodded. "And you have bear spray?"

"Nope."

"Grady Buchanan," I admonished. "Now I'm going to be sitting at that office every time you go hiking, wondering if some grizzly is eating you alive."

With a laugh, Grady snatched my hand and weaved his strong fingers between mine. For a moment, we both stared at our intertwined fingers.

It felt good.

It felt right.

I still didn't want to go on a hike.

"Can't we just ... sit in this lovely spot and look at the trees and listen to the water?" I asked hopefully.

He tipped his head back, frame shaking with the booming laughter he emitted. Grady wiped underneath his eyes as he looked back down at me.

"Yeah," he murmured. "We can do that today."

So, we did.

He built us a fire—not with his bare hands but with a starter log and a lighter—and we sat in our chairs and talked for hours.

Not about Tucker or Grace, or any of the million complications there might be between us.

But the normal things you'd talk about when you wanted to get to know the person sitting across from you.

"Cake or pie?" he asked.

"Pie. As long as it's made with fruit and has a nice glaze on top." I held up my hand. "And the crust is flaky. If the crust isn't flaky, then I want nothing to do with it."

He nodded seriously. "Noted."

"You?"

"Both."

I clucked my tongue. "You can't say both. That's against the rules."

"I'll have you know, there's a bakery in Los Angeles that was known for a piecaken."

My eyebrows lifted slowly. "I beg your pardon?"

He leaned forward in his chair, taking a minute to rotate the sandwich irons he had in the fire, currently holding our dinner. "It's a pie that's on top of a cake, all decorated as one giant dessert, and it was wonderful. It was also about ninety bucks if you wanted one, but it might've been the best thing I've ever had in my life."

I shook my head. "That is an abomination, and we will never speak of it again."

He chuckled. "So, you're not going to make one for my birthday?"

"Absolutely not."

What I found over our simple, fire-cooked meal and our sweet, sticky dessert of roasted marshmallows was that Grady never seemed to trouble himself over the things that made us so different. Even when I couldn't mask my horrified reactions, it only served to intrigue him more.

As darkness crept in around us, I hardly noticed. I was too busy noticing everything else. How the warm light of the fire played off his face in a way that made him even more handsome. When he unzipped his sleeping bag and let me use it as a blanket, I couldn't shake the feeling that every moment we'd spent together, leading up to our night under the stars, was just the tiniest glimpse of how good we could be with each other.

He made me laugh. He didn't shame me for the fact that I jumped every time I heard something in the woods, just patiently explained what it might be and why I didn't need to be afraid.

When I yawned, he smiled like he'd just seen something secret about me. I liked that. That he even wanted to.

"Tired?"

I hummed. "At home, I'd still be wide-awake, but there's something about the fresh air."

He leaned his head back and stared up at the stars with his long legs stretched out in front of him. "I think I'd sleep out here like this every night if I could."

"Well, I appreciate you bringing a tent, if that's the case."

Grady dropped his chin and stared at me over the fire, still licking quietly over the burned logs. "Tent can be yours tonight," he said. "I'll sleep out here."

I held his gaze steadily. "Grady Buchanan, I will lay inside that tent and imagine finding your half-eaten carcass in the morning and worry about how I'll be stranded here alone with a murderous pack of wolves trying to get me too. You will do no such thing."

"I'm very glad I didn't know about this bloodthirsty imagination when I hired you." He smiled slowly. "Everything might have turned out differently."

I rolled my eyes, which also made him laugh.

We stood from our chairs at the same time, and a sudden, bright burst of nerves lit in the pit of my stomach. Which was silly, honestly. We both had our own sleeping bags with zippers that practically wrapped us up like mummies. And the tent was big.

For a tent. Which apparently did not hold an air mattress. I thought of my parents', sitting nicely on the bottom shelf in their garage. I didn't grab it because the thought of someone coming without one absolutely boggled my mind.

He unzipped the tent and held his arm out. "Why don't you go ahead, and I'll be there in a few minutes. I'm going to put the fire out and store the food."

While he did that, I breathed slow and steady, unrolling my sleeping bag in the main chamber of the tent. He had some blankets, at least, and I made sure to spread my sleeping bag on top of them. Sitting down, I took off my hiking boots and set them neatly against the side of the tent. Then I shimmied out of my jeans and pulled on some soft leggings that I'd rolled up in my backpack. The T-shirt stayed on, and I quickly tucked my legs into the sleeping bag because it was cold.

I'd just started wrapping my hair with my favorite green silk scarf when Grady stood for a moment outside of the tent's entrance, silhouetted by the dying fire. I saw his broad shoulders rise and fall in a deep breath, which I mimicked.

The zipper moved slowly, and he ducked to come inside. His smile was small when he looked at me.

For a moment, we stared silently at each other.

"That green looks good on you," he said, voice low and rough.

I touched the scarf. "It was my Mawmaw Boone's."

Grady nodded, quickly unrolling his sleeping bag on the blankets next to mine. He yanked off his fleece, leaving him in a simple white undershirt that strained against his rounded biceps.

When his hands moved to his jeans, he hesitated.

"I'll give you some privacy," I muttered, sliding down in my bag and rolling to my side.

My eyes pinched shut as I listened to the zipper lower on his pants, and then the sound of him shucking them down his long legs. Next to me, the warmth from his body was immediate when he slid into his own bag.

I turned on my side and studied him in the dark. It was almost impossible to see his facial features.

"There's a flashlight by the door if you need to ... go in the middle of the night."

I exhaled a laugh. "I will wait until morning, even if it kills me."

The gleam of his white teeth shone in the dark when he smiled, and my eyes slowly adjusted.

It was almost unbearably intimate to lie with him like this. We were side by side but not touching. I could smell his skin and count the freckles across his nose. Neither of us said a word as we studied each other like that.

"You're so beautiful," he whispered.

My eyelids fluttered shut, and I pressed my face into the side of my pillow.

Grady exhaled slowly, and I wondered if his fists were rolled up tight like mine, a physical manifestation of restraint. The only one I could manage at the moment.

"Good night, Magnolia."

I opened my eyes and stared at him. He had so much more willpower than I did, but his ability to treat this as carefully as it deserved only seemed to make me want him more.

What I wanted to do was unzip my bag and do the same to his. I wanted to slide myself over his lap and see what his muscles looked like under that white shirt. I wanted to know the strength of his body as he flipped me on my back and used his hands on my body until I saw a different sort of stars.

The kind that brought a curl into my toes and a helpless arching of my back off the ground, where my whole body bent with the force of pleasure.

And I wanted to bury my face into his chest, sleep against him where he was the warmest.

I wanted to wake with his arms curled around me.

I sighed. "Good night, Grady."

He clenched his teeth, eyes knowing, seeing all those thoughts play across my face.

I rolled onto my back, and he did the same.

And just like that, eventually, we fell asleep.

CHAPTER 20

GRADY

I should have known better.

The thought skittered across my foggy brain before I was even fully awake. It was chased immediately by another one.

I knew she would feel this good in my arms.

Without opening my eyes, I took a moment to catalog every single part of how we were lying together.

Yes, we were both in sleeping bags, but at some point during the night, we'd turned toward each other. My own bag was half unzipped because I always got hot when I slept.

Magnolia was burrowed into my chest, her arms curled up between us, the tips of her fingers resting on my chest, just above my heart. My head was curled over hers, nose resting along her temple, my top arm slung over her waist.

Her legs were pressed against mine, like they were trying to push through the heavy barrier of the bag. Even through the smell of campfire that naturally plagued an outing like this, it was impossible to avoid Magnolia's scent. I inhaled deeply and recorded it in my memory.

Sweet, with a touch of floral.

If I moved my hands like I wanted, to learn more of the things I wanted to learn, I'd wake her. And her body moved with such slow, even breathing, there was no way she wasn't still asleep. So, I stayed just as I was and thought about the fact that she showed up in the first place.

I loved that she surprised me like that.

I loved that I never imagined her crashing my emergency camping trip.

I loved that I'd never seen her wear jeans, and that her ass looked just as good in them as I'd pictured it would.

I loved that she thought I'd get eaten by a bear and that she didn't want to sleep in the tent without me and that she was so much more badass than she realized, crawling into the tent without complaint.

I loved that she had come to some sort of realization about us on her own.

Tipping my nose closer to her soft skin, I inhaled her again, allowing my hand to slide up her back softly because I wanted to know how her body curved under my palm.

Perfect.

All her curves and edges, body, soul, whatever you wanted to call it, were perfect for me.

And with that, I knew I was being selfish by taking this moment. Magnolia deserved to know how I felt—and why—before she felt stuck. Before she felt like this was just another choice made for her by someone else. I'd seen the fallout between Grace and Tucker when he didn't know, and what that had done to her. I refused to pin either me or Magnolia into a place where we felt trapped, too far into our relationship without this huge piece of my truth.

I would sound crazy.

I might lose her.

But I would not take this choice from her. I didn't see how I could say that I loved her if I did.

Pulling my head back to watch her in sleep, I knew that I was in love with her.

And as I thought it, her back arched under my hand, her chest expanded on a slow inhale as she woke. But her eyes stayed closed, even as her lips curled up in a sleepy smile.

Magnolia's hand, the one that had been lightly touching my chest, smoothed out, and her fingers spread over the surface of my thin shirt. My heart sped at her touch, and I couldn't find the willpower that I'd had the night before to stop her.

Fingers wandered slowly, tracking up, up my chest, sliding along the side of my neck to trace the line of my jaw. The edge of her fingernail, which I knew was painted a soft pink, scratched lightly through the stubble on my face, lifting goosebumps along my arms.

I refused to speak, to say one single word, because this was my moment of weakness after months of restraint. And in that weakness, I'd never felt more myself. More at peace.

No mountain or view or adventure could come close to what Magnolia did to me. She was the thing I was searching for, the thing that made me yearn for more out of life.

Her movements stayed small and so did mine.

The tilt of her hips brought her closer, shuffling within the confines of where we found ourselves.

The press of my fingers along her back was slight, sliding down her spine until I caught the slightest hint of her skin beneath the hem of her shirt.

Magnolia moved her chin, and a puff of air from her mouth hit the side of my throat.

Then ... then it was her lips brushing my skin just under my jaw.

A rough exhale pushed from my mouth, and she did it again, with a hint more pressure.

This wasn't a touch of her lips. This was a suck. A taste.

My face turned toward her, a drag of my nose down along her temple, so close that the slightest flutter of her long eyelashes struck my skin.

Her fingers curled into my shirt, desperate and surprisingly strong, tugging me closer.

Without a single word spoken between us, it was like we'd agreed that nothing existed outside of this one moment, that we were allowed this because we'd managed the entire night pressed against each other without a touch.

At the same time, our faces pulled back just enough that the full force of her gaze was visible.

Swallowed whole. That was how I felt. Struck backward and knocked down.

Her desire was tangible in the slight flush I saw splashed along the top of her cheekbones. Her pupils were dilated, her lush mouth hanging open just enough.

Hot strikes of air hit my lips, her exhales short and choppy.

"Please," she whispered.

I slanted my mouth over hers, hard and fierce.

I'd give her anything, sacrifice anything. I'd tear apart the world when she looked at me like that.

In the next breath, Magnolia was pushing frantically at the half-closed zipper of her sleeping bag while I did the same.

She sucked on my tongue, which unleashed a groan from deep in the caverns of my chest.

Something about this kiss was otherworldly, deeper than I thought possible, hotter than I'd ever experienced, our lips pushing and sucking and biting on each other's.

Nothing was sweet about it, an ironic contradiction to how we'd started down this path. Our barriers gone, I prowled over her body. Her legs split instantly to make room for me, a perfect cradle for my hips to roll along hers.

Magnolia whimpered, clutching at my back, her nails raking underneath my shirt against my skin.

One hand gripped the back of her neck, directing our wet, head-spinning kisses.

My other hand pushed down her back again until I could grip her hip, hitch around her thigh, and wrench it up against my side.

Men uprooted their life for this. They sacrificed everything, launched ships, started wars. It was chasing this feeling of absolute rightness, of a pleasure that surpassed anything physical.

It might have been our bodies creating the friction and sparking white, sleek heat along our skin that made her breath hitch when I gripped her ass in my hand. It might have been our bodies that made me hiss out a breath when my hardness pressed against her, where I knew we'd fit perfectly, every place that was soft and warm on her would take me.

But with each roll, push, touch, bite, suck, that woman embedded herself into my fucking soul.

She pushed at my shoulder, and I lifted, ready to stop if that was what she wanted.

She didn't.

Another push and I was on my back, and she slid up over my lap, straddling me easily. I sat up and gathered her close while our mouths fused again, hot and fierce, my arms wrapped tight around her back.

Her scarf was half off her head, and she ripped at it, her hair spilling down around her shoulders. I gathered it in my fist, glorying at the feel of it wrapped tight around my palm.

Everything will be okay, I thought. There was nothing we couldn't overcome. In the drugged haze of her lips and tongue, the way she pressed herself down against me, I convinced myself that every reason I'd held back was minor, that every strange complication could be conquered.

My kisses shifted from her glorious mouth to each side of her lips. The line of her cheekbones. The tip of her nose, which made her exhale a laugh. I cupped her face, sliding my thumbs along the silk of her skin.

Her eyes were big in her face, those magnificent eyes—topaz and streaked with a little green—in a color I'd never seen on anyone else. It would be so easy to allow myself to get caught up in the high of touching her like this, kissing her like this, and let that sweep away all the things I'd promised myself when it came to her.

Magnolia's teeth dug into her lower lip, stemming a smile.

I allowed one of my own.

In response, she tucked herself against me, her face burrowed into the side of my neck as my arms tightened. We sat like that for a moment, and as my brain cleared, I couldn't help but sober. Everything that was sharp and bright with pleasure tempered just a bit, like a boiling pot that someone slid off the burner.

The thing I'd promised myself was that being honest about my feelings was the most important thing I could give her.

"Good morning, Miss MacIntyre."

She inhaled deeply, tightening her thighs around mine where she still sat on my lap. "Grady, when your voice sounds like that, I feel like doing positively sinful things to your body."

My frame shook with quiet laughter. She sounded so bothered by it, and all I wanted was to lay her back down on the blankets and explore all those sinful things.

"And I would love to hear about those sins in detail," I murmured, sliding a couple more soft kisses down the line of her shoulder. "But I wanted to talk to you about something first."

Magnolia sat back to look at my face, and her concern was clear in the slight bend of her eyebrows. "What is it?"

I swallowed, suddenly nervous. "Do you want coffee or anything first?"

"Do I need coffee to be able to process whatever it is you need to say?"

I met her small smile with one of my own. "No, just making sure."

Even though I couldn't blame her, I felt a sharp slice of disappointment when she slid backward off my lap so that she could see me better. The light outside of the tent was muted enough that I knew it was probably before seven as the sun slowly rose behind the mountains. There were no sounds that nature didn't produce, just birds and water, rustling trees. Magnolia shivered slightly and pulled her sleeping bag up around her shoulders as a blanket.

Her face was bare of makeup for the first time since I'd met her, and still, she was flawless.

As I stared at her, I knew I'd made one grave error in judgment. I'd never practiced what I would say to her at this moment. Because how did you explain something illogical? I couldn't point to something that made sense. All I could do was try to explain this strange phenomenon and hope that she believed me, hope that beyond that, she'd allow us the chance to see how good we could be together once she'd heard about it.

"You know how some families have like," I started, "legends. Stories that seem to belong only to that one group of people."

"I guess," she answered hesitantly.

"The Buchanans have one of those. A family legend. I don't know where it started, and I don't know the history or how it's even possible, but it's a little ... crazy when you hear it for the first time."

Her smile was wry. "I'm from the South, Grady. We have a whole lot of crazy here."

"See, that's how Grace and I wrote it off as, too, before we moved here. As some Southern nonsense because our parents didn't have it happen like that for them."

"What are you talking about?"

I let out a deep breath, licked my lips, and tried to regroup. "As far as we know, at least for the past five generations, the Buchanans have one perfect soul mate. Someone who ... completes them."

"That's ... very romantic."

Her hesitancy made me smile again. "It's more than that, though. Something about it is tied to this place. To Green Valley. When a Buchanan meets that person, their soul mate, they know. And they know instantly."

Magnolia watched me quietly, the only change in her face was a slight tightening of her mouth.

"My parents," I explained, "they didn't meet in Green Valley, right? And he's the only Buchanan male in five generations who can say that about their spouse, other than my cousin Hunter. They're the only two who didn't find true happiness with their soul mate."

"Grady," she said slowly, "that sounds insane."

I sat up on my knees because it was impossible to sit still. "I know, trust me. We never believed it was real. Because our parents were not meant to be together."

"But you believe it's real now."

I nodded. "I do."

Her throat worked in a slow swallow. "And Grace ..."

My eyes closed. It was impossible to avoid this. "She met Tucker as soon as she crossed the line into Green Valley, and it worked a little differently for her because she's the first female born in the past five generations, but yeah, she knew almost immediately too."

Magnolia's eyes took on an unfocused look. "I-I remember meeting her for the first time. She was getting ice cream with your father. She looked like she was going to pass out when she saw me with him."

"Even when she fell in love with Tucker, I didn't really believe it was true."

Those eyes focused again, razor-sharp, onto my face. "What changed?"

My hands fidgeted nervously, and when I tried to take in a full breath, my lungs weren't quite working right. But I could do nothing except answer her honestly. "You."

Magnolia's chest rose and fell rapidly. "Me."

Because I had to be touching her, I reached out and took one of her hands in mine, lifted it up, and pressed a fervent kiss onto her fingers. "I know how crazy this sounds, but you ... you walked in through the door, and I swear, something shifted into place inside me, Magnolia."

Her eyes were big again but not like they had been when we were kissing. They were full of confusion, skepticism, and something that started my first kindling of true fear. I saw her own fear, reflecting back at me.

"So, you"—she licked her lips—"you think I'm your soul mate. That we belong together."

"This sounds so crazy, I know." I kissed her fingers again. "I know. You felt something, though, right? Something different with me."

Her nostrils flared on a deep breath. "And you felt like you needed to tell me this after our first kiss?"

"Magnolia," I said, "it's possible that that was a horrible idea, the worst I've ever had, but I saw how much it killed Grace when they broke up for a bit, and he had no idea the truth of where her feelings started or how strong they were. It felt like she was keeping this huge secret from Tucker."

"Can we not talk about my ex and his romance issues with your sister?" she said, voice dangerously low, and she pulled her hand from mine.

It was the conscious disconnection that pushed my fear up a level.

"Yeah." A pit swirled dangerously in my stomach.

Shakily, she rubbed a hand down her face. "I think, I think maybe there's a reason people have waited to spring this on their ... perfect match."

"Shit," I whispered. "I'm sorry, I shouldn't have said anything. I just felt like you should know."

Her eyes flashed. "Know what, Grady? That you've got us locked in before we get so much as a first date? That someone else in my life thinks they get to make this decision for me?"

"No, no, Magnolia." I speared my hands in my hair. "I swear that's not how this is."

"It's how it feels, though." Magnolia snatched her boots, shoving her feet inside them, and I panicked.

"Fuck, please don't go like this." I laid my hands on hers.

"Get your hands off me," she said, icy cold. "I may be a lady, but if you touch me without my permission, I will feed you your testicles one at a time."

Immediately, I snatched my hands away. My throat was tight, and it was hard to breathe properly. Everything in the tent felt small and cramped by how horribly I'd bungled this.

But it was so, so much worse when the sound of a large truck got louder—then stopped—right outside the tent.

She looked at me, hands frozen on the laces.

A car door slammed. "Wakey, wakey, brother."

"Oh, my Lord," Magnolia whispered.

"If you want, just stay in here," I whispered back. "They don't have to know you were here."

For a second, I thought she'd do it when I saw the slump of relief in her shoulders.

But then her chin lifted and determination shone brightly in those eyes I loved. "I'm not hiding from anything anymore."

It was almost painful how much I wanted to kiss her at that moment. She could see it too because her gaze locked onto my mouth, and she heaved a regretful sigh.

"Be right out," I called.

Another car door slammed, and I knew Grace wasn't alone.

I pulled the zipper on the tent entrance and slowly straightened, emitting a groan at the ability to stand fully after the entire night in the tent. Grace was by the truck, whispering to Tucker as they stared at the creek. In her hands were two cups of coffee.

"You disappeared, you jerk," she said as she turned, a bright smile on her face. "You could've told someone you were ..."

Her voice trailed off, and I knew Magnolia had exited the tent after me. Tucker's mouth fell open. He snapped it shut instantly, color flooding his cheeks.

"Holy hell," Grace whispered, and both coffees fell out of her hands.

CHAPTER 21

MAGNOLIA

I'd never been so happy for my backpack because it hid the tremor in my hands where my fingers curled tightly around the straps. I'd never been so happy for something to hold my attention —the items I'd brought with me to this cursed campsite—because hastily shoving items into my backpack gave me a reason not to obsess over the shock on Grace's and Tucker's faces.

My face was hot, my hands shaking like a leaf, and it was a miracle my legs were holding me.

"She works for you, Grady," Grace whispered fiercely, like I wasn't standing three feet away from her. "What is wrong with you?"

Grady stood tall and stoic next to me and folded up my chair when I didn't reach for it. My eyes glanced quickly up at him, and his skin was bone pale.

"I'm sorry," he said quietly to me.

"Are you going to ignore me?" his sister asked.

I wanted to shove one of her big combat boots right up her ass.

In the second I allowed my gaze to flicker dangerously in her direction, I saw Tucker take a few steps forward and speak quietly to the woman he loved.

That was what made all this so ... so ... utterly and completely insane.

He knew what that flick of my eyes meant.

I didn't lose my temper often, but when I did, I was like a beach ball held under the water for too long.

Whatever Tucker said, Grace nodded, and that just made the whole situation even stranger. He knew what to say to her too. He knew both of us.

The person he knew least in this whole situation was Grady.

Who'd dropped a veritable bomb on me right after the best kiss of my entire life.

"If I felt like I needed to explain myself to you, Grace, I would," Grady said, keeping his voice even. I knelt to the ground and pushed the rest of my clothes into my backpack. He did the same, and the heat from his body made something melt inside me but not the kind of melting I wanted.

I needed a wall of iron to get through this interaction unscathed. I needed my emotional reserves, something to prop me up so I didn't blow about a dozen gaskets on these crazy people and their crazy talk of love legends.

My hands started shaking again, and I saw Grady reach out to help me, then stop, pulling his hands back.

"I'll bring your sleeping bag to the office," he told me.

Shakily, I nodded. The force of his gaze on the side of my face was so strong, so intense, as tangible as if he touched me, and my wall melted further.

I wanted it.

I didn't want it.

He knew me so well, respected me so thoroughly, yet ...

Yet he'd put me into an untenable position, the kind that I was actively running from. Feeling stuck. Feeling trapped. Feeling forced.

"Oh, Grady," Grace breathed.

Her tone had my head snapping up. It was the *understanding*. Some unspoken comprehension that snaked chills down my spine.

One hand covered her mouth, her big eyes, the same shade as Grady's, were wide with comprehension.

"Is she ..." Her voice trailed off. "She's the ..."

From the corner of my eye, I saw Grady nod once.

Tucker dropped his head and cursed, a string of muttered words so vile that I almost called him on it. I'd never heard him say anything like that.

It was that chain of unfinished words, the fragmented sentences, those slight motions of realization from them both, the slow dawning of awareness of what this was, that made my remaining reserves disappear in a flimsy puff of air.

"What is wrong with you people?" I asked, standing slowly.

No one said anything. Grace looked like someone had knocked her over with a cast-iron skillet. Tucker wouldn't lift his head. And Grady ... Grady looked miserable.

I'd never seen an expression on his face like the one he was wearing.

Agony was stamped on every inch of that wonderful face. The one I'd worshiped just minutes earlier. The one that looked down at me like I was the most important thing in the world to him.

"I'm standing right here, and you're talking over my head like I'm a child. You don't get to *force* people into a relationship with some absolute nonsense and expect that they'll just toe the line." My voice gained volume like I was a holy freight train bearing down the flimsy tracks, and all three shifted uncomfortably.

Grace's hand dropped from her mouth. "Grady, you *told* her already?"

He glared at her. "Stay out of it, Grace. I stayed out of your relationship."

Tucker held up his hands. "Why don't we all take a deep breath, all right? This is a lot of information that we're all wading into, and I think Magnolia has every right to be frustrated."

Grace rolled her lips together. The color in her face was high. I suppose if I wanted to put myself in her shoes, the color on my face would be high too if my brother was in some magical love spell with the woman who took my boyfriend's virginity.

It was that ungracious thought, so uncharacteristic of me, that had me rankled all over again.

I crossed my arms and pinned Tucker with a stare. "*Magnolia* doesn't need you to fight her battles."

He conceded that with a slow nod. "I know that. Just ... trying to keep everyone calm."

Grady's hands rolled into tight fists at his side.

That probably made him insane, Tucker stepping in to try to handle me. And to think, in the office, I'd felt so swept away by it. Possessive displays of male ownership were only swoon-worthy in very particular settings, and this did nothing for me. Simply left me bubbling and boiling with frustration.

I was not his simply because he'd decreed it so. Because he felt some strange feeling when he first saw me.

I pulled the straps of my backpack over my shoulder and snatched my camping chair from where Grady had set it on the hard ground. "Y'all are crazy," I muttered. "You're crazy if you think this is normal. That because some love switch flips in your head, because you believe it's right and true and perfect, that everyone else should just fall into line. Life doesn't work that way. It's not supposed to."

"Please don't leave like this," Grady begged quietly, turning his back so that Grace and Tucker couldn't see his face, couldn't see mine. "Give me ten minutes once they leave, please, Magnolia."

He was a shield, tall and strong, and it would've been so easy to fall into that. To allow him to protect me, to allow him to make this easier on me. But I didn't do that anymore.

If something was hard, I could face it on my own.

If something was scary, I was perfectly capable of being my own shield.

"This is too much, Grady," I told him. I pointed behind him to where Tucker and Grace stood. "All of that, them, us, whatever you just told me, it's too much to handle, and it's all being poured on my head like ... like hot oil. And not slowly either."

His face bent in utter misery, twisted in a way that betrayed just how much this tortured him. And I believed him, I did. I believed that he thought this was true, that they all did. But still, I couldn't make peace with another person trying to fit me into some predesigned space that I didn't choose for myself. My entire life had been like that to varying degrees.

And I was officially resigning from that kind of hold over my choices anymore.

Nothing would be decided by committee. By a list that someone else wrote out for me.

"I get it," he said, so quietly, so resigned, that my heart unwillingly cracked at the sound of it. This exuberant man, who embraced challenges, who didn't shy away from big, scary things, was brought to his knees. "I'm so sorry it happened like this. I wish ... I wish I'd handled it better."

Even with my backbone straight and my resolve firm, I found myself wanting to slide my hand up the side of his face. To comfort him as he'd comforted me so many times. But I respected him, liked him too much to give him false hope at this moment. "I know you do, Grady."

It was all I could give him. Faced with all that impossible, and all that hard to understand, it was the only concession I could allow.

Because it was true. I knew he would take it all back if he could, maybe even back to our kiss in the tent, so that he could rewrite the path that had unfolded. He'd do it to shield me from this moment. He'd do it to make it easier for me to understand.

Any of those choices, I knew without a doubt that Grady would make them for me.

But he couldn't.

And that was why I found it remarkably easy, though tears welled dangerously in my eyes, to turn my back and walk to my car, away from every single one of them, without another word.

CHAPTER 22

GRADY

I'd never experienced quiet like the one that descended between the three of us as Magnolia—looking, somehow, like a queen—walked to her car, hidden in the grove of trees, and left.

Like we all knew that the moment she was well and truly gone, we had a mountain of complete and utter awkwardness to address, and it wouldn't be fun.

Or maybe they were just waiting for me. Because I couldn't tear my eyes away from her car as it drove away, couldn't bring myself to process just exactly how fucking horrible that had gone.

For one kiss, I'd had her. And now I didn't.

"You know," I mused, "I really, really hate this family legend horseshit."

Neither of them replied. Probably because behind my back, they were holding hands, communicating wordlessly with longing, loaded glances as people head over heels in love were known to do.

"I'm so sorry, Grady," my sister said quietly. "If we'd known she was out here ..." Her voice trailed off.

I turned. "If you'd known, what?"

She blinked. "We wouldn't have come?"

"Do you know, or are you asking me?"

Tucker's jaw hardened at my tone, but in a wise life choice, he didn't intercede.

Grace, of fucking course, sensed his mood and ran a hand down his arm. Yes, *please*, soothe the beast who wants to defend you from your big, bad brother. The guy whose only crime was falling helplessly in love with someone he used to date.

These feelings were so unfamiliar to me. They were bitter and cold in my veins, each one building on the next until my thoughts raced in a blur.

My sister stepped closer to me, her features soft with understanding, and it made me rage inside. I didn't want understanding. I wanted to break something into a million pieces, just to release some of this pressure building up.

And somehow, she sensed that, so Grace paused, hands raised slightly in concession.

"This is super freaking weird, right?" she asked.

I laughed harshly. "Yeah, Grace, it is."

"Trust me, I know. I remember."

That was the thing, though. I didn't want to remember what it was like for her at first. She arrived in Green Valley only a couple of days before me, and in that time, she covered a lot of ground. By the time I got there, she and Tucker were circling each other warily, not quite sure what to do with the other person.

Remembering what it had been like to watch them that first day I arrived and we hiked Coopers Road Trail, I had to pinch my eyes shut.

My sister, the delicate flower she was not, was hissing and spitting at Tucker like a wounded cat. Like she couldn't help her reaction.

I rubbed at my chest. Yeah, almost everyone in my family had gone through this to varying degrees, but I wanted to know if a single person had ever found the love of their life connected with so many entanglements. With so many complications.

But that wasn't Grace's fault.

She was the only person in my life who could read my mood at twenty paces. The person who I'd count on to always have my back and come out swinging for me.

I opened my eyes and gave her an apologetic look.

Immediately, a tear fell down her cheek.

"Don't cry," I groaned.

She laughed, and it was wet-sounding. "You're not usually so snippy with me."

"Yeah, well ..." I spread my arms out. "This is uncharted territory in the moods of Grady."

Grace sighed, giving a quick glance over her shoulder at Tucker. He smiled at her but hung back, giving us some privacy. I tried to gauge his face because this was probably strange as hell for him too, but his features were inscrutable.

If I were in his position, I wouldn't know what to say either.

So ... you fell in love with my first girlfriend. Want any tips?

Kill me now.

"This is so ..." She shook her head when words failed her.

"Yeah."

Fill in the blank. Weird. Awkward. Uncomfortable. Weird. And that was just for the parts of this related to Tucker. All the other facets of what just happened could create an entirely new list.

Frustrating. Heartbreaking. Discouraging. Depressing.

Those were the kinds of words I normally banished from my vocabulary, which Grace knew. If any piece of life could be described in those terms, then I'd change that part of my life. Why sit in it? Why choose to spend your days feeling anything like that?

It chaffed against everything that made me *me*, to purposely step into a space where I might feel any or all those things.

Grace must have sensed that too because she took a cautious step forward and wrapped her arms around my middle. Her hug was welcome because this was just one of those situations when talking it to death wouldn't make it go away.

It wouldn't make it easier, even if Magnolia gave me the time of day after this.

I wrapped my arms around my sister and set my chin on the top of her messy blond hair. A curl lifted on the wind and tickled my nose.

"What'd you do to your hair? Stick your car key in a light socket this morning?"

"Screw you," she muttered into my chest.

Normally, I would've laughed, but that muscle seemed to be weak at the current moment.

"Magnolia, huh?" she asked quietly, keeping herself tucked against me.

I eased her away from me. No avoiding eye contact on this one. I'd screwed up my first foray into that possible relationship, and I didn't want to do the same to my second attempt.

"Wanna walk?"

She nodded.

I lifted my chin in Tucker's direction. "He okay waiting over here?"

"If I ask him to, yeah." Grace nudged me with her shoulder. "Plus, he knows I'll tell him everything you said as soon as we get in the truck."

My smile was small, but it was a smile. And even that felt like a victory in light of how hollowed out I felt inside.

"We'll be right back," she told him.

He nodded. "Take your time."

What a strange feeling to give him a lift of my chin and still fight against the urge to get his blessing. His permission that this was okay.

Now wasn't the time for that particular conversation, and from the looks of it, both Tucker and I knew it.

Grace and I didn't wander far because that wasn't the point of this little jaunt. It was giving us space to breathe, time to look for words to a strange situation, and give my sister—if I knew her at all—a chance to rein in her wild emotions at her twin brother loving this person who used to be her biggest stumbling block to being with Tucker.

Her deep exhale was how I knew she was ready to hear it. "Why don't you start from the beginning?"

I hopped over a log and waited for her to do the same. The only sound for a minute was the rush of the creek and the leaves rustling on the branches. The wind had a bite to it, but it felt good against my slightly feverish face.

It took me by surprise but finding the words came easily. About her interview, what she was wearing, and what a fool I made of myself. That strange unerring sense of certainty that I felt looking at Magnolia's face had Grace nodding slightly because she understood perfectly.

"I remember," she murmured. "I remember when I looked at him and all I could think was, *mine. That man belongs with me.*"

Right. She'd had that thought when Tucker was still with Magnolia. But that went unsaid. Because we both knew it.

It wasn't like I held it against her. They never crossed any lines, not until Tucker broke things off with Magnolia. And I knew Magnolia didn't hold that against them either. There was no betrayal, but there was a hard truth to face.

If Magnolia forgave me, the four of us would be inextricably intertwined.

"I get why you didn't tell me," she admitted.

It felt like a good time to slow down because we didn't really have a destination in mind. So, I stopped and leaned against a tree trunk. Knobs from the wood dug in my back, and I didn't really care.

"I felt like"—I shrugged—"like she needed to be the first one to know. It felt important."

Grace smoothed a hair over the top of her ponytail. "I get that too."

"She's already dealt with whispers and gossip and judgment her whole life," I said, peering intently at the water. "Her dad didn't make things easier on her, but ... Man, it's hard to admit this after how bad he came down on Tucker after they broke up, but I understand now why he did. After getting to know her. Learning about her family through her."

Grace blew out a breath. "He almost ruined Tucker's law firm, Grady."

"I'm not defending what he did," I told her. "I said I can understand why he did it. There's a difference."

She nodded. "There's a lot for us to work through with this, isn't there?"

"Maybe not."

"Why do you say that?"

"Because she said we're crazy for thinking this is okay and marched off? I may have lost her before I even really had the chance to have her, Grace." My voice cracked at the end, and her eyes welled up. "I've never ... I've never even dreamed that it was possible to feel like this about someone. She's nothing I was looking for, and she is every-fuck-ing-good-thing I could ever want. And I just lost her."

She gripped my arm. "You don't know that. You don't! Give her time. Just ... let her breathe a little, okay?"

"Yeah." I rubbed my forehead. I felt like I could sleep for a week.

"My brother doesn't give up, okay? This sucks, and it's hard, but if she's the one, Grady, then you two will move past this."

I pinned her with a look. "And if we do? You'd be okay with Christmases and birthdays and family vacations with you and Tucker and me and Magnolia?"

"Yes," she answered immediately. "Because if she makes you as happy as Tucker makes me? Then it's not even a question in my mind, Grady. I know what this love feels like when you come out on the other side. We can get through all the awkward conversations in the world. I'd do them a hundred times if I knew you'd have this kind of happiness waiting for you."

I dropped my head back on the tree and exhaled heavily. In theory, I knew Grace would have my back. She always had in the past. But something shifted when you found the love of your life. Even the strongest relationship outside of it was moved into a secondary position. Hearing her say it out loud, though, something unlocked, just enough that I could breathe a little easier.

No matter what, she was still my twin.

"Thank you," I told her.

"You're welcome. Just warn me next time, okay?"

I smiled. "Okay."

"What are you going to do?"

"Give her time to breathe, I guess. Whatever that means."

"One tip," Grace said slowly. "Maybe give her a little hint that while you're respecting her need for space, you'll still, you know, be waiting for her."

"The mantra of every pathetic stalker," I muttered.

She slugged me in the shoulder.

"Ouch. Fine. I will."

"Good." Grace hitched a thumb over her shoulder. "I'm gonna go back. You want help packing up?"

I shook my head. "I'm gonna stay out here today, I think. I'll be back by dinner."

"Love you," she said.

"You too."

Grace walked back toward Tucker, and I pulled out my phone, staring at my screen like it would give me answers.

After a few minutes, it was still dark. I was still missing her. I still had no freaking clue how to handle this. Maybe suffering in silence wouldn't help either of us. But neither would pushing her.

An idea unraveled slowly in my brain, and I decided to go with it.

Me: I'm going to call, and I'd like you to send me to voicemail. If you ever choose to listen to that message, I'd humbly ask that you wait until you're ready. Whatever that looks like for you.

I didn't wait for Magnolia to answer, but she still had the settings on her phone in such a way that I could see when she read my messages. I took a deep breath and hit the call button. My stomach flipped painfully at the sound of her recording, which picked up immediately, as I'd asked.

You've reached Magnolia MacIntyre. Kindly leave a message and I'll call you back just as soon as I'm able.

"It's me," I started. I took a deep breath before I said anything else, praying with every dull thud of my heart that someday she'd listen.

CHAPTER 23

MAGNOLIA

*C*lothes were armor.

I'd realized it years ago without even being able to put a name to the thought. But when I was in middle school, in those etiquette classes with that awful teacher that Daddy had fired, all I knew was that when I was dressed my best, I felt invincible.

Oh sure, some backwoods, off-the-grid-living crazy might've told me to strap a knife to my thigh or something if I really wanted to feel safe, but the honest to God truth was that when I slipped into my favorite outfits, I walked taller (which was a big deal, as I wasn't all that tall), and my chin stayed high like someone was pushing it up (also a big deal when you had a daddy like mine), and it felt, just a little bit, like nothing could pierce me through those clothes.

In all my adult years, I'd had one public slipup after Tucker broke up with me, and it involved a basic white T-shirt and—I shudder to even think it out loud—black cotton leggings, but we just put that incident into the sea of forgetfulness where it belonged.

After I got home from the Camping Trip That Shall Not Be Mentioned, after I sent Grady's phone call to voicemail like he'd asked, I hardly stopped to think about what I was doing. Clothes were stripped off and left in piles on my immaculate bedroom floor. The water in my shower turned straight to scalding, and even though it was not the correct day of the week, I washed my hair because I just knew that I'd be changing things up a bit early.

Two hours later, the clothes—reeking of bonfire and Buchanan insanity —were tossed into a load of wash, my lips were slicked with my favorite lipstick, my hair was straight and falling around my shoulders, and I'd slid into my favorite magenta dress. It hooked high around my neck, clung to my chest and torso, and floated in a glorious cloud down past my knees.

Oh, what a luxurious and ridiculous choice it was too, in January, in Tennessee.

But I had no plans to go anywhere, and if I wanted to strut around my fifteen-hundred-square-foot home wearing a halter dress and stilettos, then there wasn't a single damn person in the world who could stop me.

Ruthlessly, I locked down any thoughts about what had happened. Behind a steel door with an impenetrable deadbolt.

There was work to be done, and allowing the past twenty-four hours to cycle on an endless loop in my head would serve no one.

My dining table—a beautiful mahogany showpiece that my parents kept aside for me when Momma's parents died—was gleaming with the late morning light streaming into the front windows of my house. Today, it would serve as my office.

There would be no lounging on the couch to answer emails and sort through ads.

No. Today, I would scrape back every shred of sentimentality and keep my work under a bull's-eye.

That was the kind of armor I was talking about.

If I was still wearing those same clothes and sitting on a soft, inviting surface, Lord knows what might've happened.

If I'd looked down and saw the soft pants I'd slept in, I might have thought about Grady's hands. There was no protection in those clothes, nothing to shield my thoughts, because his hands had been big and strong. Incredibly sure of their path along my body.

When I opened my laptop, I refused to notice too closely that my fingers shook.

You walked in through the door, and I swear, something shifted into place inside me, Magnolia.

My hands curled into helpless fists, and I pinched my eyes shut.

Not a single part of me wanted to think about him as he'd said those things. Not really.

No part of me was ready to listen to whatever voicemail was now sitting on my phone, dangling like a damn carrot on a string, ready to lead me down a path toward ugly tears and puffy eyes and nowhere good.

"Get out of my head, Grady Buchanan," I whispered.

It was almost sad to realize that even the imaginary version of Grady, the one I was conjuring like a pesky ghost, respected me enough to do as I'd asked.

The words spoken out loud, and his voice—low and rough and fervent —disappeared into a puff of smoke.

My shoulders relaxed, and I got to work.

I worked on some new ads, ordered lunches for a group coming in a few days, and followed up on some inquiries that came through the website, setting them up in the schedule as I found the correct openings. Tucker and Grady would be pleased as the weather started warming a bit, into March and April, because we'd have enough business to warrant some help.

The satisfaction it brought me to see brightly colored blocks of time on a calendar that had been fairly sparse at first was why I could close and lock and seal that steel door efficiently.

It wouldn't be hard for me to do my job because if I had to go into that office at five o'clock in the morning to avoid Grady until I knew what in blazes to do with him, then I would.

My phone beeped, and I lifted the screen to see a text from Daddy.

Daddy: Drove past on my way home last night, and it was dark at your place. Just making sure my daughter isn't dead in a ditch somewhere while trying to respect her boundaries as an adult.

With a roll of my eyes, I tapped out a response.

Me: Not dead in a ditch. Safe at home. I LOVE YOU TOO.

I probably should've put down the phone when my reply was delivered, but instead, I found that my thumb had snuck out from the orders of *We do not think about Grady*. It slipped silently across the screen of my phone until my voicemail box appeared.

His name was at the top, and for a solid minute, I stared at those letters and wondered how we'd gotten to this point. Where just the sight of a capital G with a few innocent lines and curves after it had my heart quivering and my stomach knotted in a big ole mess.

It was almost like I wanted to torture myself and see exactly how far my hot-pink armor went, because before I could talk myself out of it, I tapped on his message, and the sound of his voice flooded just about every sense that I was in possession of.

No matter that I couldn't see or smell him, or that it was impossible to touch him.

His voice had that effect on me, and it was silly to pretend otherwise.

"It's me," he said. Then he paused, and the breath he let out was slow and deep, and I could imagine him gathering himself. "Magnolia, I hope—"

Ruthlessly, I hit the pause button and navigated away from whatever he'd been about to say next.

I wasn't ready to hear it.

And I refused—out of stubbornness or determination or self-preservation, however it might be labeled—to look too deeply into why.

Then I got back to work because that was all I wanted to do.

All I could do.

The alternative—shaky hands and knotted stomach and quivering heart —wasn't something I was ready for.

CHAPTER 24

GRADY

"*A*nd you're sure there's nothing wrong?"

I swung the ax, relishing the satisfying thwack as it split the piece of wood.

"Definitely sure."

Another piece went up on the block, and I hefted the ax over my head.

Thwack.

A clean line down the middle, two pieces flying off to the side where they used to stand tall and straight. Just like my heart.

Aunt Fran cleared her throat, and I knew this conversation wasn't over.

"Sweetheart," she said, "I would just like to point out that we have enough firewood to get us through an entire winter apocalypse. Maybe two."

Grimacing at the massive stack, which I'd been working on for the past week after they had a big ole tree cut down in their yard, I knew she was right.

But what else was I supposed to do with myself?

The first week had been a learning curve for me.

For instance, I learned that you could not shower for four days and still catch the faintest whiff of bonfire in your hair because, sickly, you wanted to remember what it was like when you held her in your arms and you both carried that scent.

I learned that it was possible to go three nights without sleeping much before your body caught up and proceeded to torture you with dreams of her for a solid twelve hours.

I learned that Magnolia—holy hell, it hurt to even think her name— was more than capable of running Valley Adventures without catching a simple glimpse of me.

All those handy week-one lessons were what brought me around the bend and through week two.

Hadn't seen her once, but her fingerprints were everywhere.

I led three guided hikes (that was what forced the shower on day five), and at some point each morning before I arrived at the office, she had lunches ordered and ready to be delivered just on time. She had manila folders marked and tabbed with instructions. She had everything set out for gear in neat stacks along the new table she put at the back of the office.

One morning, I showed up about ninety minutes earlier than I needed to be there, just to see if I could catch her in the act, but she was sneaky, that woman I was in love with.

The calendar continued to fill. The office remained clean and tidy and well-organized without a single, solitary sign of her.

"Grady," Aunt Fran said gently. "You've been staring at the wood for a couple of minutes now, and I think maybe you need to eat something."

My shoulders slumped, and with a resigned sigh, I allowed my aunt—a foot shorter and probably a hundred pounds lighter than me—to herd my mopey ass into the house.

I was fortunate that she and Uncle Robert had a renovated garage apartment that they allowed Grace and then me to live in while we got our feet under us. I had privacy and space to myself without spending a penny on rent. That was what family was for, she told us.

And it was also so she had someone to feed, I'd learned. Aunt Fran didn't love having an empty nest, and my stomach was the grateful beneficiary of her cooking.

While I sat on a stool at their kitchen island, she bustled happily around the kitchen, first pouring me a giant glass of sweet tea and then fixing up a plate of the brisket Uncle Robert had smoked the day before.

"Who is it then?" she asked casually.

I set my glass down. "Who is what?"

Aunt Fran didn't even blink. "The curse. Who is it?"

She scooped some mashed potatoes next to the brisket and popped them both into the microwave.

Exhaling a laugh, I could do nothing except shake my head. "H-How did you know?"

"Child, I have three sons who all suffered to varying degrees through it. I met your uncle just before I turned fifteen years old, and I know how he lost his mind over me. Lord knows we were just kids because he was just a few months older than me. But it was real." Her smile was soft as she said it, her eyes understanding. "And you have always been one of the happiest people I've ever known. Even when you were little, Lord, you just lit up the room, lit up everyone in it when you were around. You couldn't have been more than five the first time I remember thinking it. When you smiled, when you laughed, Grady, it was like you plugged that energy into the whole world."

I braced my elbows on the counter and sank my chin into my hands.

The microwave dinged, and Aunt Fran set the plate down on the counter, along with a fork. I smiled, just a little, at the fact that she used her fancy china with the flowered edges to heat me some leftovers.

"So," she continued, "I know something's wrong when you singlehand-edly chop up a hundred-year-old tree that's been the bane of my gardening attempts."

"It was a *really* big tree."

"I do not need that many shade flowers, and at this phase in my life, I can appreciate God's creation while sometimes wanting to rearrange things a little bit." She cleared her throat in a way that had me lifting my head. "And while your uncle is forever in your debt for all that work you did, Grady, you were working like the devil himself was chasing you."

It was moments like this when I missed my mom.

She wasn't Southern, so she didn't have the same turn of phrase that Aunt Fran did, but their energy was so similar. I missed sitting at my mom's kitchen counter in California while she listened to Grace and me prattle on about school or work or whatever it had been.

When I still didn't answer right away, Aunt Fran sighed, tsking her tongue in a way that cracked a wider smile on my face.

"There now," she said softly. "That looks more like you."

"It's that noise," I told her. "I swear, you Southern women have it down."

"Grady, we came out of the womb knowing how to cluck our tongue in a way that conveys every single ounce of judgment in our bodies."

I laughed, and I saw how it made her relax.

It's a weird thing to be smack in the middle of heartache and realize just how selfish it makes you.

While Magnolia and her happiness consumed my thoughts, I'd lost the ability to step back and see how my own mood was causing those around me to suffer too. And they suffered because they cared.

Grace checked in on me a lot, and each time, the worry lines on her forehead were a little more pronounced. Tucker was giving me space, which honestly was what I needed.

And because I was still a little selfish, I wasn't thinking about my timing when I spoke next. Aunt Fran took a sip of her own sweet tea.

"It's Magnolia," I said slowly.

Whatever was in her mouth came out in an undignified spray. Horrified, she covered her mouth with one hand, frantically reaching for a towel to clean up the mess.

"Lord, I am so sorry, I can't believe I just did that." She patted at the counter, her movements slow and deliberate. "I'm going to need you to repeat that, sweetheart."

"You heard me," I said dully.

"Oh, Grady," she murmured. Her face was so full of understanding, and I wanted to shove the heels of my palms into my eye sockets to block it out. I didn't want understanding as to how fucked up this was. How hard it would be to deal with. I just wanted ... I wanted her.

The tea was wiped up, but Aunt Fran kept dabbing the towel along the counter, probably so she had something to do with her hands while she processed that little nugget.

"Well," she said, "you're not the first to have a lot of complications."

I nodded. "I know."

"I suspect you won't be the last either."

"Something to look forward to with future generations of Buchanans, eh?"

She smiled. "I did have three boys. Eventually, someone will make me a grandma, and then I'll get to start this whole process over again."

"How old were your boys when you told them about this?" I asked. "Grace and I had heard about it over the years, but only as if it were complete and utter bullshit. Didn't exactly prepare us well."

Aunt Fran carefully folded the towel and set it down. "We kinda just told the boys as they grew up in different ways, using different words. When they were younger, we talked about how young Robert and I were when we met, and even though we didn't get married until he was twenty and I was nineteen, our boys grew up knowing their parents' love story. When they were older, some of that changed, how we talked about it with them. That they might meet someone and just ... bam ... feel that strike of lightning."

Lightning.

Yeah, that sounded about right.

"Levi had to be patient, as you know. Jocelyn, oh I love that girl, she wasn't quite ready for a boyfriend. Connor and Sylvia were a lot like Robert and me. They met, and that was that." She smiled. But it faded. "Hunter, he's never quite told us the full story, but ... he moved away because of what happened between him and—" Aunt Fran stopped. "Well, that's all I can say. What he did tell me, he told me in confidence, and I promised him that it was his tale to tell, if he so chose."

Her eyes were sad as she watched me process the fact that my eldest cousin moved across the country because he didn't end up with the person who made him feel those lightning bolts.

"So, he married someone else," I said. Those words, coming out of my mouth, felt like they'd done permanent damage. To every part of me. It was unfathomable. It was depressing. I wasn't sure I wanted to hear Hunter's story.

"Like I said." She eyed me carefully. "It's his tale to tell. But I'm sure he'd talk to you if you wanted to ask him what happened."

"Not sure if it would make me feel better right now."

"Do ... do Tucker and Grace know?" she asked.

I nodded.

"Okay." Aunt Fran blew out a slow breath. "And you're trying to figure out how to tell her? For as crazy as her father is, she's a reasonable girl. God bless Bobby Jo, because she's the only reason that Magnolia got the brains she did."

I rubbed at the spot over my heart. "She knows."

A soft, knowing exhale was all I got. "Oh."

"Yeah."

"Oh, sweetheart. I'm sorry." She patted my hand. "Give it time. But ... maybe just call Hunter. See what he has to say. It might help."

I nodded. Aunt Fran came around the counter and folded me in a tight squeeze. It felt nice, like someone was trying to absorb some of this from me.

"I'll tell you this," she said, arms still tight around me. "Try not to worry about what'll happen tomorrow, all right?"

"That easy, huh?"

She leaned back and gently patted the side of my face. "Worry is like trying to win a race while you're sitting on a rocking horse. You'll move, all right, but you sure won't get anywhere good."

My eyebrows lifted. "That's good advice."

"I'm a smart woman." She pointed at the food. "You better clear that plate before you leave this kitchen. You need some good food."

"Yes, ma'am."

"And don't you even think about leaving that dirty dish in the sink. Every person who walks in this house knows how to open a dishwasher."

She gave me a motherly peck on the cheek and left me with my fancy-plated leftovers.

She didn't pry, which I appreciated. Probably because it was clear enough that Magnolia hadn't liked what I'd had to say. My fumbling admission.

It still made me groan when I thought about it. But in truth, there was no good, easy way to tell someone, and I was making peace with that.

And I still had hope. The fact she chased me to the campsite, stayed overnight, then kissed me like she had, I couldn't help but have hope. But hope was hard to keep honed to a sharp edge in the face of continued silence.

Somehow, I found myself rounding the corner toward February as the days passed in the wake of her walking away from the campsite.

The hope dulled from overuse with every day that passed.

When I imagined her sneaking into the office, probably when the skies were still dark, just to avoid seeing me, it had the same effect.

When I saw her desk, tidy and neat and empty, I felt it too.

Every day that my voicemail sat on her phone, if she'd even kept it there, I felt just a bit more scraped out inside. And because that hollow feeling was so unfamiliar, I was doing things like chopping up hundred-year-old trees with a single ax.

As I ate the food from Aunt Fran, I scrolled through my phone and stared at Hunter's contact info.

I wasn't quite ready to talk to him yet—the man who'd left. Who married someone else, and from what we all knew, wasn't all that happy in the wake of that choice.

No. I wasn't ready for that yet.

I still had hope—dull and quieted—but it was there.

CHAPTER 25

GRADY

*B*y the time the tree was chopped, the pieces stacked along the back of Aunt Fran and Uncle Robert's yard, a few more days had passed. February entered quietly with some cold, sunny days that made for excellent outdoor working.

Even though no hikes were scheduled that week, I found myself in the office, watching Green Valley pass by the front window. They went on about their lives like normal, and it was hard not to envy them.

Envy wasn't something I was used to feeling. Not with anything, really.

Back in California, I used to feel pangs of it when I thought of the people who could spend their workdays wandering the outdoors. Which was what made my current situation even more ironic.

Here I was in Tennessee, a beautiful mountain range and massive national park practically in my backyard, and I was choosing to sit inside at a desk.

There really wasn't even anything for me to do there, except think about her.

The office was immaculate, which meant she'd spent some time making it so.

I found myself wishing she'd put up some of her holiday decorations. A Valentine's Day-themed Christmas tree or something. Heart confetti lining the floors. A bouquet of red and pink flowers on the table, so the people passing by could smile at them.

Anything.

Like it had since Aunt Fran brought it up, it got me thinking about Hunter. How did you willingly walk away from the person you knew was perfect for you?

Levi waited it out, and it was hard to argue with those results.

Suddenly, I couldn't not ask him. I couldn't not try to understand.

Hunter was about a decade older than Grace and me, so we'd never been close or even talked that much, to be honest. Levi I could've called in a heartbeat, but not his eldest brother.

Me: Hey, it's Grady. I have a strange question for you, if you have a few minutes. It's about the family... you know. The curse.

Gray dots appeared. Then disappeared. Then appeared again.

My phone rang, and his name appeared. My head went back in surprise.

"Hey," I said.

Hunter was quiet for a second, then he sighed. "This is the last damn thing I ever want to talk about with anyone."

That had me cracking a rusty smile. "You called me, remember?"

He grunted. "I have fifteen minutes until my next meeting, so if you're going to ask something, let's just get this over with."

Hunter was so different from his brothers, who were both a lot like me. He was gruff and a little quiet. He rarely visited, and when he did, it was quick. After about three more sentences, it would probably go down as the longest conversation I'd ever had with him.

But he was giving me time when I asked for it, and that mattered. I stared at Magnolia's desk and blinked.

"How were you able to walk away from Green Valley knowing she was still here? Assuming she is," I added.

"Good Lord, jump right in without warning, why don't you?"

"You told me to ask."

"I know," he said. Hunter took in slow inhale, a slower exhale. "Leaving was an act of self-preservation. At the time, it felt like the only real choice I had."

I clicked the button for the speaker and set my phone on the desk. "And now?"

"Now is more complicated," he admitted. "I love Seattle. I love my job. It's not as simple as just deciding to be somewhere else."

The omission of his wife was glaring, and I hesitated before pointing it out. "And Samantha?"

Hunter was quiet a moment. "My mother is going to kill me, but I haven't had the heart to tell her this yet, so if you utter a word, I will end you, do you understand?"

With a grimace, I took his growled warning exactly how he'd intended it. "Yeah, I won't say anything to anyone."

"Samantha isn't … she's not part of the picture anymore," he said, voice no longer a growl but weary. So, so weary. "And no, I'm not explaining why."

"Got it." A family passed in front of the office window, a little girl popping her head up to look inside. I waved. She waved back and ran to catch up with her parents. "I think I'm just trying to figure out the line between patience"—I rubbed my forehead—"and insanity. When it comes to waiting."

He hummed. "She not take it well?"

"Not exactly. And I maybe, no, not maybe ... I told her too soon, I think. But I thought being honest upfront would help."

Probably for the first time ever, I heard Hunter emit a low chuckle. "Navigating how you drop that particular nugget is like walking through a minefield, Grady."

"No shit."

"It didn't go over well with her either," he said quietly. "With I-Iris."

The way he stumbled over her name plucked a string of recognition so deep inside me it was painful.

"I hate talking about this," he said. "I hate thinking about it. I've moved on from it."

"How?" I shook my head. "It seems impossible."

"I will tell you this because I wish I'd had someone to talk to, but I didn't." He stopped to gather himself with another inhale and exhale. "I left Green Valley because living there and not being with her *was* impossible."

I didn't say anything, because honestly, what could I say to him? He'd left a decade earlier, carved out a life for himself somewhere different, and the entire time he did it, he knew that the woman he loved, who completed him, was doing the same for herself. It sounded like the worst kind of hell.

There was a question I didn't want to ask, but I knew I should.

"How did you know? That you couldn't ever be with her."

Hunter was quiet for so long that I wasn't sure he was going to answer.

"Trust me, there was no hope for that situation," he said evenly.

There was that word again. Hope.

"Grady," he continued, "I'll tell you this much. If you have even *one* shred of hope, the tiniest sign that she's not done with you, don't give up. Don't leave. Don't let her doubt you for even one moment, because when she starts doubting you ... that's when it will all go to hell, and you won't be able to claw your way out."

There was so much raw pain in his voice, it was hard to find my own to be able to answer. I cleared my throat. "I hear you."

"I gotta go," he said. "Good luck."

"Thank you, Hunter."

With a click, he was gone.

It was the first time in weeks that my focus truly shifted to what the future might look like. Every day since I'd seen her, I was thinking about that day, taking it as it came, keeping my blinders on to the present because that's all I could really do without losing my shit.

But Hunter's story, even though I got the skimmed-over version, forced my blinders off. Because I had to be able to look around and know that I'd even be able to see a moment of hope if she gave me one. Not only that, but how would I be able to let her know I was still here. As long as she'd let me be.

Thumb tapping on my thigh, I looked around the office, so drab and quiet without her presence or her touch on the space. And I got an idea.

I flipped open my laptop and started searching.

Ten minutes later, I was typing out a very professional email to Magnolia.

To: MagnoliaMacIntyre@gmail.com
From: grady.buchanan@gmail.com
Good morning, Magnolia,
I'm going to be out of town for most of the day today to get

some items for the office in Knoxville. I know it's unlikely that a last-minute booking would come in, but if it does, please feel free to contact Tucker for his availability. I'm letting him know this as well.
Thanks,
Grady

Before lunch, I was in Knoxville at a giant craft store, wondering if I was losing my mind. And as I expected it would, my email triggered a response from her that had me grinning.

To: grady.buchanan@gmail.com
From: MagnoliaMacIntyre@gmail.com
Grady,
Thank you for letting me know.
May I ask what items you're purchasing for the office? I wasn't aware we needed any supplies.
Thanks,
Magnolia

To: MagnoliaMacIntyre@gmail.com
From: grady.buchanan@gmail.com
Magnolia,
Just a few things I thought we were missing.
Have a great day.
G

With my phone tucked safely in my back pocket, I wandered the aisles with a goofy grin on my face, spending far more than I anticipated.

As I made the drive back to Green Valley, I marveled at how one depressing phone call about the sad truth of my cousin's situation and three fairly innocent emails could completely shift my outlook.

It made me think about one of the visits I'd made to Green Valley as a teenager to spend a couple of weeks of our summer with Pops. I must've been about thirteen, and he was showing me his sharpening stone, the one he kept for all his best knives. As a man who spent a lot of time hunting and fishing, taking the responsibility to clean what lives he'd taken so that he could use every possible part of that animal, knives were an important tool to him.

"There are easier ways to sharpen a knife," he'd said, sliding the long blade against the coarse stone, one innocuous-looking rectangle he had sitting in front of him on a folded towel. "Faster ways too."

"How come you don't use those then?"

"Because faster and easier doesn't always mean it's the best way or the right way." Tilting the knife at just the right angle, he pushed it along the surface of the stone, still visibly wet from the soaking he'd given it the night before. The back and forth motions were soothing, as was the sound it created. "Something like this knife, how important it is to you, you want to take care of it. And sometimes, taking care of something that important, it's better to take things slow and steady, even if it makes more work for you."

Maybe that's what I was doing.

The weeks of quiet were just the soaking of the stone, the necessary time for the conditions to hone that hope again, until it was bright and visible and caught the light just right, so we could both see it.

Patience had always been one of my weaknesses.

So had being willing to sit in discomfort.

But this, *she,* was worth it.

The office was just as I'd left it when I returned that evening, and as I nodded to a couple of women who passed on the sidewalk, I wondered if Magnolia was waiting for me to leave so she could see what I was up to.

I left all but one bag from the craft store in my car while I set up a couple of things. A tall frame passed in front of the window, and I saw Tucker stop and do a double-take when he saw me.

My face was hot when he slowly opened the door, taking in the sight of me up on the ladder by the black metal shelves.

"Tucker," I said evenly, like I wasn't hanging a strand of hot-pink, plastic heart-shaped lights along our inventory shelves.

His eyes were wide and uncertain. I could practically hear his thoughts. *That's it. Grady has lost his mind.*

"What'cha up to, Grady?"

"Just sprucing up the place."

"Uh-huh." He scratched the side of his face. "Haven't seen much of you the past couple of weeks. Your aunt told me you might be here, and I thought I'd chance it."

I turned back to the lights and hooked the end on the edge of the shelf, anchoring it with a box of hiking boots. "Mind plugging that in for me?"

His eyebrows popped up. "Uhh, nope." He leaned over and snatched the end of the strand, plugging it into the wall outlet.

The lights were terrible. Tacky and cheesy. And perfect. She'd love them. And if I knew her like I thought I did, she'd take them for exactly what I meant them to be. A sign. And a challenge that I knew she wouldn't be able to resist. Not if she still cared, at least. She might think I was crazy, but hell, half the people I loved were crazy in some form.

"What do you think?" I asked him, climbing down the ladder and studying them carefully.

"Bit crooked."

I tilted my head. Shit. They were. "They're supposed to be. It's artsy."

"Uh-huh." He studied my face. "She talking to you yet?"

"Not yet," I said, keeping my voice light. "We emailed about some work stuff today, and she hasn't quit yet, so I'm taking that as a good sign."

Tucker nodded. "I wanted to give both of y'all some space, because I know this isn't a normal situation." He pointed at himself, and then me and the desk, as if that one stupid piece of furniture represented Magnolia. "The three of us. My past with her."

"It's not." I gestured to the chairs tucked into the table by the front window. "Have a seat."

He slid one out and flipped it to face the desk, and I took my normal spot.

"In truth, I wasn't sure if you even needed me to come talk to you about this," Tucker admitted. "You hardly need my permission, or blessing, whatever. You're both adults if she decides she's okay with everything."

"But she's still your ex-girlfriend," I said.

"That she is." Tucker blew out a hard breath. "She's a good person with a good heart, and we grew apart very naturally. Long before your sister showed up. It's almost like we were that married couple who stayed together simply because it was easier, which sounds horrible now, but it's true. I can truly look at her and wish her well. And if you're the man who will protect that heart of hers, then I'm happy." He held my gaze. "I'm happy it's you."

I extended my hand, which he took in a firm shake. "I hope she lets me."

"Yeah." He sighed. "Maybe hitting her with that so soon wasn't the best idea."

"Ya think?"

We both laughed, and something inside me settled because this was my friend. Someday, he'd be my brother through marriage.

He glanced at the lights again. "You sure you know what you're doing?"

"Nope." I smiled. "But I'll tell you right now, with no offense intended, I probably won't ever seek your advice when it comes to her."

"None taken," he answered easily. "Your Magnolia is different than the one I knew. I can say that with utmost sincerity."

My Magnolia, I thought. The want was visceral and painful. The desire for her to have, to want that same type of claim on me. There would be no ownership that wasn't fully equal. If she belonged to me, then I'd belong to her right back.

We stood, and he waited while I locked up the office. As we passed the front window, I caught a glimpse of those lights and smiled.

Tomorrow. I'd see tomorrow what kind of hope I deserved to have.

CHAPTER 26

MAGNOLIA

*A*t just after five a.m., the streets of downtown Green Valley were hushed and quiet and dark. My headlights almost seemed like a harsh intrusion when I pulled up in front of the office, but I felt that every time I snuck in early to do my work without fear of running into Grady.

But that morning, when I rolled out of bed, I hurried to slide on some clothes and shove my feet into my house slippers (which I'd never worn in public before), and I felt a zing of excitement.

Because not once had Grady ever taken it upon himself to buy anything for the office without talking to me first.

That man was up to something, and I couldn't even be upset.

Two weeks of silence had started to feel like a stalemate that I wasn't sure how to break.

He hadn't reached out, but if he respected me, I wasn't sure he'd push me too hard either.

I missed him, terribly, but I still thought it impossible that he'd actually fallen in love with me the day he met me.

When I pulled my car into a parking spot, I saw it. The slightest hint of pink glowing through the window.

"What on earth?" I whispered, but on my face, I felt the widening of my smile. I got out of the car, keys poised in my hands and my coat zipped tight up around my face because it was cold. When I approached the window and saw what he'd hung along the shelves, I felt like a little girl.

The glass of the window was cold when I pressed my palm against it. Those lights, bright and fun and undeniably silly, made the inside of the office glow pink and warm.

Heart-shaped lights for Valentine's Day.

Maybe, just maybe, this was the break that the stalemate needed. Without thinking, I whirled and got back in my car, heading home before I could think about it too hard. I ran into my house, flinging open my storage closet at the end of the hallway where I kept all my favorite holiday items. When I saw what I was looking for, I smiled, holding it carefully.

With a stop in my kitchen to grab the other item I needed, I ran out to my idling car and drove back to Valley Adventures.

When I let myself in, I kept the other lights dim, because even if it was silly to sit in the dark, I wanted to feel like those heart lights were all I needed.

The bowl from my closet was a gift from Aunt Julianne. It used to be my Grandma MacIntyre's, something I treasured more than I could bear. It perched on the corner of the desk, where he'd see it immediately.

When I pulled open the drawer of the desk, I grimaced when I saw how few candies were left. The Piggly Wiggly would just be opening, so I ran back to my car.

Only a few people meandered the aisles this early in the morning, and as I knew right where I was going, I didn't do more than just acknowledge the ones I saw. When I made my way to the bins of candy, I stopped at the correct one and smiled. Carefully, I pulled a bag from the dispenser and used the heavy silver scoop to buy far, far more than I needed. Just as I was twisting the small white tie around the top, I felt the weight of someone's stare.

The eyes were the same color, so was the hair, and when Grace walked slowly up to me with her gaze pinned on the bag of butterscotch discs, her mouth was tilted up into a secretive smile.

"You're getting some shopping done early," I said. I straightened my spine and met her straight on.

She pointed at the black camera bag over her shoulder. "I have a sunrise shoot, and I was craving those awful little powdered sugar donuts you should never admit to liking."

I smiled. So did she.

Grace took a deep breath. "I'm sorry we ambushed you at the campsite. And I'm ..." She looked away, blinking down at the floor for a second. "I'm sorry all this is so awkward. You and I seem to have a way of meeting in this place over strange circumstances involving the men in our life."

"Thank you for your apology," I told her. "It's not easy for any of us."

"We're not exactly given a handbook either." She had the same crooked, wide smile as her brother, and it sent my stomach tight into a ball to see it. Grace stared at the candy again, and I fought the urge to hide it behind my back. "There's only one person I know who loves those gross things enough to need a big bag."

My face was flaming hot. "Just stocking the office."

"Right." She studied me intently. "I won't tell him I saw you, if that's what you're worried about."

I lifted my chin. "I'm not. He'll know soon enough that I got these."

"Good." Grace smiled again. She opened her mouth and then seemed to think better about saying something.

"Go ahead," I drawled. "I know I'd have a hard time keeping it in if I were you."

She exhaled a laugh. "I've thought about what I'd say to you if I got the chance. Practiced telling you what an amazing person my brother is."

"I already know that," I told her softly.

"I figured as much." She blew out a slow breath. "He's my brother, and I'd do anything for him. It kills me to see him hurting." Immediately, she took a step closer, understanding etched all over those pretty features of hers. "And I get why you left. I don't hold that against you. But this ... Buchanan thing, I don't know why we call it a curse. It's strange, that's for damn sure, but there's so much freedom in finding the person who'll love you through *anything*."

Emitting a shaky laugh, I couldn't help but shake my head at her. "You trying to convince me that this is less strange than it really is might have more impact if we didn't have the history we do."

"I know, I *know*." Grace was searching so hard for the right words, and in that struggle, I saw her love for her brother. I saw her love for Tucker, and right in the mix, I also saw a woman who was desperately trying to find common ground with me. I thought about the lights in the office. The bowl on the desk. All of it was important, even if it wasn't easy. And we'd only get there one day at a time.

I closed the space between us and set my hand on her arm. Her eyes widened in surprise.

"It's okay, Grace. I don't need you to tell me who Grady is because he can't help but show what kind of heart he has. And I'm not even sure I need you to make this ... legend into something more palatable. Just knowing you're willing to stand here with me and try, it means a lot."

"I am," she said on a rush. "I'm so willing. I want to get to know you, Magnolia. More than passing off wine and shooing off gossips, and ugh, showing up in the worst possible places with no notice."

I laughed under my breath.

Her facial features smoothed into something more serious. "But I will also completely respect your need for time. Just like Grady is."

"Thank you." I smiled. "I appreciate that."

"When you're ready, I'd love to meet you for coffee." She held up the horrible powdered sugar donuts. "And something better than these."

I assessed her. "People will talk."

She nodded slowly. "They will. And I'm okay with that."

This unexpected run-in added just what I needed to my morning, an edge of certainty when I couldn't see all my steps. Normally, I had every one planned out beforehand. And maybe this was teaching me that going in blind was okay too.

"I'll let you know when I'm ready for that coffee." I held up the candy. "I'd better get back to the office."

She nodded, and I saw her eyes inexplicably gloss over. Happy tears, I had to guess.

After I paid, I walked out of the Piggly Wiggly, got back in my car, and made my way back to the office to put the finishing touches on my little gesture.

By the time I left, I'd accomplished nothing in the way of work, but my heart felt a million times better than it had for the past handful of days. Maybe what Grady and I needed were little signs, little statements that we could build on. Steps that would get us where we needed to go, even if they were only baby steps and happened one at a time.

Eventually, we'd have something big to climb over, but I couldn't help but feel like this was exactly what we needed. Time apart to miss the other person, and clear signals of what we knew about them.

By seven-thirty, I was drinking my coffee, with my laptop perched on a pillow on my lap, and an email notification popped up into my inbox.

To: MagnoliaMacIntyre@gmail.com
From: grady.buchanan@gmail.com

Magnolia,
The bowl is so pretty I almost don't dare touch it, but as you filled it with the greatest candy ever, I'm afraid that I had no choice.
I'm guessing it's vintage? (the bowl, not the candy. Those were so delicious that I ate sixteen of them.)
Grady

To: grady.buchanan@gmail.com
From: MagnoliaMacIntyre@gmail.com

Grady,
It was my Grandma MacIntyre's. She inherited it from her mother. The glazing around the handles is real gold, and the roses along the inside are hand-painted, so if you break that by reaching for your 17th piece of candy (which you shouldn't because even you can't afford such eating habits), I'll have to invoice you.
Magnolia

To: MagnoliaMacIntyre@gmail.com
From: grady.buchanan@gmail.com

I will treat it with the utmost care. You have my word.
G

His response had my cheeks warm with all the subtext packed into that sentence. I knew how he meant it. He'd treat me with the utmost care. I just had to decide if I was ready to accept it.

Over the next three days, it became a game between the two of us. He'd leave something for me to find in the morning, and I'd sneak in before dawn to add to the growing collection.

When he added a giant hand-painted sign wishing anyone who could see it a Happy Valentine's Day, leaning up against the floor in front of the desk, I added a tasteful bouquet of red, white, and pink roses in a mason jar on the middle of the table by the front display.

When Grady hung a surprisingly charming wreath of pastel pink hearts on the front door, I added two giant mylar balloons tied to the desk chair, an X and an O in rose gold. I drove to Merryville to get them because I'd be damned if anyone at the Piggly Wiggly would be allowed to wonder who I was thinking about hugging and kissing.

His answer to those was a trio of framed vintage Valentine's cards so stunning in their colors that I almost cried when I saw them lined up on my desk. The first one was a red cuckoo bird popping out of a red and white clock.

It proclaimed in whimsical letters, *I'm cuckoo over you!*

With my hand rubbing my chest, I picked up the frame of the second card. A puppy was climbing up an old-fashioned style cash counter.

Let me register in your heart.

"Oh, Grady," I whispered shakily. We'd emailed after each discovery, and they'd stayed innocent, a sweet teasing about what the other had left us to discover. But these felt different.

The sun was rising outside, the office slowly lightening along with it. Normally, I didn't stay this long, but I found myself not wanting to rush through this moment. It felt very much like he was saying something important to me.

Carefully, I set the second frame back in the middle and picked up the third.

It was the simplest of the three, and the picture was stunning. I almost opened the frame to be able to study it better. Centered on the card was a giant red heart, pierced with a golden arrow. Above the heart flew two white doves.

For my dearest Valentine.

And beneath the heart were two pristine white magnolia blossoms.

Eyes watering dangerously, and my heart too big for my chest, I knew that I wanted to see him. But behind that overwhelming desire to throw open the door and run toward Grady, the chair, the desk, my fear, they all held me tethered. His feelings were so sure, so large, I wasn't sure how to tiptoe my way back into any sort of new footing with him.

This time when I left the office, I drove in the opposite direction of home.

There was only one person I could talk to about this.

I needed my daddy.

When I got to their house, he was sitting on the long stretch of front porch in his favorite Adirondack chair, drinking coffee.

I leaned down to kiss the top of his head, and he watched me carefully as I took the seat next to him.

"You're here early, daughter."

I nodded. "Momma out on the lake?"

He hummed into his coffee. That was a yes.

"Got something on your mind?"

"Yeah." I reached forward and grabbed the plaid wool blanket he kept draped over the porch rail for cold mornings and laid it over my legs.

"I need your advice on something, and before I tell you, I need you to promise me that you'll just listen first."

He opened his mouth, and I held my hand up.

"I mean it. No getting upset, no yelling, no fuss over any of it, I just need my daddy's advice about how to deal with something."

"Okay," he said gruffly. "What is it?"

I took a deep breath. "How long did you love Momma before you knew she loved you back?"

My question had a profound effect on him. With a low whistle, he rocked his chair backward, like the words actually dealt him a blow. "Lord, Magnolia, you coulda warned me."

"Sorry."

His eyes went a little unfocused, and he took an absent sip of his coffee. "If I think about it, I most likely fell in love with your mother on our first date. Wasn't hard. Wasn't confusing. Something about her just knocked me sideways, and I never truly righted myself again."

I'd heard this story so many times, I practically had it memorized. But I'd never listened to it really thinking about what that must've been like for my daddy. To set aside his pride like that and wait because he trusted so deeply that they were meant for each other.

"Every time we saw each other, I was more and more certain that she was the one for me. I'd never met anyone like your mother. She was —is—incredible. Strong and smart and so damn beautiful that it still hurts to look at her. She knew what she wanted out of life, knew what made her the happiest, and she was unapologetic about going after it."

"Fishing," I said with a smile. "Make her living so that she and everyone else can fish and do it well."

"That's right." He grinned. "And if that wasn't the sexiest thing I'd ever seen. Her ambition matched mine even though we wanted such different things. But I always knew what I felt for your mother. Right from the beginning. That's why I asked her to marry me on our fifth date."

"And two hundred more times after that," I murmured.

He squinted. "Just about."

"That didn't bother you? To ask her that many times and have her say no?"

"Hell no. Your momma is stubborn as the day is long. She told me on that first date that she had no intention of marrying anyone, and she meant it. Took me damn near fifteen years"—he smiled at me—"and one positive pregnancy test before she said yes."

I swallowed hard, imagining Grady pining away for fifteen years. Could I have done something like that to him without knowing? Was that why he told me so quickly?

"That's such a long time, Daddy."

He shrugged. "It was still fifteen years I got to spend with my favorite person in the world." He gave me a strange look. "You know all this, though. What's this about, Magnolia?"

The edge of the blanket was soft, a perfect place to focus my attention. "I find myself in a situation where someone cares for me very, very deeply." I paused, keeping my eyes trained on the reds and blues of the plaid. "He might even love me. And it took me by surprise."

Daddy's chair started a slow rocking motion again, but to his credit, he didn't flip his lid. "But you like him?"

Slowly, I nodded. "I do."

When he lifted his mug up to his mouth, I saw his hand shaking a little. "Could you love him?"

Why did that make my eyes burn with unshed tears?

Why did his restraint make me feel so wildly emotional?

Maybe because it felt, for one of the first times in my life, that my father was trusting me with this precious thing.

I leaned my head back on the chair and closed my eyes. That simple movement, my eyelids closing, had a tear sliding down my cheek and settling somewhere by my ear.

"Yeah, Daddy," I whispered. "Very easily."

Another tear snuck out, and I sniffed, unable to hide that tiny leak of emotion.

"Then why are you crying, sweetheart?"

"I don't know," I admitted.

"I'm not sure I believe that."

I opened my eyes, glancing quickly in his direction. "His feelings are so much bigger than mine."

He nodded. "But he told you what those feelings were?"

"He did." I swiped at my cheek.

"Magnolia, pride is a dangerous thing in the wrong hands. And it comes in all different shapes and sizes for all sorts of reasons. Pride in your work and your mind and your family and your things. But when you lay your heart at someone else's feet—the *right* person's feet—you don't worry about what they might do to it. You trust that the person you give that heart to will protect it. They'll value it so much that your pride is a worthy sacrifice when it comes to your happiness."

Well, whatever tears I'd stemmed started right back up again. Daddy's eyes watered suspiciously as he dug into his pocket and gave me his handkerchief.

I cried because I missed Grady.

Because his feelings still scared me a little.

But mostly, I think I cried because I knew it was okay that they scared me.

He'd laid his heart at my feet because he trusted me with it. Being scared of that, the way he'd refused to let his pride come before what he felt for me, meant that I cared too.

"Is it," he said, stopping to clear his throat, "is it that Buchanan boy?"

Emitting a watery laugh, I nodded. "He has a name, you know."

"I know what his name is."

From around the back of the house, my momma wandered up, pole in hand and a slight smile on her face.

When she saw me crying, she paused. "Good Lord, what did I miss?" she asked.

"Magnolia's got a new man," Daddy said gruffly.

She ascended the steps, a dimple appearing to the side of her mouth as she watched us. "That so?"

"He can't be too bad, I suppose," Daddy admitted.

Momma leaned her fishing pole against the rail, and instead of taking an empty chair, she slid easily onto Daddy's lap, curling her arm around the back of his neck.

"Why's that?"

Daddy slid his hand up her jeans-covered thigh and closed his eyes contentedly. "I figure any man who's smart enough to love our daughter and tell her so right away is all right by me."

I laughed, and Momma smiled.

She leaned down to press a soft kiss on his mouth. "Reminds me of someone else."

He grunted.

"It's Grady, right?" she asked, eyes resting carefully on me.

"How'd you know?"

"I met him just after you started working for him." Her smile was mysterious, just like so much was about my mother. "He made sure to tell me that I should be proud to have you as a daughter."

I sat forward. "He did?"

She hummed. "Any man who's brave enough to tell me what I ought to feel about anything, especially my own daughter, is all right by me."

Daddy blinked. "Are you wearing house slippers, Magnolia?"

All three of us looked down at my feet, which were clad in pink fuzzy slippers. I lifted my chin imperiously. "Yes, I am."

"Huh."

I stood quickly. "I need to go."

"Already?" he asked. "You just got here. I could make some breakfast."

My heart was racing. "I forgot to leave some Valentine's decorations at the office."

My parents traded a look.

"You okay, Magnolia?" my momma asked.

I nodded. "Never better."

With a peck on the cheek for both of them, I ran in my pink fuzzy slippers back to my car and jammed the key into the ignition and started it.

Before I backed out of my parents' driveway, I pulled out my phone and flipped furiously until I reached my voicemail screen. There it was, as it had been for weeks. Waiting patiently for when I would be ready to hear it, just as he'd said.

I pressed the play button, his voice filling the car from the speakers.

"It's me."

Oh Lord, how I'd missed that voice.

"I probably should have handled all of this differently, Magnolia." He sighed. "I'm sorry for telling you the way that I did. Sometimes, I get so excited about stuff happening that I don't always think through how I've got to get there." Grady chuckled under his breath, probably thinking about the way he'd begun with Valley Adventures. "But you know that. I think I'm most sorry that I made you feel stuck or trapped in any way because the way I feel about you, that's the last thing I'd ever want. So, while my intentions were good, the execution was ... lacking. What I should have done in that tent was tell you that I could kiss you like that for the rest of my life, and I'd be perfectly happy. I should have told you that even though you're the most beautiful woman I've ever seen in my life, what I feel for you goes so much deeper than that.

"Your brain and your drive and your humor, it's so sexy, Magnolia. Everything about you is perfect to me. And I should have given you time, right alongside my honesty, and trusted that you'll make the right decision for you. Not for me. Not for anyone else. And I should have known that waiting for you to get there is the best kind of waiting I could ever do. So, I hope you listen to this someday, my Magnolia, and I hope you'll come to me. I hope I'll get to love you the way I was born to because I'll do that better than anything else in this world, if you do me the honor of allowing me to."

Tears streamed down my face as he disconnected the call.

This time, I didn't wipe them away. I let them fall. As I peeled out of my parents' driveway, through my happy tears, I thought I caught a glimpse of them smiling.

CHAPTER 27

GRADY

I wished it were raining.

It was a strange thought as I brought the ax down onto another piece of wood. If it was raining, then everything around me would've matched my mood.

Instead, the day had dawned bright. The sky was painfully blue and free of clouds, the sun pushing warmth into the air as it rose higher.

When I showed up at the office, earlier than I'd ever dared, I swear I still smelled Magnolia's lingering scent.

But for the first time since we started our little Valentine's game, nothing was left behind.

She'd been there because the frames holding the cards had been moved.

My back muscles screamed with overuse as I bent down to grab another piece of wood.

No email to let me know what she thought.

Sitting at the office was impossible with my mind racing in the wake of her silence. The hope I'd felt building all week suddenly felt too big. Was she quiet for a good reason? Or were the cards too much?

I tipped my face up to the sun and felt a trickle of sweat slide down the side of my face. At this rate, I'd have the entire grove of trees next to Aunt Fran's garden chopped up. They'd have firewood for a decade, and she'd kick my ass for getting rid of her morning shade on the front porch.

The piece of wood in my hand was rough, and I set it carefully on the splitting log. My shoulders were burning before I even lifted the ax because I'd done this so many times in the past two weeks. It was one of those moments, the kind men don't really like to admit to. I knew it was dumb, and I knew I could injure myself. But I needed the outlet. Each swinging arc of the ax, each satisfying hiss as it came down, each rewarding thunk as it dug into the wood was like releasing a pressure valve inside my body.

The smaller of the two pieces flung out into the air, and I sighed heavily.

I set the other one on top of the stack, set the ax up against the splitting log, and as I was leaning down to grab the piece from the ground, I heard a car pull up.

Uncle Robert was working, and Aunt Fran was spending the day in Knoxville with Sylvia, which was the only reason my heart gave the slightest hiccup. Given that I was around the side of the garage apartment I called home, whoever pulled into the driveway couldn't see me.

I swiped my discarded shirt from the ground and wiped at the sweat coating my forehead and face. That was when I heard the knock on the door of my apartment.

My chest heaved on a massive inhale.

"Be right there," I called out. Even though my chest was still sweaty, I tugged my T-shirt on.

The default optimism built in me wavered because I didn't want to expect to turn that corner and see her. It was probably someone else. Maybe Connor. Maybe Grace. Maybe Tucker.

Except when I took that corner, I ran smack-dab into Magnolia, who was coming around the back.

My hands gripped her arms so she didn't fall backward.

"Whoa, sorry," I said.

The automatic reflex to apologize for almost running her over was such a bullshit lie because I wasn't sorry.

Having the ability to touch and see her had all my senses reeling.

She laughed under her breath as I set her back gently. "It's all right."

My eyes devoured every inch of her after weeks without a single glace. Her face was bare of makeup, her hair pulled off her face in a high, simple whatever women called it, a bun or something. Whatever it was, that bone structure of her face, her big eyes, her soft lips, nothing distracted my hungry gaze.

Magnolia did some studying of her own. "What were you doing back there?"

I rubbed the back of my neck. "Chopping enough firewood for the whole town."

"Ah." She licked her lips, and I almost groaned. In pain. In pleasure. Hell, if I knew. "I loved the cards, Grady. They're beautiful."

My heart was beating dangerously fast. "You're welcome. I'm trying to make up for my lack of a Christmas gift."

Her lips curled in a tiny smile. "That so?"

Any hope I'd been lacking that morning, any optimism that had ebbed in even the smallest amount exploded in a bright, painful burst behind my ribs. Her eyes glowed, and that glow was like an entire can of gasoline tossed carelessly onto a fire.

"I'm a hopeless wreck, if you hadn't noticed," I murmured, taking the tiniest step toward her.

A white flash of her teeth appeared as she bit down on her bottom lip. She shook her head slowly. "You're no such thing, Grady."

I let out a slow breath. "Why are you here, Magnolia?"

Before anything else happened, before anything else was said, I needed to hear her say it. I needed to know.

She looked briefly at the ground, and her chest expanded on an inhale. When her head lifted again, I saw my answer, and it took every ounce of restraint not to pounce on her, take her to the ground, and devour her.

My hands curled into fists at my side.

"I listened to your voicemail," she said quietly. "I'm sorry it took me this long."

I shook my head. "Don't apologize. I-I threw so much at you."

"I think," she started, "I think I needed to make sure that what I felt could stand on its own before I really knew what you'd said."

Let her finish, let her finish, let her finish, I instructed my body. Because it was like a snarling, starved beast, just out of reach of a fresh meal.

She took a small step of her own. Her hand lifted, those long, graceful fingers trembling slightly before she curled them into the edge of my shirt. With the slightest tug on that fabric, she pulled me to her, and oh, did I go willingly.

After that, my body, my heart, every instinct that knew exactly what to do with Magnolia took over. My hands slid around the curve of her hips and to her back. Her hands moved like silk up my chest, and her face found a resting place against my neck as I curled my body around hers.

I exhaled when she was fully wrapped in my embrace.

"Just to be clear," I said, my lips resting against the crown of her head, "this isn't some new work trust exercise you want to try out, right?"

Her frame shook with laughter, and she lifted her chin to look at me. "No." Her eyes dropped to my mouth. "This is me coming for you, Grady Buchanan. If you'll have me."

My hands tightened on her back. "*If* I'll have you," I breathed incredulously. My forehead dropped to hers, and I exhaled a laugh. "Magnolia, I'm not going anywhere unless you asked me to."

She surged up on her toes, arms snaking around my neck, her mouth settling onto mine with startling intensity. A relieved groan broke free from my chest when her tongue swept against mine.

This kiss was freedom, the unshackling from whatever had held the two of us back, and all those burdens fell to the ground when her fingers dug into my hair, and I bent at the knees to boost her up into my arms. Her legs wrapped around my waist, my hands gripping her ass while I kissed her with abandon.

The fact that we were alone was a miracle, because when I pressed her against the wall and rolled my hips, Magnolia's mouth broke away from mine with a gasp. Her head dropped back against the garage, and I sucked at the edge of her jaw, tasting all the glorious soft skin that I hadn't been able to since the last time we did this.

She tasted sweet and clean and heavenly in all the places that my lips traveled while we clutched at each other.

I was in love with her. And she was here.

With surprising force, she gripped the sides of my face and brought my lips back to hers. I smiled into the kiss until she bit my bottom lip. My head slanted, deepening the kiss to someplace dirtier, someplace darker, and my sweet Southern belle, she met me there.

This was what I'd been waiting for.

This sense of rightness. When the surety that had been planted the moment she walked through the door was allowed to bloom into something incredible.

Magnolia broke away from the kiss and took a gasping breath. "Can we ...?"

I stared at her mouth.

"Grady," she whispered, her finger lifting to trace my lips. I nipped the tip of one, sucking it into my mouth, rubbing my tongue against the fleshy pad. "If you keep looking at me like that ..."

"What?" I rasped.

She pitched her hips forward. "Can we go inside?"

I froze, watching her face. "If you want to," I answered carefully.

There wasn't a moment's hesitation. "I want to."

"As my lady wishes." I straightened, keeping her firmly in my arms.

She placed sucking kisses along my jaw as I opened the door with one hand. The apartment was dark, but thankfully tidy. The bed was big and comfortable, but that felt presumptuous, so I strode toward the couch.

Magnolia pinned me with her gaze, and holy shit, pleasure followed that look all the way down my spine.

"Not the couch."

"I love a woman who knows what she wants," I said fervently. We toppled back onto the bed, and she laughed when I sat up between her bent knees. I just wanted to look at her.

My hands slid up her legs, covered in soft cotton.

"Did you come to me wearing pajamas, Magnolia?" I asked.

She smiled. "Yes."

Slowly, I felt along the curves of her thighs, her calves, my fingers tracing her slender ankles. My head tilted when I got to her feet.

One was bare.

One was in a strange, fluffy pink shoe.

She laughed, leaning down to snatch it off and toss it to the floor. "Ignore those."

"Oh, I don't think I can." I bent to take her mouth in another kiss. "It was very bright pink. And furry."

One perfectly arched eyebrow lifted in such an imperious way that I couldn't help but laugh.

"They're house slippers," she explained haughtily. "And there is nothing wrong with them."

"Of course not." I dropped a kiss onto the side of her ankle. "I love your house slippers." My hands moved back up the insides of her legs, which made her lips roll together impatiently. "And I love these pants." My fingers trailed softly along the edge of her cotton shirt and pushed up underneath it. My palms covered her ribs, the tips of my fingers brushing the underside of her breasts, soft and warm and full behind a thin layer of silk. "And I love whatever is under here that I can't see yet."

She moved restlessly, her chest rising and falling rapidly. "Are you going to keep that shirt on all day?"

I grinned at her obvious impatience. "Do you want me to?"

"No." Magnolia stared me down. The challenge I saw in her eyes, the demand, almost had me falling on her like a freaking beast. This was a woman with no fear. No shame in what she wanted from me, what she wanted for her. And I felt like a fucking king that she was showing this side of herself to me.

Before I pulled my hands from under her shirt, I coasted my palms up and moved them in a ghost of a circle over the top of her breasts. Her eyes closed, her chin tilting toward the ceiling. With a smirk, I reached behind my neck and tugged the shirt off.

She sighed happily, trailing her fingers along my abs, which contracted helplessly under her touch. Her fingers curled into the waist of my shorts and tugged until I had no choice but to fall on top of her.

I caught my weight before it landed fully. Our noses brushed, my lips whispering over hers.

"You are so beautiful to me," I told her. "But I will not screw this up by moving too fast, Magnolia." Her eyes softened, and she cupped the side of my face. I turned, placing a fervent kiss in her palm. "You mean too much to me for that."

"You think I don't know that already?" Her fingers swept over my cheekbones and slid back into my hair. "Why do you think I'm here?"

I kissed her sweetly, brushing the tip of my tongue against hers before pulling back again.

"Grady," she whispered, "nothing about this feels fast or rushed or wrong." She kissed me, a mirror of the one I'd given her. "I wouldn't be here if I wasn't committed to this. Even if you hadn't told me what you did, I was falling for you before I even recognized what was happening."

I blinked. "You were?"

She smiled. "Who else would I go camping for?"

"No one," I answered honestly.

Magnolia was still laughing when I swept her up in a deep kiss, rolling so that we were on our sides. I wasn't exactly sure how long we kissed like that, how many minutes we spent learning the feel of each other's bodies.

She was ticklish, which I discovered when I peeled off her shirt and dragged my lips along the line of each of her ribs under her skin.

When I closed my mouth over the silk scraps covering her chest, pulled the material down with my teeth, hollowed my cheeks with a deep, sucking pull against her sinfully warm skin, it did the most amazing thing. My sweet girl moaned a curse word so foul that I wanted to beat my chest like a fool.

She liked to be underneath the full weight of my body, especially as I tugged off her clothes and spent glorious minutes discovering each part of her that I uncovered. Anytime I propped myself up to see better, she'd grin and tug me back down, wrapping her legs around my hips and trapping me in place. It was fine by me, of course, because I loved the way my skin slid across hers as I moved.

And in turn, Magnolia discovered things about me.

When she sucked on my tongue, it was like she released a lever in my hips, helpless rocking motions against her core.

When she whispered in my ear that she wanted her hands on me, wanted her mouth on me, wanted my mouth on her, my teeth found the curve of her shoulder so that I could scrape her skin, a gentle bite that had her gasping.

When she pushed my shorts off, followed by my briefs, and we were finally, finally both free of every inch of clothing, we'd worked ourselves into such a frenzied state, such a mindless build of slow pleasure, it was like she unclipped a leash, whatever harness had held me back.

Magnolia wrapped her hand around me, and I dug my fingers into her skin, dug them in hard.

I whispered her name and tugged her hands away, pushing her arms up over her head where I anchored them in place with one of my own.

My other coasted down her skin, the lithe, endless curves of her insane body, and I couldn't stop marveling over the fact that she was mine. That I could see her like this. Experience her like this.

It was my turn for my hands on her, and as I devoured her mouth, our tongues and teeth clashing, slashing, sucking, tasting, my fingers had her crying out against my lips in only a few short moments. Her back arched, her chest heaved, and I was so far gone for this girl.

"Grady," she whispered, "come to me. I need you."

The plea was so drowsy, so drunk with pleasure, and I was still so amped with unspent energy that I let go of her hands, eager to feel them against my back. She complied immediately, sliding those fingers down my spine until she gripped my ass and urged me forward.

I was trembling when I felt her for the first time, when I urged myself to move as slowly as possible, to let this go on forever.

I'd live on the knife-edge of this feeling for her because I knew she'd never make me. It was painful, how good it—she—felt.

I groaned her name when I couldn't move any farther. For one moment, we held like that, and then she arched her hips. Restlessly.

I sat up suddenly, on my knees, staying right with her, but lifting her hips with my hands as I did. I moved like that. Fully able to see her, fully able to touch her, and bring her over the crest again.

Again and again and again, I snapped my hips, gritting my teeth to hold out until she broke with a gasping shout.

Then I fell with her.

She caught me easily as I eased myself back over her. My breath sawed in and out of my lungs. Her back was damp with sweat, and so was mine.

I kissed her softly, swiping my thumb along her cheekbone.

"I'm so in love with you," I whispered.

Magnolia mirrored the way I was holding her face, staring deeply into my eyes. "And I'm so in love with you, Grady."

My eyes closed, and I wrapped her tightly in the circle of my arms.

"I think that's why your feelings scared me," she admitted quietly, lips brushing my collarbone.

"Yeah?" I kissed the top of her head. "Why's that?"

"Because I was headed there with you without even realizing it." She sighed. "You saying it out loud was like I opened my eyes, and I was standing on top of a mountain before I even knew I'd taken a single step."

I smiled. "A hike up a mountain. That's like your nightmare."

She pulled back so I could see her face. "Not anymore," she answered seriously. "Not if I'm with you."

I tugged the blanket up over us, and we stayed like that all day.

We napped. And we talked. And we made love two more times.

And as she fell asleep that night, wrapped in my arms after a quiet picnic on my family room floor, I realized that the weeks leading up to it, the day, was exactly what we needed.

Time to see, time to learn.

And what she'd said was exactly what I needed to hear. The words were the ones she needed to have the power to say. There was always a choice in doing something so big, so terrifying. But with the right person, it wasn't all that scary.

CHAPTER 28

GRADY

Two weeks later

$\mathcal{M}$y sister peered over the edge of her coffee while she watched me struggle. "You're too tall for that car."

I wrenched Magnolia's driver's-side seat back. "I'm too tall for a lot of cars, but she needed mine today for ... something."

Grace smiled. "And there you sit, cramming yourself into that too small car with a giant-ass grin on your face."

"Right you are, sister." I unfolded from the car and stretched. "You don't even want me to explain all the reasons for this giant-ass grin."

She wrinkled up her nose but didn't say anything. Turnabout was fair play because I'd watched her and Tucker moon for months, knowing they couldn't keep their hands off each other.

In the past two weeks, I'd spent every possible minute with Magnolia, learning every single damn thing about that woman that I could.

Some of those things were fully clothed activities, like cooking dinner with her in her immaculate kitchen, overlooking the small patio and bones of the garden she had in her backyard, which she promised was beautiful in the summer. She favored savory foods but had a deft hand with desserts, which she'd shown off to perfection with the chocolate cake she baked for dessert one night.

Then she smeared the frosting on my stomach and licked it off, and I'd never, ever look at chocolate cake the same way again.

She loved a wide range of movies, as long as they came with a happy ending, and we'd watched a few of those cuddled up on her couch.

We played games (she ruthlessly kicked my ass in Monopoly) and somehow ended up almost breaking her dining room table in the process.

Basically, every day, outside of work, we were at her house.

Magnolia's house equaled privacy.

Mine did not.

Privacy led to the non-clothed activities, which were just as fun.

In her, I found my perfect match. In bed, we were insatiable, each night (or afternoon, or morning) showing me a different way that you could find pleasure in the person you loved.

Sometimes, she woke me with sweet kisses, which led to slow, dreamy sex while we were both only half awake.

Sometimes, I accidentally ripped her shirt off and took her against the wall as soon as we cleared the door after an entire day of dancing around each other at the office, where we desperately tried to maintain professional boundaries.

But today, we were attempting something else new.

Trading vehicles when she refused to tell me why she needed mine and where she'd knowingly show up somewhere that Tucker and Grace would be.

I'd be lying if I said I wasn't a little nervous for this particular first.

Grace smiled when Tucker came out of the garage apartment. "What took you so long?"

He dropped a kiss on the top of her head. "Just talking to my dad. I think he may have found someone to take on some of my caseload at the office."

"That's great," I told him. "We'll certainly need you next month more. I can't believe how booked up we are."

He grinned. "You gonna get sick of hiking all day?"

"Hell, no." I winced when an ache in my back flared up. "But I do need to start working out again. I about broke my back this week moving wrong."

We all held our breath as soon as I said it because we all knew I'd hardly done anything except spend time with Magnolia the past two weeks. Tucker flushed a little pink, but he shook his head. He glanced down at my sister. "Were we that bad at first?"

She grinned. "Yes."

The sound of a car horn sounded, and I turned, shading my eyes against the sun.

"What the ...?" I breathed.

Grace let out a delighted laugh as Magnolia pulled my SUV into the driveway.

Tucker burst out laughing.

Behind my car was the shining silver Airstream from the conference. And behind the wheel of my car, Magnolia was grinning like a fool.

She slid the car in park and rolled down the window. Her eyes were shining. "Well, didn't I say I was going to win?"

"You have got to be kidding me." I leaned in a gave her a hard-smacking kiss on the lips. "You actually won it?"

"I did." She cupped the side of my face, giving one nerve-tinged look behind me at the two people trying not to stare. Then she pecked my lips. "Maybe I'll let you camp with me." She spoke against my mouth.

I growled, which made her laugh.

"Oh my gosh," Grace squealed, running her hand along the sleek side of the Airstream. "It's adorable."

Magnolia raised an eyebrow as she climbed out of the car. "That's what I said."

I rolled my eyes, and Tucker laughed.

"It's functional," I said.

"Something can be functional and still be cute," my sister pointed out.

Magnolia nudged her with her elbow. "Exactly."

"They don't even deserve to sleep in this beauty," Grace said. She leaned in toward Magnolia. "I vote girls' camping trip for the first outing."

"Whoa, hold on," I interjected. My hands slid around Magnolia's hips, and she leaned back against me while she laughed. "It is thanks to me that she was even there to enter for it."

My girl tipped her beautiful face up to smile at me, all the nerves gone now. "But it's mine. I might gut the whole thing and decorate it pink."

Grace laughed as she and Tucker wandered around the camper to inspect it.

I leaned down and whispered into her ear. "You can decorate whatever you want, I'll still want to christen every single surface with you."

Gently, I nipped at her silky soft earlobe. She shivered. "And christen them we shall."

Magnolia hummed. "You are a terrible influence, Grady Buchanan. You've turned me into something wholly unladylike."

I swatted her butt as I pulled away from her, which earned me a mock glare. "You couldn't be unladylike if you tried." I pecked her lips again. "And I love you for that."

Tucker appeared around the back again. "Does this have A/C?"

She nodded.

He whistled appreciatively.

"Keeping this a secret was harder than I thought."

I snorted. "I'll bet."

Magnolia unlocked the door and laughed when Grace rushed inside, gushing over every part of the camper.

"Look at the little toilet and the little kitchen cabinets!" She poked her head out, pointing a finger at Magnolia. "We're doing a photoshoot with this thing, and oh, can you wear that yellow dress?" Her head disappeared again. "I'm having so many ideas!"

I laughed at my sister's enthusiasm.

"She's sweet," Magnolia murmured quietly.

Curling an arm around her, I kissed the top of her head. "She's been dying to spend some time with you."

"Someone was being a little possessive of my time."

I raised an eyebrow. "You want me to give you some space?"

Magnolia's smile was slight, and her eyes so full of heat, I almost dragged her into the garage apartment. "What do you think?"

"I think I know what kind of unladylike thoughts are running through your wonderful brain, Magnolia MacIntyre."

She fitted her arm around my waist, laughing softly. "I'm glad to get to know her better. Even if we do make Green Valley's strangest double-date partners."

"Amen to that," Tucker said, watching us with a smile. He hitched a thumb over his shoulder. "Anytime you want me to pry her outta there, just let me know. She's probably planning ten photoshoots for you."

"Eleven!" Grace shouted. "It's perfect."

"She's just fine," Magnolia answered with a smile.

"Want to bring that out tonight?" I asked her. "We could stop and fill the propane tank and grab some food for a campfire on our way out of town."

She watched the camper, watched Grace leap out of it and talk excitedly to Tucker. "Maybe next week."

Something was brewing behind her eyes, and I wasn't exactly sure what it was.

I smoothed a hand down her back and felt her ribs expand on a deep breath.

"Y'all want to come over to my place for dinner tonight?" she asked. "Grady was going to grill some hamburgers, and I made my aunt's famous coleslaw."

Grace's smile spread wide and happy over her face, but she still glanced quickly at Tucker, who nodded.

"We'd love that," she answered fervently. "You're sure?"

Magnolia nodded, turning her face up to mine briefly. I couldn't not kiss her.

I loved so much about her. Everything, really. But sometimes, one thing you loved about a person stood out just a bit more than the hundreds of other things on your list.

Her courage in facing the things that might have scared anyone else away right then was what I loved most.

"I'm sure," she said. "Come on. We need to get those patties made." She smiled at my sister. "Does six sound okay?"

Grace nodded. "Perfect."

We drove away a few minutes later with our fingers intertwined, and absently, I brought our hands up my mouth so I could kiss her knuckles.

I never could have known what I really would've faced by moving to this strange little town, what was waiting for me on the other end of her phone call, that interview. I thought it was unending excitement and thrills to keep me busy.

Instead, I found the love of my life in the unlikeliest of places.

And with the mountains unfolding in a mighty path along the skyline as we drove back to her place, I knew those adventures—the very best ones—were far from over.

EPILOGUE

MAGNOLIA

"*D*on't be nervous."

I allowed myself one tiny eye roll.

"I'm serious, it'll be fine."

Grady squeezed my leg and let his big hand stay right there, that spot on my thigh that he loved to touch whenever he was driving. I loved the way his fingers, long and tan and a little nicked up from a run-in with some hedges he helped me clear out of my backyard, curled around my leg.

"I'm not nervous," I told him. And I was lying through every single one of my teeth. I'd put this off for three weeks until I trusted my daddy could behave. Every single day of those three weeks, I learned a little something about myself and this man who was in love with me.

We were so different, but goodness, we fit together in such a perfect way I could hardly believe it.

"Why does it scare you to introduce me to your parents?" He turned the wheel onto their road and whistled at some of the houses we passed. "I've already met your mom, and unless I read her steely-eyed composure wrong, she *loved* me."

I smiled. "So humble."

With ease, he smiled back, those fingers pressing against my leg. Just a hint that he could have me dissolving into laughter if he gripped me in the right way.

"She did," I admitted on a sigh. "But my daddy …" I gave him a helpless look.

"Is crazy overprotective of you," he filled in.

"Yes."

Grady glanced in his rearview mirror and then pulled the car over to the side of the road, just before the entrance to their driveway. He tugged down his sunglasses so I could see his eyes and shifted so he was facing me. The hand on my leg came up to cup my face.

"We'll get along just fine." His thumb swept gently along the bottom curve of my lip. I kissed the pad of his finger, watching the ways his eyes heated at the small gesture. "Because I'm crazy in love with his daughter. And if there's one person he can trust with your heart, it's me."

A sigh escaped my lips, and he leaned forward to capture it with his mouth. His lips moved over mine in soft, sucking kisses, and my hand curled around the back of his head, my fingers threading through his hair so I could deepen it.

I dragged my teeth over his bottom lip, and he hummed low in his chest. Oh, I loved that hum. I loved the noises he made, especially the helpless ones when I moved in a certain way and touched him just so. I'd never felt sexier in my entire life than when I discovered all the sound effects that came along with having Grady Buchanan in my bed. And kitchen. And living room. And the office (just once, with the door double-locked and the shades in the front windows drawn).

But falling in love with him was so much more than that. It was the give and take that we found in uncovering what day-to-day life would look like with each other. He respected me. Challenged me. Pushed me in the very best ways. But also backed down when he could tell I needed him to.

And most of all, he just loved me … for exactly the woman I was.

Just as Grady shifted, his hands cupping my face, his tongue brushing mine, I pulled back and smiled into his handsome face. That was precisely the problem in all of this. That was the crux of my mood all morning, as we prepared to go to my parents' house so he could sit and dine with the people who brought me into the world.

Everything was so good, and I was terrified my daddy would run his mouth, ruin the goodness, and send Grady straight for the hills.

Of course, he saw all that play out on my face.

"He can't scare me away, Magnolia," he said gently.

"You say that now."

His smile was a small one, only a slight bend in those lips, and I allowed my fingers to brush against the stubble on his jaw.

"What's this about?" His voice was a whisper. "My girl knows that I'm not going anywhere, even if your dad does his worst."

"I do know that," I admitted. My fingers trailed down his throat, and briefly, I toyed with the edge of his bright blue dress shirt. I'd never seen Grady so cleaned up, and he'd done it to impress my parents. He could've worn a simple T-shirt for all they cared. As long as they saw how much he loved me, I knew in every corner of my heart that they'd accept him fully.

It was all they ever wanted for me.

He was patient as I worked out how to put my feelings into words. Another thing I loved about him.

"I've never ... I've never brought someone into that house like I'm about to with you."

His brows turned in. "What do you mean?"

My face went all warm when I met his eyes. "You're it for me, Grady Buchanan. You're the rest of my life."

"I'm glad to hear that," he murmured, gaze tracking over every inch of my face.

"And when I walk through that front door, the one I've walked through a million times, I'll be doing it while I hold your hand. I want you to love it ... to love them. And I want them to love you," I admitted.

"Come here," he said gruffly. He gathered me in his arms, and the sigh that exited my lips was heavy with relief. Grady pressed a kiss to the side of my head.

That was when the harsh knock on my window came. We pulled apart when my dad's face lowered, his eyes taking in our tight embrace.

Smothering a smile, Grady lowered the window. I glared up at my father. "Daddy."

"Magnolia." He ducked down farther and gave Grady an assessing look. "You must be ... Grady."

Grady lifted his hand in greeting. "Sir."

I gave him as much of a smile as I could manage. "We'll be right there, Daddy."

"Why you parking on the street?" he asked.

"We weren't *parking* here," I said. "We were talking for a minute is all."

My dad's gaze flicked back to Grady, then to his hand, which had found that same resting spot on my leg. His jaw twitched.

Grady pulled his hand away, and I felt a momentary pang of disappointment until I realized he was getting out of the car. My dad's eyebrows lifted in surprise, but he straightened, setting his hands on his hips while Grady took long, easy strides around the front of his car.

He held out his hand to my father.

My breath got caught somewhere in the middle of my throat when Daddy didn't immediately take the offering. But after a beat, his hand gripped Grady's.

"It's a pleasure to meet you, sir," Grady said. His stance was relaxed, his eyes clear, and his smile warm.

Daddy glanced at me through the windshield. Maybe my pleading eyes registered in that brief look, or maybe he saw how much this moment meant to me. Or maybe my father just loved me enough to know that if I was bringing Grady here, after what I'd told him, that I viewed this man as my future.

"My wife told me not to come out here," Daddy said.

Grady exhaled a quiet laugh.

"Normally, I listen to what she tells me, especially when she says it with a certain look in her eyes." My daddy took a deep breath and let it out slowly. "But I wanted to see how you'd react when you weren't ready."

Grady looked my way, giving me a tiny wink. "Well, sir, I've been ready to meet you and your wife for a while."

"Why's that?"

He lifted his chin. "Because I'm completely in love with your daughter, and if I'm very lucky, with your wife's and your blessing, I'll be asking her to marry me in the next few months."

With a shaking hand, I covered my mouth.

My father's eyes widened and color bloomed on his cheeks. J.T. McIntyre was not often taken completely by surprise, but if I hadn't been so shocked by what Grady said, I might have snapped a picture.

"That so?" he asked gruffly. "Hardly seems you've been dating her long enough to know that."

Grady nodded. "Might seem that way. But I have a feeling you won't judge me for it." His eyes flicked back in my direction again, and he smiled. "Sometimes, you just know."

Daddy was quiet. "I suppose you're right." He slapped Grady on the shoulder. "I'll meet you down at the house. Don't park on the grass like an ingrate. I worked my ass off on that lawn."

Grady grinned. "Yes, sir."

My hand fell away from my mouth when I caught a glimpse of my daddy's smile as he walked away from the car.

Grady slid back into his seat, wearing a satisfied smile on his face. "That went well."

I stared. "You told him you're going to propose to me in the next few months."

He looked over at me. "I did."

"Are you crazy?" I laughed.

He leaned in for a soft kiss, which I gave freely. "Maybe I am, my Magnolia."

I curled my fingers through his as he drove us down the driveway. Maybe I was crazy too, because even if he asked me tonight, I'd say yes.

Sometimes, you just knew.

SECOND EPILOGUE

HUNTER

*T*he pen I used to sign my divorce papers was heavy in my hand, one of the nicest ones I owned. My dad gave it to me the night before I graduated high school, and I remember thinking that a pen was one of the worst gifts I'd ever received.

But I kept it. Used it all the time at work, stored it in the fancy box he'd presented it to me in. It wasn't heavy because I was using it to end my marriage. It was heavy because it was expertly made. The black ink flowed effortlessly across the white paper, and before I could even blink, it was done.

And my father, who gave me the black and gold pen in the black and gold box, had no idea that I'd even filed for divorce from my wife. Neither did my mother. I'd told no one back at home that it had come to this.

Even though it was the right decision—one that Samantha and I made together—and even though they'd never really gotten along with my wife, they'd view my divorce as a sign that I should come home to Green Valley.

I set the pen down and leaned back in my desk chair.

Going back to Green Valley was the last thing I wanted. Not because of the town itself. Or the people who lived there.

It was because of her. Because of Iris.

The bottom-right desk drawer, the one that held a small box that I hadn't touched since the day I got married, beckoned me to open it. Instead of indulging that impulse, my gaze moved back to the paper I just signed.

Was it that simple? Scrawl my name in expensive ink, legally end the marriage that had been over emotionally for almost three years, and then open the locked box. Look at her face and feel my heart turn painfully in my chest, simply because now … with the writing of my name … I was allowed to.

It wasn't that simple.

Because nothing in life was. Opening a box and looking at a picture would never be enough when it came to her. And soon, too soon, I'd have to face her anyway.

I pushed aside my divorce papers and carefully picked up the letter I'd received earlier that day.

No, it definitely wasn't simple at all, because with the contents of that letter, I found out I'd have to face Iris for the first time in ten years.

"Ready or not," I murmured into the quiet apartment, "here we go."

ACKNOWLEDGMENTS

The first person who gets a shout-out is Korrie Noelle. Thank you doesn't even really seem sufficient, because she was so instrumental for me in approaching the character of Magnolia—her family background, her history, her reality, and her truth as a biracial woman. Korrie was honest and vulnerable about her own truth, her own reality, and answered any question I had during the process. Because of her help in approaching Magnolia respectfully and sensitively, I hope I came close to doing her character justice.

I'm also beyond grateful for Kathryn Andrews, who helped me plot and listened to me ramble and vent and gave me such valuable feedback on this story, as she does for all of my books!

In our little corner of the world at Smartypants Romance, thank you to Brooke and Fiona (who deserve sainthood), Penny for 'giving' me the characters of J.T. and Bobby Jo (who turned out to be some of the most fascinating secondary characters I've ever written), and the SRU authors whom I just adore unequivocally.

To my husband and boys, for letting me lock myself in our bedroom to write this book during one of the weirdest summers ever, and the rest of my family for their never-ending support.

To Najla Qamber for the most amazing covers. She took the CRAZIEST description I've ever given her for what I wanted and turned them into glorious reality.

To Rafa Catala for the mad photography skills on the cover.

To Jenny Sims and Janice Owen for the editing and proofreading.

To Michelle, who helps me during release, and my readers for being generally amazing and wonderful.

"Consider it pure joy, my brothers and sisters, whenever you face trials of many kinds, because you know that the testing of your faith produces perseverance."
James 1: 2-3

ABOUT THE AUTHOR

Karla Sorensen has been an avid reader her entire life, preferring stories with a happily-ever-after over just about any other kind. And considering she has an entire line item in her budget for books, she realized it might just be cheaper to write her own stories. She still keeps her toes in the world of health care marketing, where she made her living pre-babies. Now she stays home, writing and mommy-ing full time (this translates to almost every day being a 'pajama day' at the Sorensen household...don't judge). She lives in West Michigan with her husband, two exceptionally adorable sons, and big, shaggy rescue dog.

Stay up to date on Karla's upcoming releases!
Subscribe to her newsletter:
http://www.karlasorensen.com/newsletter/

Website: http://www.karlasorensen.com/
Facebook: http://www.facebook.com/karlasorensenbooks
Goodreads: https://www.goodreads.com/author/show/13563232.Karla_Sorensen
Twitter: http://www.twitter.com/ksorensenbooks
Instagram: https://www.instagram.com/karla_sorensen/

Website: www.smartypantsromance.com
Facebook: www.facebook.com/smartypantsromance/
Goodreads: www.goodreads.com/smartypantsromance

Twitter: @smartypantsrom
Instagram: @smartypantsromance
Newsletter: https://smartypantsromance.com/newsletter/

Subscribe to her newsletter: http://www.karlasorensen.com/newsletter/

Scorned Women's Society Series

My Bare Lady by Piper Sheldon (#1)

The Treble with Men by Piper Sheldon (#2)

The One That I Want by Piper Sheldon (#3)

Park Ranger Series

Happy Trail by Daisy Prescott (#1)

Stranger Ranger by Daisy Prescott (#2)

The Leffersbee Series

Been There Done That by Hope Ellis (#1)

The Higher Learning Series

Upsy Daisy by Chelsie Edwards (#1)

Seduction in the City

Cipher Security Series

Code of Conduct by April White (#1)

Code of Honor by April White (#2)

Cipher Office Series

Weight Expectations by M.E. Carter (#1)

Sticking to the Script by Stella Weaver (#2)

Cutie and the Beast by M.E. Carter (#3)

Weights of Wrath by M.E. Carter (#4)

Common Threads Series

Mad About Ewe by Susannah Nix (#1)

Give Love a Chai by Nanxi Wen (#2)

<u>Educated Romance</u>

<u>Work For It Series</u>

<u>Street Smart by Aly Stiles (#1)</u>

<u>Heart Smart by Emma Lee Jayne (#2)</u>

<u>Lessons Learned Series</u>

<u>Under Pressure by Allie Winters (#1)</u>

Made in the USA
Monee, IL
30 September 2022